KATIE GINGER lives by the sea in the south-east of England, and apart from holidays to very hot places where you can sit by a pool and drink cocktails as big your head, she wouldn't really want to be anywhere else. *Snowflakes at Mistletoe Cottage* is her third novel. She is also author of the Seafront series – *The Little Theatre on the Seafront*, shortlisted for the Katie Fforde Debut Novel of the Year award, and *Summer Season on the Seafront*.

When she's not writing, Katie spends her time drinking gin, or with her husband, trying to keep alive her two children: Ellie, who believes everything in life should be performed like a musical number from a West End show; and Sam, who is basically a monkey with a boy's face. And there's also their adorable King Charles Spaniel, Wotsit (yes, he is named after the crisps!).

For more about Katie, you can visit her website: www.keginger. com, find her on Facebook: www.facebook.com/KatieGAuthor, or follow her on Twitter: @KatieGAuthor.

Also by Katie Ginger

The Little Theatre on the Seafront
Summer Season on the Seafront

Snowflakes at Mistletoe Cottage

KATIE GINGER

ONE PLACE. MANY STORIES

HQ
An imprint of HarperCollins*Publishers* Ltd
1 London Bridge Street
London SE1 9GF

This paperback edition 2019

This edition is published in Great Britain by
HQ, an imprint of HarperCollins*Publishers* Ltd 2019

A catalogue record for this book is available from the British Library.

ISBN: 9780008331085

MIX
Paper from
responsible sources
FSC® C007454

This book is produced from independently certified FSC™ paper
to ensure responsible forest management.

For more information visit: www.harpercollins.co.uk/green

Printed and bound by CPI Group (UK) Ltd, Croydon, CR0 4YY

In loving memory of Angie and Dan

Chapter 1

London

Felicity Fenchurch primped and preened in front of the camera, brushing her honey-blonde curls back from her face. The director shouted, 'Action,' and she gave a longing smile, dipped down to pull a tray from the oven, and gazing at the camera from under false eyelashes, pouted.

'There you have it,' Felicity announced, removing her pink oven gloves with a flourish. 'A deliciously decadent fabulous four-cheese lasagne, made with fresh homemade perfect pasta.'

'Cut,' shouted David, and the silent studio erupted into life. 'That's a wrap for the day, everyone. Felicity, darling, that was marvellous as usual. How you manage to look so damn sexy serving cheesy pasta is beyond me.'

Esme Kendrick watched as they exited the studio. As a food technologist, she'd done all the cooking this morning: chopped all the ingredients, grated the different cheeses, made a velvety béchamel sauce. She'd even made the pasta at the crack of dawn before the greedy pigeons had started cooing, getting up in the dark and padding about in the cold kitchen as a wintery wind blustered around the apartment. It was November, and as cold as

1

a penguin's flipper outside, but to Esme November meant nearly Christmas, and there was something different about London at Christmas time. Everyone was a little friendlier, a little kinder, and with parties and celebrations the city was alive with a kind of electricity. After a rushed cup of coffee, she'd made her way to work, with the great strings of Christmas lights swinging above, glittering in the winter gloom. The lasagne, complete with a perfect golden-brown finish, had then been presented to the world as the handiwork of TV goddess, Felicity Fenchurch. In reality, all Felicity had done was smoulder at the camera and mix things in a bowl.

'I'm so nervous,' Esme said to Helena, her best friend and a fellow food technician. 'Why am I so nervous about pitching Grandma's double-layer chocolate chestnut cake to Sasha?'

Helena brushed her dark brown bob behind her ear. 'Oh, I don't know, is it because it's your absolute favourite recipe of your gran's? The one you make every year at Christmas, the one you never, ever stop talking about as soon as summer's over and the weather gets even the slightest bit nippy. The one that—'

'Yeah, maybe it's that,' Esme interrupted playfully. 'Right, wish me luck. See you tomorrow.'

Sasha's office was of the new modern glass variety that looks more like a greenhouse. As their producer, she was scary but fair. Never rude or patronising, not like Felicity, but she was a powerhouse – a confident, composed, I've-achieved-my-dreams-with-effort-and-hard-work kind of woman. The type you look up to and fear all at the same time. The glass wall, with a view onto the corridor, was lined with tall green plastic pot plants designed to make the place seem homely. Esme was just approaching the door and about to knock when she heard voices from inside. Peering through the dusty leaves of a banana plant, Felicity Fenchurch sat purring at Sasha discussing something oddly familiar.

'I know it's a late edition, Sasha, but I really think my granny's triple-layer chocolate chestnut cake will be just the thing. Chestnuts are always big at Christmas and nothing screams indulgence like a chocolate cake. And what makes mine special is the addition of a secret ingredient – maple syrup. And a slightly unorthodox method of chilling the batter before baking. It'll be revolutionary.' Felicity smiled and bright white teeth gleamed in the dull office light.

Esme couldn't believe what she was hearing. These were the same things – the same words – she'd used when describing her recipe to Helena yesterday. Felicity must have overheard them and now she was passing off the recipe as her own. An unpleasant feeling grew in Esme's stomach.

'I'm really not sure,' replied Sasha, in cool professional tones. 'We'll need to drop something else and it'll have to fit into that timeslot. I really don't fancy redoing the entire schedule.'

'Of course. I was going to suggest we drop the chocolate orange tart. It's so last year anyway and with some clever cut shots from David this will be sublime.' She smiled at David who glowed at the compliment. Felicity crossed her long legs and Esme, with heat rushing through her body, spotted the red sole of a Louboutin.

'And,' pitched in David, 'I just love that it's her granny's recipe, don't you? People love sentimental cooking. It'll be a bestseller for sure.'

'Okay then,' replied Sasha, nodding. Her grey hair was cut into an elfin crop and her deceptively youthful face remained passive. 'Fine. We can do it.'

Esme stepped back and leaned against the opposite wall, her legs rubbery and almost giving way. Her whole body shook with rage. Stealing boring old day-to-day recipes, as Felicity had done before, was one thing, but stealing this one was something else. This recipe was the one she used to remember her grandma, the one the whole family ate at Christmas with a toast to Gran first. Esme had thought long and hard about sharing it and it had taken her ages to be able to do it. Only this winter had she finally reached the point where she wanted other people to taste

3

it and feel the sense of love and care it imparted, rather than holding onto it as if she was holding on to the memories of her gran. To hear Felicity passing it off as her own grandma's recipe was low. Esme bit her lip to stop the tears from falling and anger tightened her hands into fists. Should she march in and confront Felicity or let it go? Her heart pounded, her temper causing her brain to freeze. As a strong sense of injustice took over, without thinking, she raised her hand and knocked.

'Come in,' said Sasha in a loud clear voice. 'Oh, Esme, can I help you?'

Esme paused in the doorway, unsure what to say. She couldn't quite believe what she'd heard or that her body seemed to be acting of its own accord. 'Sasha, I . . . The triple-layer chocolate chestnut cake Felicity just told you about – that recipe's not hers, it's mine—'

'I beg your pardon,' Felicity replied, shooting up to standing, her face a picture of shocked indignation, but there was a flicker of fear in her eyes. 'How dare you accuse me of—'

'You must have overheard me talking about it yesterday. You stole it!' Esme turned to Sasha who was also now standing.

'Sasha, I came here tonight to tell you about my grandma's recipe for a double-layer chocolate chestnut cake – to see if we could use it in the Christmas show,' Felicity squeaked in outrage, but Esme ignored her. 'It's from a cookery book that's been handed down through my family. It's got all our favourite recipes in. I wanted to share this one because Gran was – it's so special.'

Felicity sat back down and found a tissue in her bag before pressing it to her nose, pretending to cry. 'How can you say that, Esme? You know it's not true.' In support, David, the director, glowered at Esme.

'Esme,' Sasha began calmly, her face placid. There wasn't even a hint in her eyes that she was shocked or finding this remotely uncomfortable. Esme was. She felt decidedly uncomfortable and she had a horrible sinking feeling she should have thought this through before barging into Sasha's office letting her fiery temper take over. 'Are you saying that Miss Fenchurch has stolen your recipe for a . . . what was it?'

'A double-layer chocolate chestnut cake,' Esme replied as confidently as she could, though her stomach burned. Her eyes were drawn to the deep green scarf Sasha had fastened around her neck. It was floral and pretty, and at odds with her cold, harsh demeanour.

Felicity sobbed. 'Sasha, this is absolutely outrageous. And mine is triple-layer anyway.'

'You've just added one, that's all,' Esme blurted. 'The recipe is the same.'

Sasha glanced from Felicity to Esme, her face expressionless. 'Esme, you've made a very serious accusation here. Are you sure you want to continue with this conversation? Is it possible you've made a mistake and this is purely a coincidence?'

'No,' Esme said, quickly, her voice rising. In the back of her mind something told her to stop and think but it was too late, her mouth was still opening and the words flowing out. 'That recipe was from my grandmother's cookbook. Hers is the only recipe I know of with the addition of maple syrup and a method of chilling the batter.'

'Do you have the recipe book with you, to prove that it's yours? I assume that as you were coming to see me this evening to pitch the idea you brought it.'

'Yes,' said Esme, pulling her bag from her shoulder. This would prove her right. She reached into her bag, fumbling around inside, spilling the contents onto the floor. Her hand trembled as with a sickening dread, she realised she'd left it next to the kettle last night after showing Leo something. Running late this morning, she'd forgotten to re-pack it. Esme raised her eyes to heaven and gave a silent prayer, hoping this wouldn't go against her. From the corner of her eye, she caught Felicity's face. A sly smile spread across her plumped-up lips and she held a tissue to her eyes to hide it.

5

'Do you have it with you?' asked Sasha. 'It would be useful to have a look at it.'

Esme bit her lip as a flush crept up her neck and into her cheeks. 'I'm afraid I left it at home.'

Felicity scoffed. 'Probably because there is no book. You seem to lie about everything, Miss Kendrick. Is Esme even your real name?'

'Now, now,' interrupted David, putting a hand on Felicity's arm. 'I know you're upset, Felicity, and justifiably so, but let's not get personal.'

'Personal?' she shouted, clutching her chest. 'This is very personal to me, David. That woman is accusing me of lying to the whole world. If this got out, it would be a PR nightmare for me and the studio, and I would be left with no option but to sue. I have to protect my reputation.'

Esme's mouth flew open, irked by Felicity's overacting. 'I'm not the liar here, you are. You did steal it. You overheard me say I was going to pitch it and then you jumped in before I could. You must have been lurking by the coffee machine when you listened in to us chatting.'

'Lurking? How absurd,' laughed Felicity, brushing her hair away from her face so they could see her full shocked expression, but Esme detected a hint of concern in her voice. 'You have no proof of that, do you?'

'Do you have any proof, Esme?' asked Sasha. 'Who were you chatting to?' She was so calm Esme wondered if she was a robot and the scarf hid a central control panel. How could anyone be so numb to another's suffering? Esme chewed her lip, the tears welling in her eyes. She couldn't risk Helena getting into trouble.

'I'd rather not say,' Esme replied, but even she knew it sounded feeble.

'May I suggest,' said David, the colour draining a little from his ruddy cheeks, 'if that's the case, we forget about this whole dreadful business. Esme has no proof and I'm sure that if there are any . . . similarities, as Sasha said, it's simply coincidence.'

Esme's mind whirled around. This wasn't right. Felicity should be apologising to her, not the other way around. 'Do you think we both have grandmas who left us cookery books then, David? Sasha, I know I forgot the book, but you must believe me. I haven't made this up.'

Sasha glanced at Felicity then back to Esme. 'Esme, you've accused a colleague of lying and stealing ideas. This is very serious.'

'It's slander and harassment,' added Felicity who stood up to leave. 'I will not sit here being insulted by this – this – liar any longer. Either sort it out, Sasha, or I walk.' She marched to the door.

'Now, wait a second, Felicity.' Sasha rose from her chair. 'Let's not do anything rash.' She turned to Esme, her face was softer, but her voice remained cold and matter-of-fact. 'Esme, I'm sorry, but without any evidence you need to withdraw your complaint and apologise to Felicity.'

Esme sat frozen, staring wide-eyed and bewildered. Slowly, she shook her head. It wasn't just her being cheated here, her grandma was too, and she wouldn't stand for it. 'No. No, I won't. I know I don't have proof with me. I left the book at home by accident. If you let me go and get it—'

'Absolutely not,' Felicity shouted from the door. 'I mean it, Sasha. Unless this is resolved now, I walk. I don't want to, but I will. I'm not lacking for offers, as you know.'

Sasha hesitated and Esme knew what was going through her brain. Without Felicity and the ratings she brought, the whole network could go down. Her show, *Felicity Fenchurch's Fabulous Feasts*, was the only way they were keeping up with the other channels. 'Esme, I'm sorry,' Sasha continued. 'I think we need to get this sorted out now. I'm very surprised you didn't bring the recipe with you if you were going to pitch it. Felicity could simply have a similar recipe. If you apologise to her, we can put this all behind us.'

Still at the doorway, holding a tissue to her eyes, Felicity's voice was almost childlike as she said, 'Even though this unfounded accusation has damaged our relationship beyond repair, Esme, I'm a professional and if you apologise, I'll try and move on.'

Could she apologise? Could she say she was wrong and back down now? Was she even sure she was right? Esme took a deep breath but her mind was made up. Sometimes you had to be strong and stand up for yourself. It's what her gran had taught her and she wouldn't back down now. The secret ingredient and method were too similar, she wasn't mistaken. Esme's shoulders and neck hurt from the tension, even her legs ached, but she shook her head again. 'I'm sorry, Sasha, but I won't apologise. I'm right.'

'Then I'm afraid I have no choice, Esme. This counts as gross misconduct so it's instant dismissal.' Esme felt the tears spring to her eyes but there was no way she would cry in front of Felicity and David.

'I've been sacked?' Her voice sounded strange where she had to force the words past the ball of anger and hurt lodged in her throat. It didn't seem real. Somehow Esme managed to back out of the room while her whole body sparked with suppressed rage. Visibly shaking, she edged passed Felicity and left.

*

The glittering Christmas lights of London sparkled in the evening darkness. Giant snowflake lights hung high in the air, twinkling overhead, but Esme barely noticed them through her tears. She walked into someone, mumbled an apology and carried on with her head down. The heavy crowds of tourists bustled around her and snippets of Christmas songs carried on the air from the shops she passed. Instead of enjoying the wonderful Christmas vibe – that special atmosphere of excitement Esme loved most about London at this time of year – she dipped her head and marched on as fast as she could. By the time she reached her and Leo's apartment, tears were flowing freely down her cheeks.

Unbuttoning her heavy winter coat, she hung it on the rack

then loosened her scarf, feeling drained and exhausted. Walking into the kitchen, she knew there was only one thing she could do to make herself feel better. Cook. She'd make Leo's favourite meal. A nice thick, juicy steak, rare and pink in the middle, and a proper béarnaise sauce with lots of good French butter and fresh tarragon. She'd even make asparagus roasted with sea salt as a side dish. A small smile crept over Esme's face as she searched the fridge for the ingredients but it was instantly replaced by a frown and cold teardrops on her cheeks. How could things have gone so badly wrong today? She shouldn't have acted on impulse and marched in there. She should have waited and thought about what to do. Now she'd thrown her job away and her heart was filled with regret.

Leo got up from the sofa. 'Esme, you're home.'

'Yep. And I got fired,' Esme replied, matter-of-fact, chopping the butter into small cubes before turning to see his face frozen in panic.

'What?' He looked even more shocked than she'd expected and walked to the window to stare out, gripping the hair at the back of his head. She'd hoped for a hug but as he stayed where he was, she poured two glasses of wine and took them over. When he turned back he reached for his wine, then his dark grey eyes gazed at her with concern.

'What happ—'

Esme bit back tears but took a deep breath. 'Felicity stole my recipe again. One of Grandma's. She must have overheard me talking about it with Helena at lunch yesterday and then decided to pitch it before I could. When I went to Sasha's office this evening, she was there saying it was her family recipe. I was so upset, Leo, and I don't know why, but I went in there and confronted her.'

'You did what?'

'I know, I know.' Esme rubbed her throbbing forehead. 'I don't know why I did it either. Well, I do. I did I because it was the right thing to do. She was even claiming it was from her granny and you know how long I've waited to share this special recipe but couldn't bring myself to do it.'

Finally, Leo reached out to her but didn't pull her into a hug, he touched her hand. He was clearly struggling to process everything she'd said. 'Are you sure you were right? I mean, I know you've said before about her doing this, but couldn't it just be a coincidence? You can be a bit dramatic sometimes.'

Esme wiped a tear from her cheek. Leo was always saying she was being dramatic when she lost her temper or got upset. His clear, decisive mind didn't get her passionate, emotional one, and maybe she was being dramatic, but it didn't stop her being right. 'A coincidence? No. That's what she's claiming but she even said about using maple syrup and chilling the mixture first. She could only've known that if she was ear-wigging.' Esme thrust her hand into her mop of ragged curls. 'It's one thing to steal a recipe but another to steal a grandma. She probably doesn't even have one anymore. I bet she devoured hers like a praying mantis. And she's tried to make it three layers instead of two. It won't work as triple layers, it'll just slide about then fall over, not unless you make the sponge thicker or use something other than double cream as a filling.'

'What are you going to do?' He turned to face her, his expression tense.

Esme feigned a hopefulness she didn't feel. 'I'm sure I'll pick something else up quickly, in a few months; or worst-case scenario, I'll go freelance.' Suddenly, Leo took her hand and led her to the table.

'Esme, can you come and sit down, please? I need to talk to you.' Esme paused. His face was serious as he placed his wine glass down, and her heart thudded in her chest. For the last few months he'd been secretive and she and her friends thought maybe he was going to propose. Was this the moment? Sat on the chair, next to their tiny dining table, he knelt down in front of her and Esme's heart rocketed up into her throat. She took a big breath in and bit the insides of her cheeks to stop herself grinning like a fool.

'Esme, I'm sorry, I should have done this weeks ago, the timing is terrible.' She wanted to shout that it wasn't. It wasn't at all. It was perfect timing. Leo raked a hand through his hair and she watched, hoping his hand would reach into his jacket pocket and pull out a tiny box. 'I know today's been difficult for you and I . . .' He shook his head. 'I should've done this before now.'

Esme bit her lip. She was going to get married!

'I think we should break up,' Leo announced.

Her mouth opened then closed again as she stared at him in disbelief. *What?* What had just happened? Everything fell silent except for the blood pounding in her ears and her short gasps of breath as she tried to control her emotions. Leo's eyes dropped and he stood up.

'I just feel we've become friends more than husband-and-wife material, don't you? And I think it'd be the best thing for both of us if we just moved on. Don't you think so?'

If he'd hoped for some kind of agreement from Esme, he was going to be disappointed. 'But it's nearly Christmas,' she said quietly.

'It's not even mid-November, Esme. It's nowhere near Christmas.' Leo went to the window. His slightly curmudgeonly attitude to Christmas suddenly seemed far less endearing and much more Scrooge-like, and as if to confirm it, he said, 'I can give you a few days to move your stuff out, you don't have to go right now. I'm not a monster.'

Dazed, Esme tried to think but she couldn't, she could only feel – and all she felt was that she had to get out. She stood and placed her wine glass on the table, then went and picked up her handbag from the sofa. As she retrieved her coat from the rack, Leo said, 'Esme, where are you going? We can still have dinner and—'

She closed the door softly behind her.

Esme trudged through the rain to the Singapore Sling, ignoring it soaking her hair and running down her face, mixing with her tears. She'd left her hat and scarf at the flat, but wasn't going back for them. She'd rather get wet. Every fibre of her being felt crushed. As she descended the steps to the cellar bar, leaving the world behind, a drop of rain fell from the sign and trickled down the back of her neck. She wanted to hide. To hibernate below ground and never come out.

After an emergency call to Helena, her friends were with her in half an hour. Esme's heart, pounded and punched by the day's events, felt broken and bruised. When she thought of Leo, the last thread of love snapped and her heart deflated like a burst balloon. She could even picture it in her chest all floppy, sad and wrinkled.

Mark, Lola and Helena gathered around Esme, open-mouthed and with drinks untouched as she told them all the details of her day from hell. Dance music thumped in the background and harsh neon lights lit their usual table in the corner. At least the DJ wasn't playing Christmas songs. The last thing Esme wanted right now was Wham's 'Last Christmas' blasting out while her life hit an all-time low. Having finished, Esme couldn't stop the great sob that emerged in a high-pitched puff of air, making Mark and Helena jump.

'Christ, sweetie,' said Mark, 'you need more than just a drink after all that.'

'I don't think I can stomach one right now.'

'Rubbish,' he replied. 'What you need is an enormous cocktail with a little umbrella in.' His bright blue eyes popped against his dark hair and olive skin. 'And as for that witch, well—'

Esme sobbed.

'And Leo is a complete knob,' said Lola. 'I can't believe after five years together this is how he treats you.'

'What will you do now?' Helena asked sympathetically. Esme simply shrugged. 'Tomorrow you need to go out and register with agencies,' she commanded. Helena was scarily matter-of-fact and dealt with everything with an almost military attitude. Esme watched the bubbles fizz in her glass. She had no idea what life beyond today would look like. She didn't yet know if she'd make it to tomorrow. 'You can stay with us as long as you need to,' Helena added, glancing at Mark as they were housemates. But Esme didn't fancy sleeping on their sofa for the foreseeable future. And Eric, Lola's other half, worked from home so their spare room had been turned into an office. She let out a giant sigh.

'I'll have to move back home for a bit, won't I? I can't rent in London without a job and I don't know how long it's going to take me to get another one. I haven't got any savings and I can't scrounge off you guys indefinitely.' She leaned forward and rested her head on the table as a raindrop dripped from her soaking wet hair onto her nose.

'It wouldn't be scrounging, you're our friend,' replied Lola. 'If Felicity Fenchurch walked in here right now, I'd punch her on the nose.'

Helena rubbed Esme's back. 'From what you've said, back home isn't exactly—'

'London?' offered Esme. 'No, it's not. I don't know what I'm going to do.'

'Could you freelance and commute in?' asked Mark.

'Too far and too expensive.'

'What about some catering work? You know, weddings and stuff?' suggested Helena.

Esme hesitated. 'Yeah, maybe. But I'd still need a good reference and I don't think I'm going to get one of those now.'

'I know,' said Lola. 'You could write that cookery book you're always talking about.'

Lola had been Esme's best friend since school and knew her inside out. They came from the same town, went to the same university and had moved to London when they'd finished their studies, living together in a grotty two-bedroom flat above a kebab shop. She was also eternally optimistic, which was both helpful and, at times, annoying. 'You need to see this as an opportunity, not a setback. Okay, so you move back home for a bit. Without having to pay stupidly high London rent, and without your time being taken up by Felicity, you could write your cookbook and get it published. This is your chance to focus on it.'

'Do you really think so?' asked Esme, who felt a tiny spark of hope in the darkness of the last few hours.

'Of course you could,' agreed Helena. 'You're the best food tech around. Not only that, you're great at creating recipes too.'

Mark nodded. 'You look at this mess. Felicity thought your recipes were so good she wanted to steal them. And when I think about all the dinner parties where you've cooked for us, OMG! That salmon thing you made when I split up with Andrew? Trust me, it made it all worthwhile.'

Esme smiled and nudged Mark with her shoulder. 'What would I do without you guys?'

'Die of thirst, probably. I'm going to get another round.'

'Where will you stay tonight?' asked Helena, taking Esme's hand. 'I'm sure you don't want to go back to the flat.'

'She's staying with me and Eric, aren't you?' said Lola. 'But you're not borrowing my pants like you did at university.'

'I had an excuse then,' Esme replied. 'I didn't know how to do washing.' But suddenly her face clouded in concern. 'There is one thing.'

'What?' asked Mark, pausing on his way to get more drinks. 'After everything you've been though today, I can't believe there's anything worse to deal with.'

'Oh yes there is,' replied Esme, resting her head on the table and speaking from under her arms. 'I still have to tell my mother.'

'Well, you're on your own there, love,' said Helena, smiling. 'I've met your mum and she is batshit crazy.'

Chapter 2

Sandchester

Joe Holloway made a Herculean effort to laugh at his friend Danny's joke. It wasn't that the joke wasn't funny – Danny's jokes were always funny – but laughing felt unnatural to Joe and had done for a long time.

He stared into his pint glass and swilled the liquid around, then drained it in one big gulp. Even though it was only a normal Wednesday night, the pub was full of his friends and the people he'd known all his life, laughing and chatting. He'd been back for a few years now and everyone in the small town had welcomed him with soothing noises, but it was the pity he couldn't stand. It still came out in the nervous glances directed his way and the gentle, careful conversation.

Their usual pub hadn't changed since he was a teenager, drinking underage. The only thing that was different was the music. The Britpop of the Nineties had been replaced by warbling women singing with fake husky voices, or middle-aged rock pop that made him want to grab the controls and turn it over. Danny's hand hit his shoulder and squeezed. A squeeze that signified he was becoming morbid again. Introverted and, as Danny so kindly put it, a killjoy.

Joe glanced up from his stool and studied the scratched wooden bar before giving a weak smile. Danny nodded towards the two grinning ladies with a cheeky wink and Joe made an effort to smile at the taller woman. He recognised the signs. Her glances from under long eyelashes, eye contact that lingered a little too long. It was getting late, almost ten-thirty, and he should be thinking of heading off. He had work tomorrow, but that hadn't stopped him before and wouldn't now. That 'one quick drink' had ended up being two or three, then four or five, and now he couldn't remember how many he'd had. The two women Danny was chatting up were smiling and laughing, caressing wine glasses in long slim fingers. The tall blonde glanced at Joe again, cocking her head to the side so her hair fanned out. She swept it all back over one shoulder. What was her name again? She'd told him when Danny invited them over but for the life of him he couldn't remember. Did it start with an A? Annie? Amelia? Something like that. He frowned, trying to remember as she came closer and leaned against the bar. She wasn't dressed in a short skirt or dress, or covered in make-up – the usual Saturday night get-ups. She wore jeans and a tight jumper. She was cute.

'Are you okay?' she asked. 'You don't seem to be enjoying yourself much?'

Joe glanced up and studied her face. She was pretty. At least, she was pretty after the few too many he'd had. Almond-shaped eyes, nice figure. Danny nudged him again and gave him a knowing look. Joe shook his head and returned to his drink. 'I'm fine, thanks.'

He didn't feel like saying anything else right now so tapped his finger in time with the music playing in the background. The trouble was women often took his lack of chit chat as him playing the strong and silent type. It wasn't. He wasn't brooding either. He was just so bloody depressed he often didn't speak at all, for hours, days if he could help it. From the corner of his eye he saw Angela, or whatever her name was, shuffling uncomfortably.

'Do you still work at the estate agent's in town?' she asked, running her fingers down the stem of her empty wine glass.

Joe nodded at the barman and nudged his glass forward. Fred refilled it. He scratched his stubbled cheek. 'Um, yeah. Do you want a drink?' He didn't really want to buy her one, but he had that longing again. A longing to be held, a longing for physical contact, for intimacy. For sex.

A slow smile spread over her face. 'I thought you'd never ask. Dry white wine please,' she said to Fred. Her hair was just like Clara's, the colour of straw. Joe turned away at the familiar surge of nausea that arose whenever he thought of her. His throat tightened. If only things had been different.

Fred delivered his drink and one for . . . Amy? Joe took his and gulped, numbing the pain. If he kept it locked away, he was able to make it through the day pretty much intact and in the evenings threw himself into video games. It was soothing entering another world where he didn't have to be himself.

'You're not very talkative, are you? Just like when you were at school.'

'We were at school together?' he asked, not looking up.

That was the other shitty thing about coming back. He saw all these people he'd gone to school with. All those who'd thought he was cool. Joe scoffed to himself and felt Amanda glance at him. He wasn't cool anymore. He was a loser, the biggest loser he knew, with a giant, steaming turd of a life.

The song had changed and the husky singer sang, 'In the arms of the angels.' *Bollocks*, thought Joe. Every song was about heartbreak or death these days, or something worse. He felt a sudden desire to leave but then that familiar urge for human contact pulled at him, sticking his butt to the seat. He didn't want to talk though. He hated all the questions these women had, like they could fix him if they could just have a little chat about it all.

She giggled. 'Danny remembered me, he told you when we

17

came over. Don't tell me you've forgotten me already?' She wrapped her hair around her finger.

Joe tried to picture what she might have been like when they were at school but he soon gave up. It was so hard to concentrate sometimes. Somehow his mind always wandered back to Clara, as if she was sneaking around in his head, trying to make him deal with it all. He knew she wouldn't want him to be like this, but he couldn't break out of the deep, dark black hole he'd fallen into.

'I'm Annabelle Crawley. I was three years below you at school.'

He nodded. 'Oh yeah, I remember.' He didn't remember. Who remembered kids three years below you at school? You just ignored them, you didn't acknowledge them, or worse, become friends with them.

Annabelle snuggled in closer. 'It's okay. I know you don't have a clue who I am, but I forgive you. You can get to know me now.'

Joe glanced at his watch, knowing exactly how this night would end and, from the gleam in her eye, so did she. The feel of her body pressed into his arm was enough to convince them that another one-night stand was just what he wanted, even though he'd feel empty again in the morning. But swallowing his pint he knew it was pointless thinking any further ahead than the next day, and that was pushing it sometimes. He felt like his soul was lost, roaming somewhere outside his body, out there in the world. It would come back fleetingly during the reprieve of company, only to go missing again. He knew it wouldn't stay this time, but he'd like to feel like himself again, even if it was only for a short while. Turning to Annabelle, he began talking a little more.

Chapter 3

Sandchester

Carol, Esme's mum, sat opposite her at the large kitchen table. From the strange expressions she was making, Esme knew she was fantasising about ways to harm Leo Chalmers. Stephen, Esme's father, sat quietly listening.

'So that's why I'm here, at half past eight on a Thursday morning,' said Esme, examining her mum's floral bathrobe tied around her waist. 'I didn't wake you up, did I?'

'No, dear,' replied Carol. 'We were just having sex—'

'Some tea,' interrupted Stephen, glaring at his wife. 'We were just having some tea. In bed. Watching telly.' He scratched his head and a redness crept out of his stripy pyjama top.

Esme shuddered. Since she had left home after finishing university, and her younger sister had moved out eight years ago, her parents had very much enjoyed a more active sex life. More than once when she'd been home for Christmas, or down for some family occasion, Esme would hear them and bury her head under the pillow. After last Christmas, Leo had insisted they stay at the hotel outside town, even though it would cost them more money to get taxis to and fro. But that wasn't going to happen now, she thought sadly. They wouldn't relish the prospect of having their daughter back home anymore than she wanted to be there, but they were always supportive and just what Esme needed right now. Stephen cocked his head to one side and smiled at his daughter.

'Don't worry, dear,' said her mum. 'You'll get back on your feet and if that Leo turns up here, I shall . . . I shall . . .' She grabbed a dinner knife, covered in marmalade. 'I shall stab him in the back for stabbing you in the back. I can't believe his name's Chalmers. Charm, my arse.'

Esme tried to smile, but tears were forming in her eyes again, even though she was sick of crying. That morning, climbing into the taxi at Sandchester Station, which was unstaffed because no one ever wanted to visit the boring little town, Esme had rubbed at her tired eyes. Turning up at her mum and dad's house, at the age of 33, with all her belongings crammed into one suitcase, and a Christmas pudding under her arm, was thoroughly depressing. At least it hadn't been raining. 'He didn't stab me in the back, Mum. And he didn't say there was anyone else. He just said we were more like friends than, you know.' She blushed and stared down at the table with its red check tablecloth.

'Well, darling,' Carol replied, taking her cup. 'Your room is all yours until you find somewhere else.'

'I don't know how I'll find somewhere else. I need a job first.' She ran a hand through her un-brushed hair and her fingers caught in the knots. She'd never felt so low.

'About that,' said Stephen, pouring another cup of tea. 'We were saving up some money for your wedding.'

'Wedding,' repeated her mother, nodding. She'd always had this weird habit of randomly repeating the last word of other people's sentences.

'But as things have changed, you could use it to put down a deposit on a rental if you like. I'm sure you'll find some work soon, you're so good at your job. But just remember one thing,

Esme.' She paused at her dad's sincere expression. 'Don't ever go backwards. Always move forwards. Going back never helps.'

'Never helps,' repeated Carol. 'That means no going back to that scumbag. Even if he comes crawling on bended knee with the biggest diamond you've ever seen. Men like that don't change.'

'How much do you have saved?' asked Esme.

'About three thousand pounds,' Stephen answered.

Esme raised her head. 'Really? Thank you. Thank you so much. 'It was more than generous and enough to cover not just a deposit but the first few months' rent too. Tears escaped from her eyes and she studied her parents. The wrinkles on her mum's kind, round face crinkled and her dad's mouth lifted into a grin. They were always so kind and supportive. Even if her mum did have homicidal tendencies and her father was now talking in pop-psychology book clichés, they were great parents.

'Have you told your sister yet?' asked Stephen.

'No.' Esme dipped her eyes as if she was six and had been told off.

'Why not?'

'She'll be upset with me for losing my job. She'll think I should've—'

'She will not,' interrupted Carol, now waving the marmalade knife at Esme. 'Alice will be pleased you're home and proud that you stood up for yourself, just like I am. We'll go and see her after breakfast. Little Daniel will be so happy to see his Aunty Ezzy.'

After breakfast, Carol drove them to Alice's house as if she were a Formula One driver in the last race of the season. Esme's fingers ached and her knuckles were white from holding onto the seat. It had been like a terrifying ride at an amusement park. Her ears were ringing from the angry shouting Carol had given every other passing driver. The old Ford had taken ages to heat up as well. They'd sat on the driveway waiting for the windscreen to de-mist while rain began to pour. As November took hold, the weather was wet and cold but without the buzz that December brought. Christmas lights were on here too, but with far less glitz and pizzazz than London. The local radio station insisted on playing the odd Christmas song, and though Leo used to hate it, Esme didn't. She loved Christmas and despite everything, this one at home with her family would be great. They'd eat, drink, laugh and just be together. She wouldn't have to rush back early on Boxing Day morning because Leo couldn't put up with her mum any longer.

Alice opened the front door and stared wide-eyed at her sister. They had the same red hair, inherited from their mother, though Carol now dyed hers platinum-blonde in an ill-advised attempt to reverse the aging process. If her hair had actually gone platinum-blonde it would have looked amazing, but it still went a bit orangey-yellow in places and no one was brave enough to tell her. Alice's figure had grown plump since having Daniel, while Esme's was slim and toned from regular trips the gym, but it was clear to anyone they were family. The London gym Esme and Leo had gone to had been swanky and exclusive – she'd have to start running again or something now she was home. She couldn't afford a gym membership anymore. Yet Esme envied her sister for her absolute contentment with herself and her life.

'Hello, sis,' said Esme, as she approached.

'What are you doing here?' asked Alice, wiping her hands on a tea towel. 'I didn't think we'd see you till Christmas Eve.'

'It's a long story.'

'Aunty Ezzy!' called a little voice from behind Alice's legs.

'Hello, little man,' she replied, whisking her 4-year-old nephew up into a huge hug. Daniel was gorgeous, with red hair and large blue eyes rimmed with thick lashes. Esme squeezed him tight. 'I've missed you so much.'

'Me too. Are you staying here?' he asked, staring up.

'Not in your house, I'm with Granny and Grandpa for a bit.'

Alice frowned and peered at their mum. 'You two better come in and tell me what's going on.'

*

22

Three cups of tea later and everyone in Esme's life was now up to speed on what a disaster it was. Esme stared around the kitchen where every cupboard door and each side of the fridge was covered in her nephew's artwork.

'I can't believe it,' said Alice. 'I just can't believe it.' She glanced from Esme to Carol, until she too began wielding sharp implements clearly imagining harm to Leo.

'I know,' said Carol, 'that's what I said.'

'And we all thought he was getting ready to propose. You said he'd been secretly shopping and organising stuff. You said he'd been looking at jewellery. I just assumed—'

'Me too,' Esme replied. 'And all the gang did as well.'

'As well,' Carol repeated. 'Another woman,' she said after a pause sitting back in her chair at the breakfast bar.

'I don't think there is, Mum,' said Esme. 'He told me he felt we'd just grown apart.'

Alice raised her eyebrows. 'Well, you can stay here as long as you like, you know that. Though I can't promise little man won't wake you up at five-thirty every morning. Oh, and he likes to do that by jumping on your head.'

'Thanks,' replied Esme, grinning. The central heating was on and the house was lovely and warm. Being there with her mum and sister was like being given a great big hug. 'Mum and Dad said they have some money I can use to get a little place while I find a new job.'

'Do you think that's a good idea? Taking on a place while you try and find work?' Alice bustled around the kitchen cleaning the surfaces and loading the dishwasher.

'Don't worry, Alice, I'm sure it'll be fine. I'm going to write my cookbook while I look for work. If I don't try now, when will I ever have the chance again? I need a kitchen to work in and I can't use Mum and Dad's all day with them pottering around me. It'll drive me crazy. And them,' she added, smiling at her mum. 'I was hoping I could pick up a cheap little flat and freelance while I write.'

23

Alice paused and checked on Daniel who, at that precise moment, was trying to fit the television remote control into his mouth. 'Darling, please don't put that in your mouth, or anywhere else for that matter.' He put it down and picked up one of his dad's video games. 'And don't play with that, please? It's Daddy's. Why don't you draw Aunty Ezzy a picture?'

'Ooh, pictures,' said Carol, excitedly. 'I'll go and watch him while you chat to Esme.' She disappeared into the living room happy at the prospect.

'Dad said rental prices are quite cheap at the moment,' Esme continued. 'Mum and Dad gave me enough to cover the deposit and about three months' rent. I really think this is the time to at least try. I don't have commitments like you and I need to make the most of this opportunity.'

Alice wiped over the worktop again. 'You sound like Lola,' she teased.

'I know. Annoying, isn't it?' Esme watched her mum sitting happily with Daniel, kissing his head every few moments. 'Don't tell Mum, but I'm just trying to look on the bright side so she doesn't worry too much. I'm pretty much falling apart internally.' She gave a loud sniff.

Alice, who was just about to fill the kettle again, left it and came over, giving her sister a squeeze. 'I know, Ezzy, but it'll be okay, I promise. And if you're sure this is the right thing to do, I might know someone who can help. Are you really determined to get a place?'

'Definitely. If I live with Mum and Dad for more than a few days, I'll turn suicidal.'

'Okay, well, Joe Holloway might be able to help us.'

'Joe Holloway?' Esme stopped and cupped her hands around her mug. 'Joe who we all fancied like mad at school?'

'Yeah. He's an estate agent.'

'An estate agent? I always thought he'd end up like a spy or something.'

Alice rolled her eyes. 'Anyway, *you* fancied him like mad when we were at school, not me. Rumour has it he's still a bit of a ladies' man. Loves a one-night stand.' She sat opposite and took Esme's hands. 'Are you sure getting a place isn't too risky?'

'If the worst happens, I'll only be renting so I can just move back home. I won't end up in lots of debt. And what have I got to lose? I'm 33, Alice. I need to take this chance now. If I don't, I'll get back into the nine to five, and keep putting it off. You know what it's like, there's never a perfect time, is there?'

Alice didn't have a chance to answer as Esme's phone started ringing. It was Helena. 'Hey, Hels, everything okay?' There was a pause on the other end of the line. 'Helena? Are you all right?'

'Umm . . . not really, love, I've got some bad news.'

Esme's heart sank. What else could've happened? It was only ten o'clock. What else could have gone wrong already? Was she being sued by Felicity? Oh, please God, don't let her be sued by Felicity. 'What is it?'

'I'm so sorry, honey, but Mark just told me he thinks Leo's moving in some new woman.'

'What?'

'I hate telling you this over the phone but Mark just rang him to arrange coming to get your stuff. He thought the quicker we get this all sorted the better. Leo said he needs as much out as possible in the next few days and Mark said, "Why? Have you got someone moving in already?" and he went really quiet and mumbled something, then said he had to go and hung up. We just thought you should know.'

Esme felt numb and her mind stopped working. 'Oh, right.' The trouble was it had been Leo's place originally and she'd moved in three years ago, but it had never completely felt like home. Without thinking, he'd refer to it as *his* place and it had stung. Now he'd tossed her out and moved someone else in. The scumbag.

'Mark's going to get the stuff tomorrow; I think Eric's helping. I'm so sorry, honey. It might just be a guilty conscience, but you know what Mark's like. He's got second sight when it comes to this sort of thing. He doesn't normally get signs wrong.'

Esme nodded, but forgot to speak, her mind frozen. Like a fool she'd believed Leo when he said he thought they'd become more like friends and had sat here defending him to her mum and sister. Esme had hated the idea of their relationship ending but could accept it if growing apart was the reason. It felt more respectful somehow for them to have simply changed over time. But this? Cheating? This was just nasty.

'Esme?'

'Can I speak to you later, Helena? I'm with Alice right now.'

'Yeah, of course. I'm so sorry, honey. We all love you and he's a shit. Say hi to Alice for me.' Esme hung up and told Alice.

'That dirty rotten bastard,' Alice shouted, then glanced over her shoulder to check Daniel hadn't come into the kitchen. 'He must have been seeing her behind your back for ages. You don't just move someone in a day after you've chucked your current girlfriend unless something has been going on for a while. He must have had it all planned. What an absolute . . . ' She trailed away seeing Esme's face.

A sharp pain shot though her temples and her head ached. Her heart thumped hard in her chest. At least it was still beating, she reminded herself. Even with all this. It was broken, but beating. Alice took Esme's hands in hers and looked her straight in the eye.

'I'm so sorry, Ezzy. But we'll make this work, I promise. All of us together. We'll make this work. And soon this'll be the best thing that's ever happened to you.'

Esme placed her hand on top of Alice's, sniffing back tears. 'I love you, sis. But we'd better remove all the sharp objects before we tell Mum.' Alice nodded and quickly hid the knife block behind the bread bin.

As expected, Carol went off like a rocket and when later that day Esme told her dad, he pursed his lips in outrage, which was quite a lot from him. That night, in the little box room at her parents' house, in her old single bed, Esme cried and cried until she could hardly breathe. A pile of tissues lay on the floor beside her and were scattered over the duvet. Her old Nirvana posters stared at her, Kurt Cobain's eyes making her feel watched and judged. Finally, in the early hours of the morning, in the still, quiet house, in the still, quiet cul-de-sac, Esme fell asleep, wondering how she'd gone from living her best life to being at the bottom of the scrap heap without a hope in hells chance of climbing back up to the top.

Chapter 4

Sandchester

Joe scratched the back of his head, checked around for customers, and gave the photocopier a swift kick. The damn thing was playing up again and had been for ages. If the paper wasn't getting stuck, it decided it had run out of toner and he had to get down on his hands and knees and wiggle different bits about until the annoying red light stopped flashing. It wasn't that he knew what he was doing. It was just that being the youngest of the office staff by a good twenty years, it was supposed he knew more about technology than the rest of them. He didn't.

Fridays at the estate agents were always quiet for some reason. Maybe people didn't want the hassle of tidying their houses and making them presentable for viewings, and those who were buying left all the looking for Saturdays, when they could do so without worrying about taking time off work. Either way, he was fed up. He'd completed all the admin he had to do, and the four games of solitaire he'd just played on his computer had done nothing to alleviate his boredom.

The photocopier spluttered into life and kicked out the paper he had been waiting for, as well as a few extra sheets for good measure. He took them and ran a finger round the collar of his shirt. He was sweating. In November. The radiators were on full blast and old Mr Rigby, who owned the business, insisted on having a couple of heaters on as well. It was only about eight degrees outside, but it was as hot as Dubai in here – a place he would definitely rather be right now.

Even though he'd been back for a long time, he was still getting used to working nine to five back in England. After moving to Australia with his girlfriend, Clara, he'd worked a normal working week. But with long lunch hours, swims before work, and barbecues on the beach after, it had made the slog of the daily grind so much easier to bear. He stared out of the window at the threatening grey sky and pouring rain, and sighed. The landline on his desk rang and he hurried over to answer it. 'Good morning, Rigby Estate Agents, Joe speaking. How can I help?'

'Hi, Joe?' said a singsong female voice.

'Hi, how can I help?' He didn't recognise the voice.

'It's Annabelle.'

'Annabelle?'

'Yes, Annabelle.' She sounded annoyed now. 'We met in the pub the other night and then we . . . we went back to yours.'

'Oh yes. I remember.' He did, just about. He'd made sure they hadn't swapped numbers, he didn't want to lead her on, but if she'd found the work number and rung that, she clearly wanted more than he could give. He realised he'd been quiet for a while and glanced up to see Mr Rigby smiling at him. Keeping his voice professional, he asked, 'What can I help you with?'

'I was wondering if you wanted to have dinner sometime?'

'Yeah, um, no, thanks.' There was a sharp intake of breath at the other end of the line. 'What I mean is . . .' He leaned down behind his desk, pretending to look for something in the bottom drawer. He didn't want the whole office to hear him and brushing off a lady could be quite difficult sometimes. He knew that from experience. Joe kept his voice low. 'The other night was great, but

I'm not looking for anything more right now. Nothing serious.' It was a bit of a corny line but he'd used it before and it had worked fairly well. Plus he meant it. He wasn't leading anyone on. He wouldn't do that. He mentally crossed his fingers, hoping it would work again now. Annabelle said nothing and he could feel the anger emanating from her and travelling over the air waves.

'Oh. Okay.' Her voice was curt and clipped. 'Well, I guess I'll see you around then?'

'Yeah, okay. Bye.'

She hung up and Joe sat up from behind his desk. Calls like that were the worst part of one-night stands. The fact that they weren't fulfilling didn't bother him. He didn't want to be fulfilled. He couldn't anymore. Sometimes, like with Amy – no, Annabelle – he felt bad for a while, but he never promised them anything more. He wasn't a complete bastard. Joe was adjusting his tie when the office phone on his desk rang again. 'Good morning, Rigby Estate Agents, Joe speaking. How can I help?'

'Hi? Is that Joe Holloway?'

He didn't recognise the female voice on the other end of the line, and his brow wrinkled. He hoped this wasn't another one-night stand wanting more. Before Annabelle, his last one had been a few months ago, so it would be odd her calling now. Why did he do this to himself? It never helped and it just caused more trouble. If they were going to start phoning him at work, he could lose his job. 'Yes, this is Joe. How can I help?'

'It's Alice Potts. I'm looking for some properties for my sister, Esme.'

'Alice?'

Oh God, was this Annabelle calling back pretending to be a customer? Trust him to pick a psycho. He gazed at the rain battering against the large glass windows and pictured her suddenly standing there, wielding a knife. Joe shuddered but tried to remain professional. Mr Rigby was typing slowly with two fingers and hadn't seemed to notice.

'Alice and Sean Potts. You helped my husband and I find our first house.' Alice laughed. 'You'd know me better as Alice Kendrick. We were at school at the same time. My sister, Esme, was in your year, I was a year below.'

A small smile pulled the corner of his mouth upwards. 'Alice and Esme Kendrick? Yeah, I remember you guys now. I thought Esme moved to London?' She'd been the talk of the town having worked hard to get to a good London university and then found a job working for a television company. 'She was one of the major success stories of our school. Not like the rest of us normal folk.' He sat back in his chair and played with the telephone cord.

'Yeah, my sister was always super-focused. So, she was hoping to see some places tomorrow. Is there any chance you could line up a few viewings?'

'Yeah, sure,' Joe replied, grabbing his notebook and pen. It didn't give him much time, and he wondered what the rush was, but still, business was a good thing. 'Is she renting or buying?'

'Renting.'

'Any particular times for the viewings?'

'Nope. She's free all day.'

He made a note. 'And what about budget? What type of properties does she like?'

'Budget needs to be as small as possible. She doesn't want to spend much per month and as beggars can't be choosers, just show her anything that's cheap.'

That was odd, but he made a note anyway. 'Okay, I'll call you later with the details. Can you give me your number? Or should I take Esme's?'

Alice hesitated for a moment before replying. 'No, take mine. She's not really ready to . . . no, never mind. But if you could call me, that'd be great.'

Joe took the details and hung up. Esme Kendrick? Now there was a turn up. But what was Alice going to say? *She's not really ready to what?* He rested his elbows on the desk, tapping his pen against his notepad. Looks like things were going well for Esme and her boyfriend, presuming she had one, if they were getting a place down here as well as having one in London. Of course she'd have a boyfriend. She was probably married by now, or at least engaged. She was always the most intelligent, not to mention the prettiest, girl at school. Joe could picture her now as a grown woman all pale-skinned and wide-eyed, with that mop of red curls like some Highland beauty from the Middle Ages.

He went to the filing cabinet and pulled out some brochures for the cheapest rental properties. If it was a holiday or weekend place, why rent? And why the tight budget? It all seemed very strange, but before he could think about it any further, an old male voice from the other side of the office said, 'Joe, this bloody printer is messing about again. Can you come and unblock it?'

Filing his questions at the back of his mind, Joe closed the drawer, took a deep breath and replied. 'Yes, Mr Rigby. On my way.'

Chapter 5

London

Leo paced the streets of London, taking long confident strides amongst the crowds of people leisurely ambling along. The rain was pouring down in great, heavy sheets and the dark sky was solid with cloud. He tutted as a couple came to a sudden stop in front of him to look in a shop window at the elaborate Christmas-themed decorations. With a sarcastic, 'Excuse me,' he edged around them and carried on, wishing he was indoors, dry and warm, staring out of his apartment window at the priceless view beyond. He loved looking out of that window at the skyline, a mixture of grand buildings and tall grey skyscrapers.

It wasn't a priceless view though, was it? he mused. It had cost a hell of a lot of money – too much money, some had said – but that was London, and London prices. Leo pulled the collar of his coat in tighter. You had to invest in yourself and your future – that's what people didn't understand. No one liked to admit it, but the address on your CV could make all the difference to getting that job or not. Take Esme. She'd struggled with finding permanent work until she moved in with him and then, wham, she got that amazing job with Felicity Fenchurch. He'd always prided himself on helping her career like that, encouraging her to be as ambitious as him. It was such a shame it ended the way it did. Esme's job and them. But then, she'd always been headstrong and now she'd thrown away her career.

Leo overtook a group of tourists and in his pocket, he tightened his grip on the ring he had bought Veronica. It wasn't an engagement ring, though he had secretly looked at those too, but he didn't want to rush too much. *Poor Esme.* From the look on her face that night, it was almost as if she thought he was going to propose or spring a romantic holiday on her. She'd always been fanciful though and would often let her imagination run wild. The day after they'd split, she'd come at the crack of dawn, even before he was up for the gym, and packed a suitcase, clearing out her clothes and special mementoes, like her memory box. She hadn't said a word, just moved silently around the room. At first, he'd pretended to be asleep but, realising he couldn't do that forever, he'd gone and hidden in the bathroom, thankful she had cleared that first. It wasn't cowardly, he told himself. It was tactful and made things easier for her. It was the least he could do. She must be devastated. But she'd be fine. She was one of those people who'd always be fine. Later, she had texted saying Mark would come and get the last few bits when it was convenient, and he was to contact Mark directly to arrange it. She didn't want to speak to him, or see him, and to be honest, he couldn't blame her. He knew deep down he should have given her more time, but it was difficult to say no to Veronica.

Swerving to the right and cutting up a middle-aged man who was trundling along at a snail's pace, staring up at all the Christmas lights, Leo charged down the tube station steps. The warm air rose up to grab him, a sudden contrast to the cold air outside. He was meeting Veronica soon and he couldn't wait to give her the ring. He was sure she'd love it. Still, as sad as things were with Esme, at least now he was now able to move on and be with someone who got him. Someone who was just as ambitious as him. The type of person he was meant to be with. Leo smiled to himself. Veronica was equally as driven, strong and determined, but if she had one fault, it was that she was a little bossy. She had to be, he supposed, being his boss and leading the team, but sometimes she forgot to turn it off when they were together. Since yesterday morning, when he told her Esme had gone, taking most of her stuff, she'd been demanding Leo chase Esme to confirm when she'd remove the last of her things. He'd told her he couldn't do it yet – it had only been two days since he'd ended it. To phone now would be callous in the extreme, but it hadn't stopped her mentioning it again in the office this afternoon. Leo suspected Mark knew that he'd allowed someone else to move in already and would no doubt have told Esme. He was glad he didn't have to face her at the moment when it would still be raw and hurtful for her.

A train pulled in and he jumped on. Leo was looking forward to going back to his flat and pictured the piles of Veronica's things already dotted here and there – a spare bag, a book – happy that he'd done the right thing. Esme's lack of ambition had been holding him back from his life goals for a long time now. Another reason why Veronica was the perfect partner for him. That and her insanely long legs. Together they could achieve anything. They'd started their affair six months before he'd broken up with Esme and a fleeting regret for cheating on her passed through him but quickly faded. Sometimes these things happened.

He was meeting Veronica at the flat and then they were going to a fancy restaurant where he'd give her the ring. Every time he tried to take Esme to a fancy restaurant she had this annoying habit of trying to figure out exactly what was in a dish and how she could cook it. It had been endearing at first but as things had started to go wrong, he'd found it boring. There was no way Veronica would do something like that. The new watch on his wrist shone as he reached his arm up to hold onto the bar. Whilst at the jeweller's he'd bought himself a new watch. Well, why shouldn't he? He'd been through a lot lately, he deserved a little treat.

Chapter 6

Sandchester

'So, I've got these three properties that are in your price range,' said Joe, handing Esme the details on a freezing cold Saturday morning. 'They're all vacant so we can see them today.'

Esme took them and peeked at Joe over the top of the paper, pretending to read. He had been gorgeous at school, in that bad boy kind of way, with black hair worn long at the front so it flopped into his sea green eyes. He'd looked like something from a boy band. His untucked shirt always hung loose and his school tie was short and fat, like the cool kids wore them. Esme would go the long way round to science so she could pass him on her way and see him leaning back against the wall with one leg bent. Now, he was handsome in a mature I-know-what-I'm-doing kind of way. His hair was cut short and his eyes, though ringed gently with crow's feet, were intelligent and kind. His grin was still wide, pulling up slightly more at one side, but he had straight white teeth and a chiselled jaw. Esme had met him at the estate agent's at nine o'clock and been nervous since she got up. And not just at the idea of finding a new place to live. Doubts were still ringing in her brain that she was making another huge mistake, going from one terrible decision to another. But she was also anxious about seeing Joe again. She'd wondered if he was still as handsome and if his face had aged well, but he wasn't on Facebook and Esme hadn't wanted to ask Alice for fear of teasing.

'Which one did you want to look at first?' Joe asked, putting his hands in his pockets. He was wearing a well-cut navy suit with a pale blue shirt and dark blue tie.

'Oh, umm . . .' Esme checked the details again and tried to ignore the blush creeping up her cheeks. The first property was a small flat on the seafront in a converted Georgian house. It had sconces and high ceilings, and great views onto the beach. The second was an even smaller flat above a takeaway pizza place at the horrid end of the high street – Esme put that one to the back. The third and final property was a shabby-looking cottage on the outskirts of town, with views over the fields.

'Shall we go to the seafront flat first?' said Esme. 'It looks fabulous.' She imagined large sash windows with a built-in seat where she could sit and read her cookery books or watch winter storms roll in from the sea.

'Sure thing.' He grabbed his coat and opened the door for her. Esme retied the belt on hers as a cold wind blasted in.

The sky was a dense pale grey from the rain clouds gathering to bring another damp, cold day. A strong wind blew her curls over her face and she tugged her hat down onto her head to keep them at bay. She'd been back home for three days now and her head and heart still ached for Leo and the life she'd left in her favourite city on earth – London. Would she ever get that life back again?

Last night she'd disappeared to her room after dinner like a sulky teenager, and dredged through her phone, staring at the photos of her and Leo together, hoping to spot signs of when things had begun to go wrong. No clues had been forthcoming. He was always smiling and had his arms around her. She'd been completely blind-sided by their break-up; had no idea it was coming. She'd trusted him when he'd said he was working late because they were busy at work. She'd even been pleased for him, knowing how much his career meant to him. But now she knew he'd been lying. They'd been together for five years and she'd been so sure he'd propose soon. Then last month, after checking their internet history when looking for a recipe she'd come across but forgotten to bookmark, she found he'd been looking at jewellery, engagement rings to be precise, and had assumed it couldn't be long. She'd thought that his secrecy was him planning something big. She'd been so stupid.

Glancing towards Joe as he strode to his car, Esme gave herself a mental shake. Today she had to try and look forward, look to the future. And there was always something fun about nosing around other people's houses. This excitement, mixed with her nerves at being in such close proximity to Joe, knotted her stomach as she climbed into his waiting car.

*

Joe watched Esme yank the green beanie hat down onto her head and wondered what on earth she was doing back in boring old Sandchester. Usually couples looking for holiday homes viewed everything together – quite nauseating. All the lovey-doveycuddliness as they 'ummed' and 'awwed' over period features or places that were within easy reach of the motorways or train station. Perhaps her other half was one of those uber-busy, suited and booted, successful types. A doctor saving lives, or a surgeon elbow-deep in brains curing epilepsy. Maybe he was a scientist building space rockets, or perhaps creating a vaccine for space flu. Whatever he did, Joe bet it was essential or pioneering, or life-saving. Something epic that made his being an estate agent seem normal and boring. There wasn't a ring on her finger, though. No big shiny diamond or wedding band, so they hadn't got that far yet. Not that it was any of his business, he reminded himself.

Keeping his eyes on the path avoiding the puddles, he unlocked the car. He'd forgotten how pretty Esme was. In fact, she was even prettier now than she had been back then. In her teens she'd been gangly — all arms and legs that didn't seem to work properly. She'd been clumsy, he remembered with a smile. Now she was much more in proportion, had grown into herself. 'So, how's life?' he asked, climbing into the driver's seat.

Esme hesitated. 'Oh, you know . . . fine.'

The radio kicked out a Christmas song and Esme shivered. Joe reached over and turned the heater on. From the pause, he guessed she didn't want to talk about it to him which he could understand. He was a stranger.

'What about you?' she asked, staring out the window. 'What have you been up to since school?'

His mind flew to Clara and a sharp pain shot into his heart. 'The usual stuff,' he replied, ensuring his voice was level and calm. 'Uni, a bit of travelling. I went to Australia for a while.' That was it. That was all he could manage. Before she asked anymore questions, he said, 'So you want to see the seafront property first? It's great, but it's not super-huge. With the budget you've got, I'm afraid you won't get lots and lots of space.'

'That's okay. I just need a decent-sized kitchen, that's all.' Her voice carried a slightly resigned tone. Joe glanced at her. She had a pretty profile and the mass of red curls were poking out from under her green beanie hat, emphasising the beautiful deep colour of her hair.

'So you still love cooking and all that sort of stuff?'

'Yep, I do.' Esme smiled. 'Cooking always makes me feel better. You *were* the only one who paid attention in home economics.'

'I don't know why you lot hated it so much.'

He shrugged. 'We were 15 and knew about microwavable burgers. To us, there was no point in cooking anything else.'

Esme laughed. 'I suppose not. Though microwavable burgers are super-gross.'

'They really are,' he said, laughing too. 'I have no idea why I ate them. It was like meat-flavoured cardboard in actual cardboard.'

As they sped through the town, from the corner of his eye,

Joe saw her watch out of the window. 'The town hasn't changed much, has it? Esme asked, glancing towards him.

Apart from some new-build housing developments, it hadn't. The streets were lined with boring bungalows and quiet suburban cul-de-sacs. A few new coffee shops had opened up on the high street but that was about all. It wasn't a match for Oxford Street. On the radio the DJ announced another Christmas song. Some people had already started decorating. and here and there large inflatable Santas loomed out of front gardens or from behind hedges. He thought it was a bit early, personally.

Joe drove along the seafront, following the sea to the far end of town and pulled up in front of a beautiful Georgian house that had been divided into flats. Esme climbed out of the car and stood back to admire the large black front door and sash windows. 'All you have to do is cross the road and you're right on the beach,' said Joe. The grey clouds had followed them from the town centre and a light rain began to fall. He pulled out the keys and opened the main door. 'It's the top flat.'

Esme climbed the stairs two at a time, almost beating him to the top and he was hopeful she'd like it. He found the front door keys and led them inside. They walked down a small hall, so small in fact, they nearly had to go sideways like a crab, emerging into a tiny sitting room, off which was an even smaller kitchen. Esme's face clouded. Joe knew that look but gave her a moment to look around. 'What do you think?' he asked, when she came back into the sitting room after checking out the rest of the flat, but he could already guess the answer; her eyes weren't sparkling as they had outside.

'I don't think the kitchen area is quite big enough for what I need.'

'What do you need it for exactly?' asked Joe, looking confused. He'd assumed this was some kind of weekend or holiday flat where even the most ardent of bakers would lay off the self-catering.

'I'll be doing a lot of cooking. So I need some decent workspace.'

'Right.' Joe nodded. That was weird. Most people did the

minimum amount of cooking in their holiday homes, preferring to eat out. But then Esme had always been different. Looking around, the cooker was squeezed into a corner, the fridge stuck out and there were only three cupboards and a tiny bit of workspace. They'd called it a galley kitchen in the details but even that was pushing it. 'Are you going to be here a lot then?'

Esme looked down at the floor, her cheeks colouring. 'I'm, umm, I'm having a bit of a change of direction.'

That didn't sound too good, but he didn't want to pry. 'Oh, okay.'

She was walking around the tiny kitchen opening and closing the cupboard doors. 'I, umm, I left my job in London and then . . . then my boyfriend and I broke up, so I'm back here for a bit. I'm trying to make a new start.'

Joe raised his eyebrows. He hadn't imagined it was anything so bad and was even more surprised that she'd told him so openly. Then he remembered that she'd always been honest and outspoken at school. 'Sorry. That's really tough.'

Esme scratched her head underneath her hat. Her eyes were so sad and her pale skin resembled porcelain. A part of him wanted to make her feel better, to let her know she wasn't alone in her heartbreak, but he couldn't get the words out. 'Which one would you like to try next then? I'm guessing this is a no-go?'

Esme gave a polite smile. 'If this were bigger, it'd be perfect. I'd love to live by the sea.'

'The only thing I've got like this that's larger is double the price.'

Esme frowned. 'I know I've got limited options.'

'What about the flat in Palmerston Road? The one above the pizza shop?' He tried to sound cheerful but was pretty sure it wouldn't be her thing.

'I have to be honest, I'm not keen on the pizza place.'

'It's not actually in a pizza shop,' replied Joe, smiling.

'Above it, then. I bet it smells of greasy pizza all the time,' Esme said, aimlessly walking to and fro.

'It doesn't. It's quite nice inside. It'll just get a bit noisy when the pubs kick out. It's the best pizza place in town.'

Esme's eyes widened and a smile lit her face. 'Are you speaking from experience?'

'I am.' He grinned.

'Well, I'll make a note to try it, but I don't really want to live above it. Besides, I make a mean pizza myself with fresh tomato sauce, basil, olives and sautéed artichokes. It's really good.'

The thought of it made him hungry. 'That sounds amazing. I've never had things like that on a pizza before. I stick with pepperoni, or tuna if I'm on a diet.'

Esme giggled. 'I don't think pizza is a diet dish even if it has tuna on it.' A slight glow came to her cheeks and she turned one of the brochures over in her hands. 'What's the deal with this cottage?'

'Ahh, now, that's a bit of an oddity.' Knowing the state of it, he hesitated. 'It's only just come onto the books, so we haven't had a chance to clean it yet. It belonged to an old woman who passed away. The family are looking for a buyer, but they're happy to rent it too, just so long as the building's in use. It doesn't have central heating, but it is full of character. It's surrounded by the countryside and I think it's one of the most unusual properties we've ever had. Want to have a look?'

Esme nodded. 'It sounds interesting.'

'It just needs a little bit of TLC.'

'Don't we all?' A shadow came over Esme's face. How she was so positive when she'd had such a terrible time, he didn't know.

A moment's silence fell between them and Joe read the brochure for the flat above the pizza shop. To be fair, it did look a bit grubby and the kitchen there was tiny. The owners obviously thought their tenants would survive on pizza from downstairs. He made a mental note to redo the photos when he was finished with Esme. She wandered to the window and took one last look out to sea before following him out of the flat.

Joe drove them to the outskirts of town, leaving behind the unremarkable new-builds and ordinary streets lined with terraced houses. The roads gave way to a narrow country lane, widening here and there for cars to pass. Before long, field upon field lined the sides of the road. Some held horses covered with heavy blankets and they seemed happy enough roaming about in the cold; others were bare and the smell of damp mud followed them. They turned off the main lane and drove down a narrow dirt track until the cottage came into view. They drew closer and Joe saw a smile creep over Esme's lips.

As decrepit as it was, it was pretty and picturesque, as it said in the brochure. A rose bush climbed up either side of the front door and though no flowers were growing at this time of year, it didn't look bleak. Small, hardy bushes of rosemary grew around the walls of the house here and there, haphazardly marking the boundary. A couple of tiles were hanging at odd angles on the roof, and the nearest neighbours were a mile and a half east. If she was going to be clattering around in the kitchen at all times of the day or night, which he suspected she would be, there would be no one nearby to bother her. 'What do you think?' asked Joe, pulling on the handbrake.

'It's like a fairytale.' Esme grinned at him and climbed out the car. She walked to the door and pulled back some of the bare branches of a rose bush climbing up the outside to reveal a name plaque. Mr Rigby must have missed it when he came to value the property and take the photos. 'Mistletoe Cottage,' Esme read aloud. From her tone he wasn't sure if she liked it or not, then turning back, she grinned.

'Yeah, that's the name of the place. Listen, I know it's quite isolated but all the local supermarkets deliver out here, as well as the takeaways, not that you'll be needing those.' He pulled up the collar of his coat as a gust of wind swept around them, but at least the drizzle had eased off. 'Also it's only a twenty-minute walk into town.'

'What's over there?' Esme asked, pointing to a large wood on the brow of a nearby hill.

'That's Parkin Wood. It's a great place to walk. There are tracks to follow and streams and stuff. There's nothing scary over there.'

She nodded and turned again to look at the cottage. 'I like it.'

'Just remember what I said about the inside, okay? It's not modern and new and shiny. It's all a bit old and dusty.'

Esme frowned. 'That's not very estate agenty of you, is it? Aren't you supposed to be glossing over all the terrible things and telling me it's a great opportunity or something like that?'

'It's a bit late now,' he said with a smile. 'You already know about the ancient decor and no central heating.'

'That's true.'

His voice softened. 'If you like it, then great, but I'm not going to give you the hard sell. You need to know warts and all what's going on with this place.'

She turned to look at him and he was caught by the sincerity in her eyes. 'Thank you, I appreciate it.' Just as a blush rose up her cheeks, she looked away. 'Can we have a look inside?'

'Of course.' Joe fumbled in his pocket and found the correct keys. He opened the front door and held it for Esme to enter, then switched on the light as it was so dark. Esme gasped.

The open-plan living room was full of old furniture. Two large comfortable-looking sofas sat around a Seventies coffee table in front of an open fire. In the corner, an old lamp with a rose-patterned fringed shade stood next to the window. Only a wooden workbench separated the kitchen and living room. On the other side of this, a long unit with an old-fashioned butlers sink sat underneath a huge window with views out to the back garden. Esme went and peered out. It was hard to see where the garden finished and the fields began; all around there was nothing but green.

Esme glanced at Joe and he saw the light in her eyes. They

were a beautiful amber colour, like golden syrup, and her pale skin glowed luminescent in the winter light. Something happened to his heart and he felt it beat for the first time since he and Clara had split up. He shook his head to chase the thoughts away. 'Do you like it?'

'It's amazing,' Esme replied, looking around her.

'It comes with all this stuff, too. You wouldn't need any furniture.' Esme focused on the tiny fridge making a strange humming sound. 'Well, maybe a new fridge. Is this enough workspace for you?'

'Yes, definitely,' she answered, running her fingers over the heavy wood of the worktop. Her elegant fingers traced the nicks and dents made over time.

'Did you want to see upstairs?'

Esme nodded and followed Joe up the rickety wooden stairs. The top floor had two bedrooms and a small bathroom. To say it was dated was an understatement. The bathroom furniture, while clean, was avocado green, and the tiles were salmon pink. The two bedrooms were on the small side; it would be a squeeze to get anything other than a double bed in them. Giant cobwebs lined the corners of every ceiling. The place needed a good clean but was structurally sound. Esme darted here and there while Joe struggled to keep up. 'What do you think then?' he asked when, on the landing, she finally stood still.

'I love it,' she muttered more to herself than him, then cleared her throat. 'I love it.'

'Are you sure?' Joe asked. She'd had such a rough time, he didn't want her making a mistake.

'I am,' she nodded, enthusiastically. 'It just feels right. It's hard to explain.'

Joe stood watching her. The look on her face showed how much she loved it. Her eyes gleamed and she was unable to stay still. She walked back downstairs and he trailed after her. 'You do remember it hasn't got any central heating, don't you?'

'It's fine. I'll just wear lots of jumpers.' Esme read the brochure again. 'I'm going to do it. I'm going to take this one.'

'This one is much cheaper than the rest,' said Joe, reminding himself he was working. And yet, he wavered, not wanting to add to her already difficult life. 'Are you sure? You can always have a second viewing another day, if you want?'

Esme gave a wry smile. 'Why are you trying to dissuade me?'

He clutched the keys and dropped his eyes to the floor. 'I just want you to know what you're getting into. We can make some bad decisions when we're recovering from a broken heart.'

Esme smiled. 'I'm sure, okay? If there's one thing you should know about me, Joe Holloway, it's that I know my own mind. Heartbreak or no.'

'Yeah, I remember from home economics,' he replied, smoothing down the back of his hair. 'You used to argue with the teacher *all* the time.' Her using his full name, like the teachers had at school brought a strange tingle to his chest and without really thinking he placed his hand there. 'Come on then, let's get the paperwork sorted.'

Chapter 7

Sandchester

The paperwork was signed that afternoon and by the time Saturday evening came, the sky dark and the wind beginning to groan, Esme was officially the new tenant. When she went home and told her mum, she felt a small bubble of excitement about life for the first time since it had all come tumbling down around her. As much as her heart was still shattered into a hundred pieces, she wasn't one for sulking or staying still. She was lucky to have the money from her parents; not many people would get such a chance, and she was determined to make the best of it. Having said that, her mum still had some reservations.

'So you're becoming a hermit?' asked Carol, furiously cleaning the kitchen table, her features tight with worry. And considering she didn't furiously clean anything unless she really had to, it showed the depth of her concern.

'I'm not, Mum. I can still walk into town from there. I just need a torch when it gets dark.'

'You'll get murdered,' Carol replied, her voice rising a little.

'No, she won't, dear,' said Stephen. 'There was more chance

of that happening in London than there is here in Sandchester. She'll be fine. Well done, love. Good work.'

Esme smiled.

'Are you sure about this?' Carol asked, calming down a little. 'I don't like the idea of my baby girl being out there in the middle of the woods all on her own.'

'Oh, Mum,' Esme had replied, getting up from the breakfast bar and giving her mum a big hug. 'It's not in the middle of the woods, it's just on the outskirts of town and I am sure about it. Even if I wasn't, it's too late now. I signed the paperwork earlier.'

Leaving the cloth, Carol stood up straighter, a smile beginning to light her face. 'Well, I suppose we'd better have a drink and celebrate then.' Stephen opened a bottle of fizz and Esme couldn't help but count her lucky stars at having such supportive parents. 'To new beginnings,' Carol said.

'To new beginnings,' Esme repeated and felt a little of her heartbreak soften.

*

Esme moved in the next morning with her few meagre possessions and set about cleaning everything. Everyone had offered to help, including Alice, but for some reason she wanted to do this on her own. When she'd moved in with Leo, he'd been so set on where everything had to go, and knowing how organised he was, she hadn't argued. He'd always been fastidious and she didn't want to disrupt his life as she was moving into his place. She wanted to slot into it gently because he'd said it became *their* place that day, but in reality, it had always been his. This was hers, and Esme wanted to clean the place herself with music blaring out, in a bid to stamp her authority on the cottage, and on her life. Somehow, it felt like an important marker, the start of a new phase, even though she hoped it was only a temporary stop, and she'd be back in London before too long.

When her friends arrived late Sunday morning, when the sky was pale and filled with the watery winter sun, she could see their panicked faces through the windscreen before they'd even got out of the car. Mark, Helena and Lola climbed out, muttering to each other, but Esme couldn't make out what was said until she opened the solid wood front door.

'Sweetie, what have you done?' asked Mark, walking over to give her a hug. A dark scarf was wrapped high around his neck making the bright blue of his eyes stand out against his beautiful olive skin. 'You're going to live in a gingerbread house in the middle of nowhere. Like a witch.'

'It's not that bad,' Esme replied, crossing her arms over her chest trying not to shiver. She stood next to him facing the cottage and cocked her head. 'Okay, so it is a bit crazy old lady, but it's so sweet and cosy inside. And you'll never guess what it's called?'

'What?' asked Lola.

'Mistletoe Cottage! How cute is that! It grows in the trees around here as well. Look.' Esme pointed to a tall tree to the right of the cottage and the bright green mistletoe encircling its branches.

Mark paused. 'Are you telling me you know different types of plants already? You're getting countrified.'

'I'm from the country, Mark. I've always been countrified. It just wore off a bit in London. Believe me, I still found myself saying things like "Ooo, it's going to rain," every time I came home and saw a cow sitting down.' Mark stared, astonished.

'Well, I love it,' said Lola, smiling. 'And us country folk always say weird things like that. My mum used to say wind from the east for two weeks at least when we were facing a cold snap—'

'Or saluting magpies,' added Esme.

'Sweet Barbra Streisand,' Mark mumbled, then smiled broadly. 'But it is actually very cute, even though it's in the middle of nowhere. Did you know we couldn't use the satnav to get here? It tried to take us into a field. We got a very strange look from a horse when we pulled up at its gate. It's a good job you texted us directions.'

Helena's eyes were wide as she tried her best to smile. 'Who was the last person to live here?'

Esme stared at the ground and mumbled, 'A crazy old lady. But it's much better now I've cleaned up.'

'I'm telling you now, my sweet,' said Mark, 'you are not buying any cats.'

'Deal,' Esme replied, and led them inside.

Esme sat on the old worn sofa, now covered with pretty throws and cushions donated by Carol and Alice. Leo hadn't liked cushions. He found them annoying, so Esme hadn't ever really bought any, but as this was *her* home, she could decorate it however she wished. Joe had even said she could paint if she wanted too; the landlord didn't mind at all. The owners didn't care what she did as long as the rent was paid and someone was in there so it didn't get damp. Mark brushed the seat with his hands before sitting and Esme tutted at him before bringing over a tray with steaming cups of tea.

'It does have a certain something,' said Lola. 'It's old-fashioned and homely.'

'I think it's called shabby chic,' Esme replied.

'Definitely shabby, sweetie, not so much chic.' After gawping around, Mark gave Esme a reassuring grin. 'But I agree, it does have a certain something. It's bloody cold though.'

'It doesn't have central heating,' Esme replied.

Mark's astonishment returned and Esme had to stop herself laughing at his incredulous expression. 'How do you keep warm?'

'I've got a log fire but I don't know how to light it. So it's lots of jumpers and this little four-bar fire-thing Dad gave me. I might even treat myself to some thermals.'

'Jesus wept,' he replied, shaking his head.

Lola sat forward and took a cup of tea. 'I've been thinking about this whole cookbook thing.' Esme worried she was going to say she'd changed her mind and now thought it all a terrible idea, or that Esme was mental. 'I think you should start a blog while you do it and record the recipes you test.'

'Me? Write a blog?' Esme fiddled with the corner of a cushion. Technology wasn't her strong point and whilst she was quite outgoing, did the world care what she had to say?

Helena brightened. 'Lola, that's a great idea. Esme, you should totally write a blog, you'd be amazing. And if you're cooking and stuff, testing recipes, you could post all the ones you're not going to use in the book.'

Esme considered this new development. Lola did work in marketing, which meant she knew more about this stuff than any of them. If she said it was a good idea, it probably was. She could start a blog with no outlay, but could she write stuff that people actually wanted to read?

'I think that if you want to publish a recipe book,' said Lola, 'it'd be good for you to build your own brand first. Then you'll be well known, or at least known, when you're approaching publishers; you'll have an audience ready-made for them to sell to.'

Esme pictured her name on a website with people writing kind comments about her food, then she'd be mentioned in magazines and on TV shows and soon they'd be referring to her as a blogging sensation now launching her own recipe book. Okay, so maybe that was getting a little bit ahead of herself, but if she was going to embark on fulfilling her dream, she might as well dream big. 'Okay,' she said, nodding. 'Yes, I will. I'll do it. We need a name though.'

'You have a name,' said Mark, teasingly.

'You know what I mean,' Esme replied. 'For the blog. I can't just call it Esme's Blog. Even I think that's boring and I know nothing about marketing.'

'How about The Easy Cook?' said Mark. 'Don't you say all your recipes are easy to make?'

Helena laughed. 'No way.'

'Why not?'

'It makes me sound like a slapper,' Esme cut in.

'What about The Outback Cook?' offered Lola. 'You are in the middle of nowhere.'

51

'Oh, no.' Mark shook his head. 'She's not Australian and the back of beyond isn't the same as the outback. People will expect recipes for kangaroo meat or something.' Esme's mind shot back to Joe. He'd mentioned travelling to Australia. Then he'd suddenly switched the conversation back to business. It was a stupid thing to say but he'd grown up a lot since she'd seen him last. Not just physically. He'd seemed too old in a way, weighed down almost, but then, being a grown-up did that to you sometimes.

'Recipeasy?' asked Helena.

'I like it, but I think it's taken,' said Esme. She regarded the old furniture and the ancient kitchen, her grandma's recipe book already sitting on the worktop waiting for her. 'How about Grandma's Kitchen? I'll be using my grandma's recipe book and you guys know how special she was to me.' Thinking about the blog, she wanted the world to know how special her grandma had been. So full of advice and love, and with the most caring, nurturing nature. Esme had loved her with all her heart.

Esme's friends turned to her and for a moment, said nothing, then their faces erupted in wide grins. 'It's perfect,' said Mark, clapping.

Helena nodded. 'I love it.'

'Definitely,' said Lola. 'It's just right.'

'That's got to be it, hasn't it?' Esme bounced in her seat with excitement.

'To Grandma's Kitchen,' said Helena and they all clinked their tea cups as a toast. The living-room light flickered for a few seconds and Mark and Helena eyed each other.

'Ghosts, or dodgy electrics?' he asked.

'Neither,' Esme replied. 'It's just that bulb is a bit loose.'

Mark shook his head. 'I do hope you know what you're doing, Ezzy.'

Esme chuckled. 'Yeah, so do I.'

After they finished their tea, Esme gave them a tour of the house and enjoyed watching Mark's expression when he saw the bathroom.

'Are you fucking joking?' he asked. 'Salmon and avocado? It's like something from *The Good Life*.'

'Now there's an idea,' said Helena, winking at Esme. 'You could grow your own veg, keep some chickens ...'

'Great idea,' Esme replied, suppressing a grin. 'I could even get a greenhouse.' Mark's jaw dropped.

'You could keep a goat too and make cheese. It'd all be great for your blog,' chipped in Lola.

'Stop it,' shouted Mark, covering his ears. 'I'm going downstairs.'

In the afternoon, they put their coats on and strolled around the fields in the crisp winter air, chatting about work. Esme missed the buzz of the studio and the excitement of the city as Lola told them about a play she and Eric had been to see. But as Esme breathed in the fresh, chill wind, her skin felt cleaner for its freshness and even Mark commented on how peaceful the place was. As the sky began to darken, she cooked them dinner and they ate huddled on the sofa, discussing the break-up.

'I have to say,' said Helena. 'You're doing very well, honey.'

'I'm trying,' Esme replied. 'I still cry. A lot. I miss you guys though.' She reached out and took Helena's hand.

'We miss you too,' Lola replied. 'And your puddings.'

Esme tutted. 'I know what you're getting at and don't worry, I made pavlova.'

'Yay!' everyone shouted and Esme giggled as she went to collect it from the kitchen. She missed her friends more than she could say. They'd always been there for her, celebrating every success and commiserating with every failure. They'd helped her sell her stuff when she moved into Leo's. She'd had to let go of her beloved second-hand furniture because Leo insisted there wasn't room for it and it didn't go with the sleek, minimalist style he preferred. He wasn't one for clutter and considering she could be so clean and organised in the kitchen, Esme was rather messy out of it. Esme hadn't minded clearing out some of her old junk, being so in love and happy, but sometimes, when she was upset, she did miss the familiarity of those old worn knick-knacks.

Even though she offered for them to stay over, her friends all returned to London that night as they had work the next day. It was only an hour and a half's drive and she couldn't blame them. The spare room at the cottage hadn't been cleaned yet and was so full of stuff you couldn't actually move. The gang had all agreed a drive back to London was better than sleeping on the sofa in the freezing cold living room. As she waved them off, Esme felt tears sting her eyes. She hoped her friends hadn't seen them; she didn't want them to worry. But she wished she was in the car with them returning to the sights and sounds of the city she loved. It was so alive and vibrant, and Christmas time in the city was the best. A different sort of buzz lingered in the streets. One of joy and fun, rather than focus and concentration. But standing here in the middle of nowhere, in the darkness, the trees swaying in the wind, she felt very much alone.

That night, in the silence of the house, Esme snuggled in bed. Wrapped in three layers of clothes, she shut her eyes and tried to sleep. She hadn't slept that well since returning home. Her bedroom at Mum and Dad's felt too cramped and claustrophobic, and here, in the open fields, Esme missed the constant hum of traffic she had grown so used to. The silence of the countryside felt heavy and dense and she tossed and turned, hoping sleep would come. When it didn't, Esme sat up and picked up her laptop from beside the bed. If sleep proved elusive, there was no time like the present to start her own blog. She clicked on some cooking blogs for inspiration and anticipation tingled through her body. She pored over images to use, giving just the right feel of cosiness and class. She didn't want it to look anything like Felicity Fenchurch's awful super-cute, twee blog that was all pink with giant pictures of her face looming out at you. Esme wanted hers to be about the food, and about love.

Before long, Grandma's Kitchen was up and running. And as

the sun came up and shone through her window, she closed the laptop, the battery out, and fell into a peaceful sleep.

*

Grandma's Kitchen

Hi everybody, I thought I'd better begin my blog by introducing myself to you! My name's Esme Kendrick and I love, love, LOVE cooking! Sorry for using big shouty letters but I do really love cooking! I've been working as a food technologist on some TV shows since I graduated university, but have always wanted to cook my own food and write about it, so that's why I've started Grandma's Kitchen.

It's named after my lovely grandma who left me her ancient and amazing recipe book. It even has recipes from her mum and grandma in it, so it's a real family heirloom. It means the world to me, and I hope that through sharing my successes and failures with you, you'll enjoy trying out some new recipes and begin to love cooking as much as I do.

So what more can I tell you? My grandma, Pearl, was a brilliant cook and taught me everything I know. I think that, after discovering what a liability my mum was in the kitchen, she focused all her energy on me and my sister, Alice. Mum won't mind me saying that – she's an amazing mum, but she never really liked cooking and much prefers a takeaway or having dinner in the pub to slaving over a hot stove. One of my earliest memories is of Mum trying to cook a sausage casserole and it going so horribly wrong that Grandma had to step in. I remember she turned this burnt, crazily spiced mess into something delicious she called Cowboy Casserole. I'll share the recipe with you later. You're sure to love it!

I've just moved back to my hometown after my life took an unexpected change of direction. It's been a bit of a knock, but you have to keep moving forward. My dad always says never go backwards, so I'm taking the plunge and starting this blog. The recipes you'll find here will be family-friendly (my sister insisted! She said cooking different dinners for the adults and kids would drive her insane!) and are easy to follow with no weird ingredients. I can't wait to share my first recipe with you soon!

*

After a couple of hours' sleep, Esme awoke and went downstairs to write her first proper recipe for the blog. It was the first Monday she should have been at work and it felt strange to be her own boss and not have anywhere to go. Esme wrestled with a restlessness that filled her muscles with unspent energy as she flitted around the kitchen making herself a cup of tea.

So much had happened in such a short space of time. Less than a week ago her life had been ticking along as normal, her routine engrained in her mind and body. She could have walked to the tube station blindfolded and told you exactly what Leo would say in any given situation. She wondered what he was doing now. He'd have been to the gym and be at work already. Resisting the urge to cry, Esme clicked through her blog– her future – and sat back on the sofa, waiting for the number of hits to start pinging. Deep down, she knew this wasn't going to happen, but couldn't resist watching for half an hour anyway.

She picked up her grandma's recipe book. The black leather cover was worn and frayed at the edges. The red ribbon she had inherited with it was beginning to fray as it forced numerous pieces of paper covered with scribbles and scrawlings back inside. She took off the band and opened it to leaf through its pages, examining each one and the delicate handwriting listing the recipes.

Affection and tenderness warmed her through. Her great-grandma's fingers had touched these pages, as well as her grandma's and her mum's. Carol's attempts at cooking from her youth were weirder and wilder, involving a lot of Seventies aspic-based recipes and random swearing. But her grandma had been an amazing cook and family legend had it that Esme's great-grandma had been incredible too, creating exciting dishes even through rationing. This was why Esme loved cooking so much. It was history, their history. It meant her grandma who had helped her through so much, whose loss she had felt so deeply, would never be forgotten if her recipes were still being cooked, and the love that went into them still existed.

An old torn piece of paper fell from the side and she picked it up, turning it over in her fingers. It was a recipe for vanilla biscuits and in the margin, in a small, elegant hand, she could see the words, 'Carol loves these'. Her grandma had written it and Esme smiled at the thought of her mum as a little girl, begging for biscuits just as she and Alice had done. She carefully placed it back inside and glanced again at the counter on her blog. It still registered zero hits. She checked the clock. It was now just after lunch and boredom gnawed at her brain. Esme made herself a bowl of cereal and sat back down on the sofa, still in her pyjamas, two jumpers and her favourite big, fluffy bed socks. Pulling one of the throws off the back of the seat, Esme tucked it around her as the cold of the cottage tried to seep into her bones.

Spooning soggy cornflakes into her mouth (she hated them all hard and crunchy), she opened the book to her favourite comfort food recipe. Just reading the words 'orange tea bread' made Esme's mouth water. Maybe this could be her first recipe for the blog? After leafing through the book and scanning the index in her brain, Esme decided this was definitely the right one to begin with, and even though she'd made it so many times before, she wanted to test it one last time, just to make sure the measurements were all correct. Esme moved to the kitchen and began weighing out flour, butter, sugar and boiling oranges for the tea bread.

The rickety old cottage was soon filled with the sweet smell of oranges and when the loaf was cooked and cooled, Esme cut a piece and smothered it with butter. Taking a bite was like being 5 years old again, home from school at her grandma's house while her mum worked. Esme remembered being hungry and happy sitting with her grandma at her old fold-out table, talking about the things she had done at school that day, or playing Happy Families with Alice. It was one of her favourite recipes of all time.

Esme re-read the instructions she'd written down, changing some of the wording and some of quantities to suit her own palate. Instead of white sugar, she had added light brown sugar for a hint of toffee and though she could use orange juice or flavouring, real oranges were better. Two hours later, she helped herself to another slice of the delicious bread and typed up her findings, posting for the second time.

*

Grandma's Kitchen

Hi again, everybody. For the first-ever recipe here on Grandma's Kitchen, I wanted to share one of my favourites and one that means a lot to me. This is great for a tea party (if people still have those) or kids' parties, or just as a snack for yourself. I'm presenting my comforting and delicious Orange Tea Bread! Ta da!

This is delicious warm or cold and you can even have it as dessert with some ice cream, crème fraiche or mascarpone. I used to eat this when I was little and it's still my favourite comfort food recipe today. And I don't mind telling you, I need a little comfort at the moment. If you're going through a bit of a hard time, like me, this is just what you need. It'll give you a warm fuzzy feeling right through to your soul.

It's really simple to make, so don't worry. All you do is: gently simmer an orange or two small clementines in a small amount of water for about an hour until soft. You don't even have to peel them! Once they've boiled and cooled, whizz them up into an orangey mush. The last time I made this with my mum, which

58

was shockingly a couple of years ago now, she kept stealing most of my orange mixture to add to a glass of Prosecco. It makes a wicked posh Buck's Fizz. Needless to say, mum got sozzled and I finished the cooking alone. Now . . . cream the sugar and butter together then add everything else and spoon in the orange mixture.

To see if it's cooked, test it in the middle with a skewer. If the skewer comes out clean, it's done.

Enjoy! And let me know how you get on!

*

After the snack, Esme checked the counter again. Still nothing. It was four o'clock and the bright afternoon sun was beginning to set, casting the brown fields in a warm orange light. Writing the post had been difficult. Esme struggled with how much to say and how much to hold back. She didn't want the world to know every little detail of her life, but she wanted to be open and connect with her readers on a personal level. Some of the blogs she'd read were so cold; just a list of direct instructions that read like orders. She wanted people to read hers and feel like they were with a friend. That they weren't alone. But sitting staring at the counter wasn't helping her mood so Esme changed into her running clothes and laced up her trainers.

She'd missed running when she was in London. Leo always used the posh gym, saying it wasn't safe to run outside. Esme hated it. A treadmill just wasn't the same as the ground beneath your feet. As Esme left the house and began running through fields with nothing and no one around, she felt a strange sense of freedom. As she ran, the wind blew away the few stray hairs that had escaped from her ponytail and it cooled her cheeks, even though she was hot and sweaty. Her lungs filled with clean air and her heart, beating hard, reminded her she was alive, fit and healthy, even if that heart still ached for the man she'd loved so much.

An hour later she opened the front door, her lungs burning from the effort, her body fired up and igniting. The smell of the orange tea bread still hung on the air, making her smile. With the energy that had been pulsing through her body now spent, Esme ran a bath, washing her long red hair with a jug. After changing into clean pyjamas and adding four more long jumpers to keep out the cold, she checked the counter again. Still nothing.

This was excruciating. How long did she have to wait for someone to read her blog? There were millions of people in the world – surely one of them wanted to read about cooking? Esme sighed and grabbed her phone to call Lola.

'Lola, this is horrible. I've posted some stuff and no one has even looked at my blog. What do I do to get people reading it?'

'Don't be such a baby,'Lola laughed. 'Why don't you do some research? There's loads of stuff online all about blogging. Have a look and write yourself a marketing plan. You can find templates for those online too.'

'Can't you do it for me?' asked Esme in mock petulance.

'No, I can't. I have a job to do.'

Esme winced. 'Sorry. I didn't mean that the way it sounded.'

'I know. It's okay.' It had just been a slip of the tongue but it stung. Right now, if things were normal, Esme would have been working with Helena and Mark on Felicity's TV show. She wondered if they were shooting her recipe today. The one Felicity had stolen. And all the hurt and injustice that had sent her back to Sandchester in the first place came flooding back. With an empty evening ahead of her, Esme sighed. 'All right then, I'll start reading up on how to get my name out there.'

'Atta girl.'

'But can't you be my marketing manager or something? I'll pay you in cake.'

'Hmm . . . tempting, but no. You can do this. I know you can. I'll advise, but you need to learn all this stuff.'

Esme picked at the threads of the blanket next to her. 'Oh,

all right. I guess I'll get started on all this research you won't do for me then.'

Lola laughed. 'Do you remember that time you did my maths homework for me because I didn't understand it and you said you did then got it completely wrong?'

'Oh, yeah!' Esme laughed.

'The teacher knew what had happened and we both got detention for a week.'

Thinking back to their school days, she suddenly realised she hadn't told Lola about Joe. 'Oh my God, I didn't tell you, did I? You'll never guess who the estate agent was who got me in here.'

'Go on, who?'

'Joe Holloway.'

Lola's voice grew louder and Esme heard her intake of breath. 'No way? He was absolutely gorgeous at school, wasn't he?'

'He still is,' Esme replied. She gazed around the living room, remembering him showing her around.

'Is he now?'

'Don't be cheeky. I may be recovering from a broken heart, but I can still appreciate a nice face when I see one. Anyway, rumour has it he hasn't changed.'

'Oh yeah? Says who?' Esme could hear Lola fidgeting in her seat. She loved a bit of gossip.

'Alice. She said he's got a bit of a reputation for one-night stands.'

'Oh well, some men never grow up. Do you remember when me and everyone else were crushing on New Kids on the Block, you were madly in love with Joe because he listened to Nirvana and was all deep and moody? What do you think of him now?'

Esme considered. 'He was nice.'

'Nice?' Lola didn't sound convinced.

'Professional. We didn't really chat, but he was . . . I don't know, understanding when I told him about my situation.'

Lola's voice was gentle and Esme knew she'd be playing with her pen as she spoke. 'How are you, honey? About Leo, I mean?'

'I'm okay. Honestly.' It was a lie; she wasn't okay. And hearing someone else say his name out loud, the stinging in her chest returned. 'Shouldn't you be getting back to work? We've been talking for ages.'

'Nah, I sold loads of advertising space this morning so I can doss this afternoon. Are you really doing okay? You sound like you're trying to avoid the subject.'

'I'm not avoiding it, it's just there isn't much to say. I'm kind of okay. I've stopped crying *all* the time. It's just most of the time now. It's quite embarrassing bursting into tears at the supermarket staring at a steak because that was the last meal I cooked for him. People start edging away from you thinking you're crazy.'

'Yes,' laughed Lola. 'They would, I suppose. They might think you're an ardent vegetarian mourning the cow.'

Esme laughed, but then her eyes darted down to the finger she'd thought would soon be sporting an engagement ring. 'I thought he was going to propose that night, Lola. Was I a complete idiot?'

'No, of course not. He should have proposed. You'd been together for ages and with that shopping thing and the secretiveness we all thought he was planning some big proposal too. Leo's the idiot, Ezzy. He's lost the best thing in his life and sooner or later he's going to realise it and come crawling back.'

'Let's wait and see on that one, shall we? Mark said his new woman's got long legs and blonde hair.'

'So?'

'It sounds like his boss, Veronica, and she's gorgeous. I met her once. She's one of those super-focused, ambitious people. I thought she was amazing. Now I feel stupid for admiring her too.'

'You don't know that it's her. It might not be. It could be some random blonde who has long legs but a face like a butt. You're gorgeous and amazing. And even if it is Veronica, work things don't always end well. It sounds dangerous to me.'

'You have to say that, you're my friend.' Esme picked a hair off the outermost jumper. She was fairly warm now with three others underneath. 'Thanks though. Anyway, I better get on with my research.'

'Esme,' Lola said cautiously. 'I'm really proud of you.'

Tears welled in Esme's eyes, and she blinked them away. 'Are you? Why?'

'Because you've been so strong and dignified through all this. You haven't let it beat you and you haven't gone all psycho killer like your mum would. I think you're amazing.'

'I bet I'm still in shock. At some point I'll come out of it, realise what's happened and walk to London to destroy Leo's flat and put raw fish behind his radiators.'

'Yep, that definitely sounds like your mum,' laughed Lola. Esme groaned. 'You won't do anything like that. You're a much nicer person. That's why we love you.'

'Love you too, sweetie,' Esme managed before wiping her nose on a tissue. There would be no more crying in her new house. Not if she could help it.

Chapter 8

Sandchester

Joe changed into third gear, thinking what a successful viewing that had been. The young couple had loved the two-up, two-down and he was sure they would put in an offer. They said it was perfect for them and their little boy. Joe loved the sense of fulfilment when he matched someone to a house and helped them move on to the next stage of their lives. Ironic, considering he couldn't.

The bare branches of the trees resembled long, thin fingers stretching out into the ashen afternoon sky. The privet hedges lining the fields were still green, but the colour was dulled and dark. He drove down the long winding road on the outskirts of town and saw Esme running. Her beautiful red hair, scraped back in a ponytail, bobbed behind her, her eyes focused on the ground. Even in sweaty running clothes she looked amazing. Something in him stirred and reminded him of Clara. She'd been sporty. Though she had blonde hair, like all lithe Australian women you saw on TV shows, and blue eyes that matched the colour of the clear stretch of sea near their house. Her limbs had turned a deep golden brown within a week of them moving to Australia and for three years they'd been happy, but then, things had started to change. Joe's heart sped up as he thought of her again. When he'd flown back after the break-up he was broken, but he'd hoped that being at home would help him get over it.

He concentrated on the road, on the music playing from the radio – anything to break his mind from the path it was going down. The path it always went down. He recited the first few lines from the new song the DJ had introduced and the cold sweat started to abate. Joe glanced in the rear-view mirror and saw Esme running back towards the cottage. She was braver than he was. She'd been dealt a rough hand but wasn't crying and feeling sorry for herself all the time. She was keeping her head high and tackling life head on, trying to make a new future. He wished that, somehow, he could too.

Even his photography obsession wasn't helping. He loved taking photographs of the world around him. The way light and dark played together, creating shadows, capturing a perfect moment or place, especially places unspoilt by man, like Parkin Wood. But his tendency to sulk had stopped him going out again.

Clara always said his sulking was his worst trait. He'd tried to pull himself out of it, but it was no use. Nothing seemed to help. Deep down he feared it was more than mere sulking but didn't know how to tackle it. His parents didn't either. Neither did his friends. And because he gave the world an image of a smiling Joe who seemed to be coping, everyone thought things were okay, or at least, pretended they were. His mother had suggested counselling a few times, but Joe knew it wouldn't help until he felt ready to talk. Sitting in a room with a sympathetic therapist charging him goodness knows what an hour while they sat in silence would only have made him worse. It still would. He was waiting for the day to come when he could sit down and describe how he felt, but that day hadn't arrived yet.

Joe took one last look in the rear-view mirror at Esme and pressed the brake, pausing at the junction. Checking the road three times, his hands gripping the wheel and his mouth dry with anxiety, he continued on his way. But then he felt a strange urge to turn his car around and go and see Esme. Why, he wasn't sure. As a new tenant he should probably see how she was settling in, especially as the place had no central heating. He'd give her time to get back and sorted out first, but he would definitely call in later, on his way home, just to see how she was.

When closing time approached, Joe couldn't wait to drive out to the cottage. Even as the rain battered the window of the car and he flicked the wipers up faster, his mood was lifting. He pulled up outside and noticed there was nothing coming out of the chimney. Surely she'd learned to light the fire? She'd been in for a couple of days and it had been freezing all this week – literally. It had actually hit below zero last night. How the hell was she keeping warm?

After huddling down out of the rain and giving a firm knock, Esme opened the door and he realised exactly how she was managing to keep from freezing – she was wearing about twenty layers of clothes and seemed three times bigger than she actually was. She was even wearing a hat and gloves. A grin broke out on his face and the tightness lifted from his features. It felt like a long time since he'd experienced such a weightlessness. 'Hi.'

'Don't laugh,' Esme said sternly, but a smile was lifting the corners of her mouth too.

'What? I'm not laughing.'

'Yes, you are. Or at least you're trying not to.'

He rubbed his chin as if it would help hide his grin. 'I take it you haven't learned to light the fire yet?'

Esme's eyes flicked down. 'No.'

'Do you want me to show you?' Without speaking she opened the door wider and let him in. It was arctic in the old cottage and the orange glow from a tiny ancient four-bar fire looked dangerous rather than warming. 'Geez, it's absolutely freezing in here.'

'Is it?' she said, nonchalantly. 'I hadn't noticed.' A teasing smile brightened her eyes. 'Do you want tea?'

'Yes, please.'

Joe went over and surveyed the fireplace. Esme had cleaned it out but left it bare. 'So, shall I teach you to light a fire then?'

'When did you learn to light a fire?' she asked, filling a teapot with actual tea leaves. Joe didn't even own a teapot; he simply threw teabags into a mug and added the water. He should have known Esme would do things properly.

'I was always bunking off school, remember? My mates and I used to go to Parkin Wood and hide up there. We'd light a fire in the winter to keep warm. My mum used to do her nut when I came home stinking of smoke.'

Esme shook her head disapprovingly. 'Well, I didn't think you'd learned in the Boy Scouts, you know.'

'Ha, ha! Do you know where the wood store is?'

Esme nodded and brought over the teapot, a strainer, cups and some biscuits she'd made. He took a bite. They were delicious. So much better than anything he'd ever bought, even from Marks and Spencer.

'I found it when I was exploring the other day. It's really lovely around here. I'd forgotten how much space there is and how nice it is to be surrounded by fields.'

'Well, after this I'll go and grab some and show you how to light the fire. It's quite simple when you know what you're doing. These biscuits are delicious.'

'Thanks,' she replied, pouring the tea through the drainer, then removing it and adding milk. She passed a cup to Joe.

'Do you have any newspaper?'

'There's millions over there.' She pointed to a pile in the back corner. 'I found them in the spare room. Why anyone would keep that much newspaper I have no idea.'

'Maybe they knew we needed them for the fire?'

She grinned. 'Maybe. That was very thoughtful of them.'

A silence descended and Joe glanced around the cottage. It wasn't especially different, but there was something homely about it now. Esme's presence was bringing it to life. Then he pushed the thought away and reminded himself any tenant would have brought it to life, filling it with knick-knacks and personal things. 'Are you settling in okay?' he asked to get the conversation moving again.

'Yeah, I think so. It's a lovely little cottage. Central heating would be nice though.'

He popped his half-empty cup on the table having necked it to try and warm up. It had been the tastiest cup of tea he'd ever had. 'You'll feel better when we get the fire working. Come on.'

Esme stood and he gestured for her to lead the way to the wood store at the back of the house. Luckily there was still a lot left. Grabbing some logs and handing a couple to Esme they hurried back inside as the icy wind whipped around the cottage and the rain grew fierce. 'Can you get some paper, please? And some matches.'

Esme went to the kitchen and Joe lay the logs down on the hearth then shook off his coat. Esme came over with the newspaper and knelt beside him, handing him the sheets. Each time he'd scrunch one up and place it down, then he added some kindling and stacked the logs on top. From the corner of his eye he could see Esme's head craning, watching how he built the fire. The smell of her coconut conditioner filled his nostrils and he felt an overwhelming urge to touch the silky strands of her hair. He turned slightly away, forcing the idea out and busying his hands by folding a sheet of newspaper to make a taper.

'Why are you doing that?' asked Esme.

'Well, you don't want to shove your face into the fire to light it so best to make a nice long taper and not burn your eyebrows off. You might want to get some firelighters too.'

'Oh, okay.'

Before long the fire was roaring away and the room was losing its glacial feel. Esme pulled down two cushions from the old sofa and they sat on them next to the fire as it crackled and roared into life. Joe began to feel his fingers and toes again. Esme even turned off the terrifying and useless four-bar fire and began removing some of the jumpers until she was down to just two big sweatshirts.

'This feels amazing,' she said, her eyes twinkling in the glow from the flames. 'You know what we need, don't you?'

'What?' he asked, smiling at her excited tone.

'Hot chocolate!'

Joe laughed as she leapt up and went off to the kitchen. 'What are we, five?'

'Don't be grumpy! Everyone loves hot chocolate.'

'Do you have marshmallows?' he asked, warming to the idea. He couldn't remember the last time he'd drunk a hot chocolate.

'No, but I do have a secret recipe you're going to love.'

Joe watched as Esme moved around the kitchen finding bars of dark and milk chocolate, cocoa powder and milk, and measuring things out. She began melting it all together in a saucepan and he watched her face as she stirred. Her brow furrowed a little as she concentrated but then her features relaxed as she tasted it. Could he ask what she was thinking about or was it too intrusive, to intimate even? He wasn't ready to be intimate with anyone, not emotionally. He turned away and added another log to the fire. Esme sat down next to him again and handed him his chocolate. Joe sipped and it was the most amazing thing he'd ever tasted.

'This is one of my favourite recipes. My grandma used to make these for me and Alice every Friday in winter as an end of the week treat.'

He sipped and the hot, velvety chocolate slid down his throat. It wasn't sickly sweet like most hot chocolates were. It was rich and intense and delicious, coating his throat with a silky warmth, warming him from the inside. 'So, how are you settling in?'

'Better now,' Esme replied, nodding at the fire. 'But it's quite nice here. I like it.'

'Don't you miss London?'

A flicker of regret passed over her face, followed by a look of longing. She clearly did, but all she said was, 'Sometimes. How do you like being an estate agent? I have to be honest, it wasn't the career move I thought you'd make.'

'What did you think I'd end up doing?' He took another sip of the delicious hot chocolate. Against the light from the orange flames, Esme looked like a Renaissance painting, even in her baggy sweatshirt. Her red hair was illuminated and her pale skin stood out against the depth of its colour. Joe flicked his eyes away, worried that the emotion mounting in his chest would become too much if he kept looking at her. Just as he did, her eyes met his for a second.

'I don't know, really.' She shrugged and let out a heavy sigh. 'I don't know what I thought. When we were teenagers, the world seemed so big and like we could do anything we wanted. Reality isn't like that though, is it?'

Joe gave a slow shake of the head. She'd had a kicking just like him and he could see the hurt on her face, still fresh, still painful. His had been hanging around for ages now; he was unable to shift it from his soul. They said time heals all wounds but it hadn't for him. It hadn't lessened the load he carried or reduced its burden. Esme's strength at trying to move forward already was astounding. 'Reality sucks, doesn't it?'

'So, is there no one special in your life?' Esme asked. Her tone was light and he knew it was a genuine and normal question. Strangely, even though his feelings were always heightened at this time of year, her asking didn't fill him with the same fear it normally did and he felt his brain answer before his heart could stop it.

'There was someone. I met an Australian girl a long time ago and moved out to Oz to be with her.' He paused. 'But it didn't work out.' Joe cleared his throat as a wave of sentiment engulfed him, so strong it nearly choked him. He hadn't planned on saying anymore, but the words kept coming. 'It, umm, it all went wrong and I ended up back here with no job or . . . anything, really.'

'I'm so sorry,' said Esme. 'It sucks, doesn't it?'

Joe watched her, wondering if she was being sarcastic. She probably still saw him as the bad boy from school, still trying to be cool, but then he saw the tenderness of her expression. 'It does,' he replied, nodding. Then he laughed, self-consciously. For the first time in a long time, a surge of real emotion grabbed him and he wanted to reach over and kiss her. Not for the fleeting moment of reprieve it could offer, but to connect with someone – her – Esme – on a deeper level. Connect with who she was on the inside. It was a feeling that scared him, not enough to make him run away, but enough that he felt a sudden need to lighten the mood and hide back in the shadows of his mind. 'Anyway, I quite like being an estate agent. It's more fun than you'd think.'

The conversation moved on as he spoke about Mr Rigby and some of the people he'd worked with over the years and Esme chatted about her work on different television shows. She was funny and had a quick, dry wit. He noticed though, that she often kept the conversation away from her personal life and, ever professional, she didn't name the celebrity chefs she talked about unless she was saying nice things. After what felt like five minutes, he checked his watch and was surprised to see almost two hours had passed and it was nearly eight o'clock. 'I'd better get going, Esme. Thanks for the hot chocolate. It was amazing.'

She gave a cheerful smile. 'You're welcome. Thanks for checking on me and helping me light the fire.'

Joe shrugged his coat up onto his shoulders. 'No worries. If you need a hand again, just shout. You've got my number, haven't you?'

'I don't think so, actually.' Esme looked around as if checking to see if she had.

'Well, here.' He dug in his pocket and handed her a business card with his mobile number on. 'Ring anytime, okay.'

'Okay.' She took the card in her long slender fingers and Joe made his way towards the door.

'Goodnight, Esme.'

'Night, Joe.'

As Joe walked back to his car, the cold night air biting at the back of his neck and cheeks as he pulled up his collar, he turned to the pretty cottage and watched the smoke from the chimney curl into the sky. He smiled to himself, pleased that he'd been able to help Esme, and safe in the knowledge she'd be much more comfortable now. But the feelings that had stirred in his heart were worrying – terrifying even, now he thought on them again. He wasn't ready. And as he'd feared, the guilt that washed over him caused his fingers to tremble as he turned the key in the ignition. Taking a deep breath, he put the car in gear and concentrated on the road, hoping that the moment would pass, but knowing deep down it wouldn't. The black hole from which he could never fully crawl out was beckoning him in again and he was powerless to resist it.

Chapter 9

London

Leo flopped onto the sofa and turned on the television. How come Monday night TV was so boring? He flicked over to Netflix and clicked on his profile, next to Veronica's. On Saturday night, the first night they'd spent in together since Esme had left and she moved in, she'd made him change Esme's profile to hers. But not before grabbing the remote and having a flick through to see what programmes Esme had liked. He hadn't realised how much trash she must have watched when he was working late and she wasn't out with her weirdo friends. It was a wonder her brain hadn't turned to mush and dribbled out of her ears. Leo chuckled to himself at his joke and made a mental note to use it again in conversation with Veronica – it would definitely make her laugh. Thinking of which, where was she?

He checked his phone to see a text message. It must have pinged while he was lost in thought. He worried for a moment it would be Esme, begging him to let her come back, for them to try again, and the muscles in his legs tensed but relaxed down as he saw it was from Veronica. Oh, she was working late again. As he wasn't due to meet any clients tonight and his friends had been a bit iffy with him since he'd announced his relationship with Veronica (jealousy no doubt), that meant another dinner in on his own.

The only trouble with Veronica being senior to him was that she had more nights out with clients than he had. He knew that tonight Veronica was seeing her biggest client, an American who needed a lot of schmoozing, and she'd warned him she probably wouldn't be home till late. At the time it had been fine. He'd planned to go out with his friends, but it turned out his friends were busy again. A niggling in his mind told him it was an excuse. He knew they thought he was playing with fire, dating his own boss, but they didn't know Veronica. Not like he did.

Leo found a programme to watch. A bit of Bear Grylls always cheered him up. After a few minutes he sighed and reached behind him to remove a mauve scatter cushion. He hadn't wanted them ruining the sleek lines of the expensive grey leather sofa, but Veronica couldn't get comfortable without them. Esme had never gone in for all these extra bits and bobs but Veronica had started sneaking them in. Leo had dropped some subtle hints, but she'd argued with him and the pesky things kept appearing in all manner of colours and with strange adornments and tassels. After piling them at the far end of the sofa, he was able to get comfortable. The programme was an hour long, so surely she'd be home by the time it ended.

The show finished at just gone nine o'clock and his stomach was rumbling even louder. He thought about giving it another five minutes, but it was no good, he just couldn't concentrate when he was this hungry. He texted Veronica asking when she'd be home and she responded straightaway, a bit stroppily in his opinion, saying she didn't know and accusing him of being clingy. *Clingy?* He wasn't clingy. He just wanted to know what was going on so he could plan his own evening. It wasn't much to ask. Veronica might be a dab hand with clients, but she needed to work on her communication. Still, it was early days of living together, they could work it out. Things were moving quickly, and that was good, wasn't it? It showed they were meant to be. Veronica was so like him — career-oriented, ambitious. They were sure to go places. Though Leo did still feel a little disappointed she hadn't liked the ring he'd bought her. She'd called it loud and insisted they go and find something together so she could choose for herself.

Huffily, Leo went to the kitchen. It would have been nice if her response had come an hour ago – even that one – so he could've eaten. He wasn't used to waiting around for people. Opening the fridge, Leo perused the contents. A mouldy tomato, half a soggy lettuce and some eggs were all that remained. Veronica wasn't a shopper or a cook, not like Esme. When Esme had lived here the fridge had been stocked with all manner of delights from exquisite cheeses to delicious meats from all over the world. She always made him the tastiest leftovers too, so all he had to do was throw them in the microwave. He'd have a quick chat with Veronica about doing the shopping. Leo remembered one night when he'd been really late home from work and Esme had been out with her friends, he'd arrived home just after her and was starving. In her jolly and slightly tipsy mood, she'd pulled together an amazing picnic that they ate on the floor in front of the telly. They'd met at a picnic, weirdly. In Hyde Park with her friends. They were playing some silly game and she'd fallen backwards laughing, only to crash into his path and trip him up. He'd been mesmerised by her straightaway and when she was still there when he returned from his meeting, watching him walk past. He knew she was interested and doubled back to ask her out. Things had been so much better back then. And it wasn't her fault he'd got bored with her. That was life.

Leo eyed the eggs and squared his shoulders. He'd make an omelette. He could do it. French people made them all the time so how hard could it be? Ten minutes later and feeling a bit like a student, Leo glared at the soggy scrambled egg on barely toasted bread. He wouldn't hear from Veronica again this evening he knew that much, and who knew what time she'd be in. But he wouldn't interrupt her meeting. He used to hate it if Esme did that to him.

Taking his disappointing plate and going back to the sofa, Leo decided to watch one more episode of Bear Grylls before going to bed. He ignored the thought that this whole evening should be working out the other way around, with him out all night and Veronica sitting at home waiting for him to crawl in at a ridiculous time, perhaps a little pissed, and slide into bed beside her. A sudden image of Esme's blazing red hair splayed out on the pillow next to his shot into his brain. He ignored it and scooped up some runny egg only to watch it promptly fall off the fork.

Chapter 10

London

Felicity Fenchurch turned to David, who only managed to annoy her even more by giving an unhelpful shrug of his round fleshy shoulders. Bending down, she studied the triple-layer chocolate chestnut cake that was leaning precariously to the left. She had no idea why the food technologists hadn't been able to make it work. She'd told them what she wanted, including the secret ingredient and special method, and no, she didn't have an actual written recipe, it was a concept. Her dear granny hadn't written it down. She'd told them to make a basic chocolate cake, add a slug of maple syrup and some chestnut puree, then pop a layer of whipped cream in the middle. Felicity straightened up and put her hands on her hips. She had no idea what they'd done wrong. They were clearly idiots.

David edged in closer. 'Umm, darling Felicity, it's looking a little, shall we say, tired at the moment, isn't it?' Felicity glared at him and he shrank bank. 'I just mean it needs a little extra support and a tad more decoration. I'm sure it'll be fab when it's finished.'

'It is finished,' she replied, through gritted teeth. Even with the light set up to be as flattering as possible, it was uneven and messy. Maybe they hadn't whipped the cream stiff enough. She'd watched the food techs turning out the cakes. They were fine. A little crumbly perhaps, but no one would know at home, as long they didn't start falling apart. Felicity felt herself growing hot as she glanced at the top layer of sponge and saw a crack appearing. 'I don't know why it isn't working.' She glared at one of the food techs standing nearby. 'You? What's your name?'

A petite woman in her early twenties with lavender hair winced. 'It's Lucy, Miss Fenchurch.'

'Well, Lucy,' Felicity said, drumming her long, polished fingernails on the table top. 'Why isn't it working?'

Lucy stepped closer and examined the cake that was toppling further and further westward. Nervously, she said, 'I think the cake layers are too small and the filling is too gooey for it to be triple layers. And the cream's starting to melt under the lights as well. The sponges were a bit dry when we turned them out. I think the chestnut puree threw off the whole flour, cocoa, milk ratio, and we might have added too much maple syrup, it's made it taste a bit . . . ' She hesitated. 'Umm, bitter. We should probably make the layers thicker as well as it's three layers. We could re-bake?'

Felicity caught Sasha, the producer, prowling at the back of the studio, and worse, she kept peering over and checking her watch. Felicity didn't often lose sleep over anything, but since the incident with Esme Kendrick, she'd felt watched. Sasha didn't normally bother coming to set and yet, here she was, the day they were shooting the recipe she'd borrowed from Esme. It couldn't be a coincidence and Felicity was beginning to worry that she wasn't going to get away with this one. She hadn't slept much last night, or the night before, even with her special sleep mask and the relaxation tincture she had specially made for her by a very expensive herbalist. 'There isn't time,' Felicity replied to Lucy, her voice a low growl. 'And don't worry about the taste. Can't we buttercream the outside? Or put a ganache on it or something?'

'A ganache would need to cool or it'll melt the rest of the filling and I don't think—'

'You don't think what?' Felicity crossed her arms over her chest.

Lucy mumbled, 'I don't think a buttercream would work. It'll make the cake far too sweet.'

Felicity eyed her. 'You're not paid to think, though, are you? You're paid to bake.'

David edged forwards and ushered Lucy behind him. 'Now, now, dear Fliss, I'm sure we'll be able to sort something out. But we do need to hurry, we're running out of time. The batter is ready and waiting for us to film the next segment and Sasha's decided to pay a surprise visit today.'

In her three-inch heels Felicity was so tall she could see the few lonely hairs on his pink sweaty head. *Damn that girl*, she thought. She was sure now that Esme had played a trick on her. She must have known three layers were too many and she must have had a special recipe for the batter. From the corner of her eye she saw Sasha begin to walk towards them. Why did she have to come to set today? She never came to set. Felicity clenched her jaw and turned to Lucy. 'Just shove some batons in it and put it in the blast chiller for a few minutes.'

Lucy's eyes widened. 'But the cake's so crumbly it'll just break up. I really think we need to re-bake and make the sponge thicker, or take a layer off.'

'I will not take a layer off,' hissed Felicity. 'Just stick on any bits that fall off then cover the whole thing with chocolate buttercream. Dust the top with cocoa powder and shove on some gold leaf to make it sparkly. And I really don't give a flying fig what you think. I just need this ready to be presented on camera in fifteen minutes. David?'

'Yes?'

'We'll have to do some cut shots of me and not focus so much on the cake.'

'But,' he hesitated. 'But Sasha said—'

'I don't care what Sasha says.' Felicity flashed her eyes. She could feel herself growing hot under the pressure. 'The cake isn't going to work. Don't ask me why. We must have had a bad batch of chestnut puree or something.' She brushed her hair back from her face. 'It is notoriously difficult to work with. Just shoot me with all the individual elements and do a quick shot of the finished thing. Light it with candles or something and I'll do a voiceover at the end.'

'We don't have the money for a voice—'

Felicity shot him a look that said 'Disagree with me and I'll kill you.' David shuffled away just as Sasha approached.

'Everything all right?' she asked, her eyes boring into Felicity.

'Oh, Sasha, there you are. I was just wondering if you were coming into the studio today. I so hoped you would. This episode is going to be so fantastic. I can feel it.'

'Right.' Sasha stared at the cake, then at Felicity. 'Make-up?' she shouted, and two ladies with brushes came over. 'Felicity needs some more coverage; she looks tired and sweaty today.'

And with that, Sasha turned and walked away while Felicity was left clenching her fists below the counter and gritting her teeth behind the hardest smile she'd ever had to give.

Chapter 11

Sandchester

Esme lifted her head from the screen and sighed. The week had passed slowly and it was now Friday morning. Without a job, she'd baked, shopped for food, baked some more and wandered around the house without brushing her hair or bothering with make-up. She'd found the local radio station on her laptop and the DJ talked about Christmas shopping between songs. Esme sat back and scanned the kitchen hoping something would fire her imagination. She was going to have to plan these blog posts more thoroughly instead of writing when she was bored, including whatever recipes she fancied or could think of at the time. Esme blew out her cheeks and grabbed her grandma's book for inspiration.

Having already posted a recipe for something sweet, comforting and old-fashioned, Esme thought that this time she should include a more up-to-date recipe inspired by the cookbook but with a modern twist. It was almost lunchtime and her stomach rumbled. She hadn't eaten all morning, so a brunch recipe would be perfect. Nothing too fashionable, like pancakes. Everyone was making pancakes at the moment, using different flours, packing them with protein and other odd things. No. She would make something delicious and filling. She flicked through the recipe book and discovered her grandma's recipe for Welsh Rarebit. Granny had always added mushroom ketchup to hers instead of Worcestershire sauce and Esme had followed suit, but Esme made hers slightly differently, adding crème fraiche and making the rarebit almost as a sauce. Her stomach gurgled even louder. Esme wanted something more substantial than just posh cheese on toast though, and mentally perused the contents of the pantry, hitting on just the thing.

*

Grandma's Kitchen

Hi everyone, how did you like the Orange Tea Bread? Have any of you been able to try the recipe yet? Today's post is for a delicious brunch recipe. It's inspired by my grandma's Welsh Rarebit, but with a twist. My grandma made this for me the first time I had a real proper hangover. I was seventeen and decided that trying tequila on top of drinking I don't know how many bottles of Hooch (do you remember Hooch?) was a good idea. Believe me, it wasn't! But this recipe, plus a good dollop of sympathy, sorted me out. Our grandma was living with us at the time, and I think my mum was happy to escape off to work and leave me in her care. I might have moaned once or twice that I was dying.

Anyway, this isn't a rustic, country dish, this is a sophisticated take on a traditional recipe and I hope you enjoy making my Welsh Rarebit Butter Bean Bruschetta. I made this once for my ex-boyfriend when he was on some high-protein diet and he loved it. I hope you do too! By the way, it doesn't have to be posh artisan bread, or anything fancy, a normal bit of toast is fine!

Do you know, this is exactly the thing I love about cooking: taking an old recipe and making it right for you. There's something really special about cooking for someone you care about and seeing them appreciate the effort and love you've put into it. I hope that the special person you cook this for – which could even be yourself – takes the time to appreciate it!

*

Typing the words ex-boyfriend had hurt like hell and she'd nearly removed them a couple of times, but there was no point in lying, and Leo wouldn't read this anyway. Esme tapped her feet as her favourite Christmas song, 'Fairytale of New York', played out. Even though it was mid-November, it was never too early for Christmas songs. She stopped typing and sang along as loud as she could. The music filled her body and she wriggled in her chair wanting to dance. Esme placed her laptop down and looked out of the windows scared someone might see. As usual there was no one around except for the birds in the trees. Slowly, nervously, she stood up.

At first it felt alien to move in a way that was purely for pleasure. She collected some cups from the coffee table and danced as she took them to the sink. Before long, Esme was bopping around, tidying as she went. The last time she'd danced to this song had been with Leo at a work do of his. He'd smiled at her from time to time, but spent most of it scanning the dancefloor trying to catch his boss, Veronica's eye. She hadn't suspected anything then. Leo always saw social dos as networking events. A chance to impress his bosses and make connections. Had she been stupid? Her heart lurched, but as Kirsty MacColl's voice listed all the things wrong with her man, Esme smiled. Now she thought of it, some of the things Leo did were quite annoying. He'd changed a lot over the years and the little foibles she hadn't minded at first had become increasingly unattractive. But there was still so much about him she'd loved. And she did miss her old life. Driving Leo from her mind, she sang along with the song.

When it finished, Esme sat back down, her mouth watering as she added some further instructions and finished reading it back. She closed her laptop, jumped up and made herself the same dish. Before eating, Esme lit it as best she could using the dull kitchen light and holding a torch in her teeth, and took a photo on her phone. She clicked publish and added the photo, which ended up dark and blurry. She was definitely going to have to practice that bit.

Afternoon slowly turned to evening and Esme found herself completely bored and fighting back tears. If she was in London she'd be able to call her friends and they'd meet up in a nice bar, drink cocktails and make her feel better. She could call them, she knew that, but it wasn't the same as them being physically near. She missed the noise of London, all the different sounds and smells that hit you depending on which area of the city you were in. The silence of the cottage could feel strangely oppressive sometimes.

Worst of all, Esme didn't have a television and was missing Netflix like crazy but had found her love of reading again, so that was something. At least, thought Esme, she'd managed to light the fire and the place was warm and cosy; she just wished that inside she didn't feel so cold and alone. A light flashed across the living-room window as a car drew up outside. She hoped it was Joe and shook her head for even thinking it so soon after her break-up, even though their little chat by the fire had been nice. She was clearly on the rebound, searching for affection and fun to lift her spirits and make her feel wanted again. As she stood and went to the door, her mother's dulcet tones echoed through the darkness, breaking into her thoughts.

'But Stephen, look at this place! She's in the middle of nowhere.'

As Esme opened the front door she heard her dad reply. 'It's fine, darling. I think it's quite sweet.' Esme paused; weirdly, they were both carrying gift bags.

'Hello, Mum, hello, Dad. You two all right?'

'Yes, darling,' Stephen replied, placing a kiss on each cheek. 'We've come to take you to the pub.'

'The pub,' her mum echoed, cheerfully.

'Oh, right. Thanks, but I don't really feel up to it tonight.' She shivered in the cold air. 'Plus, I don't think I should be wasting money in the pub.'

'Nonsense, darling,' said Carol. 'It's Friday night and I'm not letting you sit inside all the time being sad about that bastard. We can share a bottle of wine.'

'But you don't like wine,' Esme offered as a final protest. She really just wanted to hide away from the world tonight.

'Not much, no. But it's the sort of sacrifice I'm willing to make for my child. I'm that good a mother. So, let me in. I'm freezing my tits off out here.' Stephen rolled his eyes and Esme smiled as they all walked inside, shutting the door behind them.

'What's in the bags? Are you meeting someone at the pub?'

'No,' Stephen said, 'they're for you. They're moving in presents.'

'Moving in presents,' repeated her mum, wiggling her eyebrows.

'What?' Her parents were bonkers but she loved them dearly. She took the bag offered by her dad first. Opening she saw it was a bottle of champagne. 'Thank you, Dad. I'll drink it soon.' When she found the right time and had something worth celebrating.

'Here you go,' said her mum, handing hers over and grinning madly.

Esme's eyes widened in confusion. Gingerly, she reached in and pulled out . . . 'A cucumber?'

'It's not a hand-grenade, Esme,' her mum chided. 'You can slice it and pop it on your puffy eyes. I know you've been crying over that tosser but you don't need to have puffy eyelids over him. He's not worth it.' Moving in front of Esme, Carol gently flicked her daughter's hair back over her shoulders. 'You're too beautiful and too clever to waste time on that man. Time to put yourself first.'

Esme felt a tear fall down her face and Carol gently wiped it away. Her mum was as mad as a box of frogs, but Esme was grateful. 'Thanks, Mum. Right. I just need a minute to get ready.'

After Esme had changed into a nicer pair of jeans and a pretty jumper, they parked in town and walked to the pub. The blast of warm air that hit Esme's face when they went in was a welcome relief from the bitter gale blowing outside. She was grateful her mum and dad had already said they'd share a taxi home.

The pub was already busy, but rather than in London, where bars were jam-packed until the early hours, there was still room to move and they were able to find a table in the corner. A large open fire was burning and the music playing was a mix of Christmas songs and wedding-reception-type classics. Esme found herself bopping along as she settled into her seat, remembering how the morning's dancing had lifted her mood. After Stephen returned with their drinks, Carol choosing not to share a bottle of wine after all and leaving it all to Esme, her mum and dad began chatting to a friend at a nearby table, catching up on local news.

As Esme glanced around, spotting a few people she'd known at school and hiding in her chair as the burning shame of being dumped and sacked hit her again, her eyes caught on Joe who had entered with a large group of friends. He was smiling and laughing, and though it lit his face, there was still a dullness to his green eyes. She wondered whether to wave but didn't, not wanting to draw attention to herself. Then his friends crowded round him and he was lost in the middle of the group.

'So,' said Carol, turning back to Esme. 'How are you, darling?'

'I'm okay, Mum,' Esme replied. Carol eyed her daughter. 'Honestly. I promise. I'm doing okay.'

'Hmm. Let me ask you a question. If Leo walked through that door right now and got down on bended knee, asking forgiveness, saying he'd been an idiot to break up with you and it was all a big mistake, what would you say? Would you go back?'

Esme's eyes dropped. Part of her head was screaming yes. She'd loved him and thought he loved her. She'd loved their life together. Being in London made her feel alive and she loved the buzz of the city, the faster pace of life. Having everything you could ever need at your fingertips twenty-four hours a day. And though she knew now why Leo had become so distant over the last few months, before that they'd been happy. If she could go back to the times when they were in sync together, she would. 'I don't know, Mum,' she said honestly. Carol took her hand.

'Your dad doesn't often talk much sense—'

'Thank you, darling,' he said, teasingly.

'But he is right that you can never go back. It doesn't solve anything. It's only been a week since you came home and it's all still too fresh to think about clearly. Give it a little while longer and you'll feel different. I never liked him anyway.'

Esme's head shot up. 'Didn't you?'

'No. Far too arrogant and self-centred.'

'Oh.' Now Esme came to think about it, her mum had always been very nice to Leo but she'd never fully committed to it like she had with Alice's husband. Carol had always been unusually careful in the compliments she paid Esme when talking about Leo. How had she not noticed it before?

Joe and his friends were talking to a group of young women and Esme felt her brow furrowing as one of the women moved in closer to Joe, touching his arm as she spoke. Joe seemed a little unsure at first, but after a while was speaking to her more and more. He hadn't mentioned anything about having a girlfriend the other night and from their previous conversations, she'd got the impression he was still pretty cut up about his ex. Esme reminded herself he was single and it was nothing to do with her. He was able to do as he pleased and yet, she couldn't stop glancing over.

As the evening wore on, her mum became slowly more drunk and her dad laughed and joked with his friends, but Esme couldn't help but watch the scene playing out at the bar. The woman had continued to flirt with Joe and he'd reciprocated more and more. Then he lay a hand at the small of her back as she leaned in to say something. Esme was sure they were going to kiss and felt a strange stirring in her stomach: something akin to jealousy but mixed with a fair amount of confusion too. Joe's head turned to the woman and just as Esme had feared, their lips met. Suddenly Esme felt even more of a failure. Everyone had someone except her. Downing the last of her drink, and watching Joe and the woman grab their coats and leave the pub, all she wanted was to go home. To go back to her little cottage and cry. Her heart felt like a heavy weight crushing her chest, squashing her lungs. Fighting back tears she leaned into her dad and suggested they get that taxi back, and seeing the look on her face, he agreed without argument.

*

Grandma's Kitchen

Hello, lovely readers! How are you all doing?

Do you know the biggest thing I miss about London? I know I should say the theatres, the comedy clubs, or the museums and art galleries. You know, all the arty farty things. But actually it's being able to get any type of food I'm craving delivered directly to my door at any time of the day or night. No matter what type of takeaway I fancied – Thai, Mexican, Lebanese, Chinese, Indian, Italian, Japanese – I was always able to order it. And the silliest thing is, I never did! I always wanted to try and cook it myself, to see if I could get the same taste.

Do you know how many takeaways there are in my little home-town? Not many, I can tell you! And all they do is either pizza, Chinese, Indian, or fish and chips. Now I'm not in London and for once don't fancy cooking myself, I really miss it.

So, as it's Saturday night, and I'm staying inside and hiding away from the world, I'm going to share with you my recipe for Easy Pad Thai.

Chapter 12

London

Juanita polished the old mahogany table in the hall near Felicity Fenchurch's study. She wanted to stay as near to the doorway as possible without being seen. She wasn't listening to Miss Fenchurch's private conversation, of course. She wouldn't do that sort of thing. But Miss Fenchurch had told her more than once that she was a real celebrity, always being followed by some paparazzi or other, and Juanita wanted to find out if she was worried about anything. After all, she was talking to a solicitor at nine-thirty on a Monday morning. It must have been important.

In the study, Felicity sat in the large ergonomic chair she had recently purchased. Her shoulders were high and tense, and she leant forwards, her elbows resting on the desk with one finger pressed to her lips. She was definitely rattled about something.

Juanita moved the cloth across the wood of the table in slow, concentric circles. Her arms ached from the work already completed that morning. It wasn't that she was making as little noise as possible so as to hear more clearly, it was that Miss Fenchurch made sure she got her money's worth and Juanita was feeling a little tired today. Felicity's voice, an octave higher from the stress, rang out.

'Listen, I just want to know where I stand if this girl continues to lie and say I stole her recipe.' She paused for a moment. 'The truth? Well, of course I'm telling you the truth. She says I stole it and I didn't. Any similarity is pure coincidence.'

Another pause.

'My granny? Well, yes, but most of her recipes were word of mouth passed down through the family. Taught at the stove, so to speak. They weren't written down. Yes, of course I'm sure,' she said sharply.

Juanita edged to the doorway pretending to dust the frame and peered into the room. Felicity had moved from the desk now and paced in front of the window watching the busy London street outside. Her mobile phone was gripped so tightly her fingertips were white and stood out against the deep red of her nails. A long grey hair fell from the bun tied at the nape of Juanita's neck and tickled her skin. She brushed it back.

'So you think I'll be fine? Good. Good.' The evident relief in Felicity's voice put Juanita on her guard. Miss Fenchurch thought that just because she was a cleaner, she was stupid. Well, she wasn't. Something was definitely going on and it sounded like self-obsessed Felicity Fenchurch might have landed herself in real trouble this time. 'No!' Felicity shouted again. 'Like I said, pure coincidence, I assure you.'

Juanita screwed up her eyes. She thought of her own recipe book. The one she was keeping for her children. She'd always planned to teach them the traditional Spanish recipes of her hometown, but the opportunity had never arisen and they were grown now, with children of their own. Still, it wasn't too late. She wanted her grandchildren to know the rich, vibrant culture they came from. To know what real Spanish food was like and try real Spanish recipes, not just eat tapas in the restaurants their parents took them to. She sighed and peered one last time at

Felicity who, the call now finished, touched up her lip gloss and left the study. Juanita took a quick step to the side and began dusting another antique side-table, the strong scent from the vase of lilies filling her nose.

Felicity peered down at Juanita. 'What are you doing?' she asked with her normal accusatory tone.

'Dusting the hallway, Miss Fenchurch, including the door-frames, as you asked.'

'When did I ask you to do that?' Felicity hadn't told her to, but Juanita knew she wouldn't remember.

'Last month you told me to dust the doorways more often after you got some dust on your white gloves.'

'Oh. Right,' she replied. 'Did you hear any of that?' She pointed back into the study.

Juanita kept her eyes on the dust cloth in her hand. 'Any of what, Miss Fenchurch?' Felicity eyed her for a moment and Juanita worried she was about to be sacked. Felicity liked to threaten it whenever something was going wrong in her life. Juanita held her breath.

'Nothing. Never mind.' Felicity swept past her and collected her expensive woollen coat from the antique coat stand. 'I'm going out.'

'Yes, Miss Fenchurch. Goodbye.' Felicity didn't answer as she slammed the door behind her.

Once Juanita was sure Felicity had gone, she went into the study, but kept the duster and polish in her hand, just in case she needed an excuse to be in there. She wondered over to the desk and nonchalantly glanced down. Disappointingly there was nothing written on the pad, and the only thing that dominated her desk was the half-finished draft of her new recipe book. Juanita hadn't given it much thought before, but as she glanced at the first couple of pages of *Felicity Fenchurch's Fabulous Fiestas*, a strange prickle crept down her spine. The use of the word fiesta made her think of home and she felt the need to see her own notebook and remember her life there. Juanita really was feeling tired today. Tired of the dull grey, English weather, tired of working herself to the bone, and she wanted to read, smell and think of Spain. She stuffed the duster in the pocket of her apron and went to the kitchen, descending the stairs in the far corner to reach her basement flat. Felicity didn't need a live-in housekeeper, she just liked to have a general dogsbody. It made her feel important.

In her bedroom, Juanita knelt by the large wooden trunk she had brought with her all those years ago when she first moved to England. She ran her fingers over the rich, gnarled wood, scratched and cut with the story of her life, and opened the lid. Beneath the different mementos she had collected on her various travels, she found what she was looking for. Juanita sat on her bed and opened the old notebook book, smelling its pages. Years of cooking had soaked into the paper and she could almost taste the saffron and chilli emanating from it. Immediately, Juanita was transported to the olive trees of her youth, the imposing stark mountains outside the village and the smell of rich red wine. Aches and pains began to release from her muscles as she held it.

One of the pages had a strange mark on it. She tried to scratch off the dark red splodge but it wouldn't move. It wasn't jam or tomato sauce. It looked like nail varnish. The same red nail varnish Miss Fenchurch wore. The one she said made her feel like a vamp. Juanita studied her own wrinkled, raw hands and the blunt, broken nails at the ends of her fingers. She didn't own any nail varnish.

Chapter 13

Sandchester

Esme stared again at the screen of her laptop, clicking refresh every few seconds. It had been just under two weeks since the break-up and since she'd moved home. It wasn't that long and yet, it felt like so much had happened. Watching the screen, she huffed out a breath. There'd only been eight hits on her blog and she felt utterly defeated. No one had left any comments or signed up to her mailing list. The few that had looked hadn't bothered reading anything at all.

She knew she needed to add more content and was spending today picking and choosing recipes. Some of the older recipes were too bland for today's sweet palates, or had weird ingredients from the days of rationing. And there was absolutely no way she was cooking horse. Where did you even get horse? It was probably illegal to eat it these days and she wasn't going to try it anyway. She wanted to show some of the old dishes off, but they needed a lot of care and attention before they were introduced to the modern world.

Recently, Esme had begun to enjoy being apart from normal life, but her confidence was scant. Her cottage offered some refuge from the outside world, being as isolated as it was, but it was still quite cold even with the fire on and that, combined with a sudden lack of routine, made her despondent. It was the last week of November, but her usual excitement and Christmas cheer was gone. She'd managed to get dressed today into proper clothes and had put on three extra jumpers, but the strong wind outside blew the trees almost horizontal and whistled through the house.

Esme sat back on the sofa and pulled her legs up to her chest. She felt too old to be starting a new career. A little voice in her head told her this was all completely pointless and the whole world was shouting at her to stop being silly, stop playing at being a blogger. She might as well just plod on to retirement doing what she'd always done and then die. She picked up her phone and dialled Lola, confiding in her the moment she answered.

'It's not working,' Esme cried down the line. 'No one's reading my blog and I don't know what to do. I don't understand search engine optimisation, or key phrases, and Twitter is, quite frankly, beyond me. You can't say anything remotely interesting, or important in 280 characters. What do I do, Lola?'

Lola spluttered a laugh. 'I know it's hard, honey, but you have to keep at it. Websites don't grow overnight. You have to plug away getting your name out there.'

'But I don't know how.' Esme flung her free hand in the air and the sleeve of her oversized jumper flew out, hitting her on top of her head. 'Oh, Lola. Is this all a terrible idea?'

'No, it's not. You're an amazing cook and you just need to persevere. Try linking to other websites, or guest blogging. Oh, there is one other thing you could try.'

Esme scrunched up her face. She wasn't sure she wanted to hear this. She wasn't going in for anything gimmicky. No cooking naked or finding the next must-have ingredient and including that in everything from coffee to ice cream. 'Oh yeah, what's that?'

'Vlogging.'

'Vlogging?'

'Yeah. Video blogging. Recent evidence shows that people are searching way more for videos than they used to. It might be worth a shot. But like I said, building a following doesn't happen overnight. You have to put lots of time and energy into it. Keep adding posts and people will start looking.'

Esme wasn't sure. It was a great idea for other people, but could *she* do it? She didn't want to be yet another Felicity Fenchurch. Another fake TV cook who didn't stand for anything. Those shows were all about fancy dinner parties with matching crockery and showing off, without any real heart and soul, or even actual cooking.

Esme examined her recipe book. Her blog, her as yet unwritten cookbook, her new career, she wanted it to have a meaning she could pass on. To her, recipes were all about sharing and learning. She'd always learned from watching and others could too. She'd learned from watching her grandma cook as Mum couldn't be trusted in the kitchen. But with Grandma, Esme had watched, tried and tasted, gradually falling in love with cooking.

'Like YouTube?' Esme asked, still a bit confused by how it would work in practice.

'Yes, you could start your own channel – I'd follow you!'

Esme loved the idea of being an internet sensation. It had led to so much more for so many people, but things like that didn't happen to people like her. Still, it might be worth a shot just to get people reading her blog. 'I wouldn't need much, would I?'

'Just a decent camera that you can attach to your laptop. How's the money situation going?'

Esme shifted in her seat. Her mum and dad had been generous, but she needed to keep as much as she could aside for living expenses. Could she afford to buy a camera? 'Things are tight. I'm not making any money at the moment and I need to save what I've got.'

'I really think you should do this, Esme,' encouraged Lola. 'I know you're being careful, but you need to invest in your future and that's what you'll be doing.'

Esme cocked her head to one side. A little camera couldn't be that expensive. 'Okay, then. I will.'

'Do a trial run first and record it, then you can make sure you've got everything right.'

'Good idea. I'll let you know when and you guys can come down and review it with me.'

'Sounds like a plan. I do love a nice trip home. Maybe we'll pop in and say hi to Joe Holloway while we're there.'

'Stop it. How are you and Eric?' Esme asked to distract Lola from probing further.

'We're good. We're going to see a movie tonight,' Lola replied.

Esme missed saying 'we' sometimes. She played with the tassel on one of her cushions. 'Have a good time you two. See you later.'

Esme hung up then searched online for a camera. Before long she had placed her order and, filled with excitement, her camera was on its way.

Chapter 14

Sandchester

Joe drove to the camera shop to collect the new lens for the posh camera his parents had given him last Christmas. Whilst taking snaps of the properties for the estate agent was all right, what he really loved was to go wandering with his camera down to the sea, or out into the woods and capture all the weird shapes, shadows and scenes only found in nature. As he opened the shop door, a Christmas song started playing on the tiny radio behind the counter. A small, depressed fake Christmas tree with stringy tinsel wrapped around the base stood next to the till where the owner, Ian, stood. 'Hey Ian, how's life with you?'

'Not bad, Joe, thanks. You?' He was tall and well-built with a thick black beard, like a gothy Father Christmas.

'Yeah, all right. I've been busy this week. We had a couple of offers and a couple of lets. Not bad for this time of year.' Joe unbuttoned his coat, adjusting to the warmth.

'That's good.'

'You busy?'

'Yes, mate.' Ian nodded. 'Very. Lots of Christmas orders.'

97

'Speaking of which, has my order come in yet?' Joe loosened his scarf too.

'Yep. Hang on.' He disappeared into the back of the shop and returned with a box with Holloway written on it in thick black pen.

'Fantastic. It's a new lens for my camera. I can't wait to get out into the woods with this. There's this great twisted tree I want to capture.'

The bell sounded behind him and Joe turned to see Esme with a bright red coat tied at the waist emphasising her hourglass figure. She had a bit more colour in her cheeks now and under her hat he could see her wild messy hair. He inspected a nearby shelf, remembering their conversation by the fire and the feelings it had started within him, and how he'd secretly fancied her at school. Back then she hadn't noticed him, of course. She and that friend of hers – what was her name? Lola? – were always scheming and giggling like teenage girls do. She'd been out of his league then and she still was now.

'Hello,' said Esme, walking to the counter. 'Have you got an order for Kendrick?' She turned to Joe. 'Hi. What are you doing here? Christmas shopping?'

Joe felt himself grow hot and hoped it was the lack of air conditioning. 'I, umm, I just bought a new camera. Well, a lens, anyway.'

'Really?'

'Yeah. Photography's a bit of a passion of mine.'

'I didn't know that.' She smiled.

'What about you?' asked Joe.

'I bought a camera for my computer.'

'Oh, right.' His brow furrowed, confused as to why she needed one.

'I'll be making videos of recipes and teaching people how to cook. I'm going to post them online.'

'That's awesome,' replied Joe. He was excited for her but again found himself shocked by how she seemed to grab at life and not let it slow her down. He glanced at her face. It gave the impression of other-worldliness, and he felt something he hadn't in a long while – a kind of hopefulness. Esme radiated positivity and energy, and some of it had seeped into his soul. He wondered if she knew the effect she had on other people. The way she lit up a room with her laugh and her smile, the way she never judged. Esme glanced around the store and Joe shuffled his feet.

'I hope he's got it,' she said, beginning to worry. 'I ordered it on Monday and he said it would be here by Friday.'

Joe leaned in and whispered, 'I'm sure he has. It's just that his filing system's quite chaotic.'

She giggled. 'I meant to ask, is the King's Head still going?'

Joe nodded. 'Yeah. Surprising, I know. It doesn't serve underage drinkers anymore though.'

'Like we were, you mean? I think you'll find I never did anything like that.'

'Oh, I know, I'd never cast aspersions on your good character. I only went because we could play pool.'

'I don't think anyone will think I'm underage anymore,' Esme replied. 'I can't remember the last time I was ID'd. Sometimes I think about asking them to do it just to make me feel better.'

Joe laughed but bit back the compliment floating on the tip of his tongue.

They fell into an uncomfortable silence and after a moment Esme broke it by taking off her hat and saying, 'Do you know about cameras and stuff as well as houses then?'

'Sort of.' He moved his box from under one arm to another. 'I'm not an expert.'

Esme face was thoughtful, considering something. 'Listen, do you fancy a quick drink and helping me with which leads plug in where? I'm not very good with tech.'

Joe hesitated at the prospect of spending real time with someone. Time that involved talking and connecting. Clara was there again, drifting about in his mind, and he pushed the memory of her away. He was much better at no strings, but the look in Esme's gentle eyes pierced his heart. 'That'd be nice. Sure. The King's Head is just down the road, shall we go there? I've only got an hour though – I'm on my lunch break.'

Ian emerged with the parcel and Esme collected her order. Joe held the door for her and they made their way outside. It was raining when they left the shop and the sky had darkened to a sheet of bleak, steel-grey. They walked down the high street to the pub and passed the giant Christmas tree in the centre of town. A large star had been placed on top and strings of lights were haphazardly wrapped around. Children gazed up at it, holding their parents' hands and pointing to the top. Underneath, fake presents wrapped in bright red paper were piled on top of each other. A Salvation Army band were lined up beside it playing traditional Christmas carols and Joe saw Esme wonder at the scene before them. As the rain beat down, tapping their skin, they quickened their pace until they were safe and dry inside.

Joe took off his coat and lay it over his arm then took Esme's for her. She brushed the rain from her hair. 'What would you like?' he asked as they approached the bar.

'I'll have a cola, please. I'm going for a run later.'

'In this?' Joe peered out of the window and as Esme stood next to him, he could smell her coconut conditioner again.

'Yeah, it helps clear my head. I'll just wrap up.'

Joe turned to the barman and ordered two cokes while Esme found them a table. More and more people came in out of the rain, and Joe had to navigate through them with the drinks in his hands. Amongst the rising voices he could make out Nineties music he remembered from his youth playing in the background. It was a nice change from Christmas songs. He never looked forward to Christmas anymore and these days Christmas songs brought him down rather than lifting his spirits. Joe placed their drinks down on the table. 'So, what made you decide to start a blog?'

Esme combed her fingers through her hair. 'It's a long story.'

'Oh, okay. Sorry. Did you want to talk about something else?'

'I don't mind,' she replied, with a gentle shrug. 'It is what it is. Basically, I got fired from my job because my boss didn't believe me when I told her someone had stolen one of my recipes and was pitching it as their own.'

'What?' asked Joe, his coke held in mid-air. 'Someone stole your recipe and you're the one who got fired? That's outrageous.'

'I know.' She nodded, her eyes wide. 'Then, because I didn't have any proof, she wanted me to apologise. I refused, so she sacked me.'

Joe stared, then let out a great loud chortle. Shocked, Esme sat still and she felt her cheeks redden. 'Sorry, I wasn't laughing at you. It's just, that's the most awesome thing I've ever heard. You're incredibly brave sticking to your guns like that. Not many people would.'

When Esme relaxed and grinned at him, his stomach fluttered. 'Do you think so?'

'I do. I think it's awesome.'

They took a sip of their drinks in companionable silence.

'So, you're a secret photographer?' Esme asked.

'Amateur photographer,' he corrected, gently. 'Secret makes me sound shady. But, yeah.' He noticed what a pretty shade of pink her lips were.

'What sort of things do you take pictures of?'

'Nature mostly.'

Esme smirked.

'Not like pervy nature, I don't sneak around taking photos of naked women, if that's what you think.'

'It hadn't crossed my mind, actually, but now you've said it . . .'

Joe laughed. 'I like scenery and animals and stuff. I like capturing the world where it's been left alone by civilisation and technology. Where it's truly wild.'

'That sounds great. Do you think you could do some snaps

of food for my blog one day? I've tried but I'm not very good.'

'I'd love to,' replied Joe, as the rain battered against the windows. He was enjoying her company. That hadn't happened in a while. There were women but they didn't meant anything. Sex was just a release and he was flattered by being wanted. There hadn't been much talking involved. He was enjoying talking and laughing with Esme. Suddenly, he found himself wanting this meeting to last and said, 'Do you fancy a bite to eat as we're here? I'm sure it won't be as good as anything you could cook, but as it's so bad outside . . .'

When Esme hesitated, Joe worried he'd gone too far but then she smiled. 'That'd be nice, but only if your girlfriend won't mind.'

'Girlfriend?' Taken aback by the question, Joe's brow crinkled.

'Oh, it's just I was in the pub Friday night and I saw you with . . . someone.'

Joe felt a flush of heat rise up from the back of his neck. It wasn't just embarrassment, it was shame. He'd never before really cared about his reputation and the consequences of his actions. He'd never needed to think of anyone else or think about a future where anyone might care. But now, here with Esme, he did. 'She was just a friend,' he said quickly, and swallowed down the lump in his throat. He grabbed the menu wanting to order before Esme changed her mind and, as he hid behind it, he realised that it was the first day he hadn't felt the heavy great shadow darkening his life.

*

The rain eased off and Esme walked back from the pub in the afternoon wind. Joe had offered a lift, but Esme wanted to walk. To lift her head and look around her, to see the countryside with new eyes. Dark grey clouds clustered overhead and the wind was cold on her face. She'd always thought that being home, back in pokey little Sandchester, where she'd spent her teenage years longing to escape, she would feel trapped. But as she walked along the country lane surrounded by fields, breathing in the fresh air and enjoying the coldness on her skin, it was turning out to be the opposite. She felt free. Freer than she ever had in London. There she was trapped by a boring working week, by the crowded tube, by the constant attempts to get home and inevitable delays, and most of all, by the expectation to do everything. To cook, to clean, to keep herself in shape, to keep herself as polished as possible so she was the same as the elegant, chic London women. They weren't all Leo's expectations, to be fair. There was just a general expectation to be a grown-up and have her shit together all the time.

If she'd sat around the flat in the clothes she sat around in these days, Leo would've disapproved. He wouldn't have said anything. Not straightaway. He'd have given her half an hour, then started making comments about people popping round and what they might think if she looked like that. Now she came to think of it, life with Leo had been exhausting, but she'd been too wrapped up in perfect London living to notice.

Was she happy it had ended the way it did? No, not really. It could have been a lot easier if it had happened at a different time, if he hadn't so quickly moved onto someone else, or moved them in. *Dirtbag*. Lousy Leo would be his name from now on. Esme smiled at the thought.

And now there was Joe back in her life and he was . . . confusing. In a lot of ways he was nice and kind – not at all what she thought he'd be. The bad boy from school who all the girls mooned after was much more introverted than she'd expected. He'd said he'd moved back from Australia after a break-up, but was that all there was to it? He'd seemed so vulnerable when he'd talked about it briefly during the viewings and later by the fire. He must have loved this woman a lot. But then Esme had seen him the other night in the pub and it didn't take a great deal of imagination to know what had happened after they'd left. He'd said it was just a friend but she didn't treat her friends like that. It was obviously a 'special' friend. And yet, lunch had been fun. They'd chatted and she'd seen flashes of his personality. She shook her head. She really couldn't figure him out.

Esme walked down the winding lane to the cottage and watched the fields and hedges swaying in the wind. The late afternoon sun cast strange shadows through the leafless trees but they didn't frighten her, she enjoyed them. Esme took a deep breath. There was nothing to fear here, she was safe and at home. As she unlocked the front door and took off her coat, she glanced at the kitchen, and her grandma's notebook, picturing which recipe she would make next.

Chapter 15

Sandchester

On Saturday morning Esme set up the camera, attaching the leads to her computer as Joe had shown her. She placed it on the countertop, then ran backwards and forwards to make sure it was in the right place and at the right height. She wanted to be certain it would actually record her as she cooked.

Having gone through her grandma's recipe book four times, Esme had decided on a delicious take on the double-layer chocolate chestnut cake that started this whole sorry business. She could have made something else, but a part of her couldn't let the recipe that had meant so much to her be tainted by the memory of Felicity Fenchurch. She needed to reclaim it as her own, but with some changes. Grandma wouldn't mind. She'd always said that recipes should change, just as people did. The reason Grandma had loved cooking and recording everything in her recipe book was because as the recipes got passed down through the family, they changed and represented the new generation. It meant they were never forgotten. Esme swapped the chestnuts for hazelnuts, and the chestnut puree for chocolate hazelnut spread. With fluffy whipped cream it would be mouth-watering, gooey and utterly delicious. She couldn't wait to get started.

Mark and Helena were coming down that afternoon so she would be able to serve them some delicious cake while they watched her recording. Lola couldn't make it as Eric had whisked her away for a surprise romantic weekend in Paris, which unbeknownst to them, he'd planned months ago. Esme was disappointed not to have Lola there for her first recording but loved how happy Eric made her, so she couldn't be mad at either of them.

Nerves swirled in Esme's stomach and her shoulders were tensed. That niggling voice of doubt in her brain had started whispering in her ear again, asking her why she was even bothering. It was going to be a disaster. She wasn't the next Felicity Fenchurch. Who did she think she was kidding? Not that she wanted to be like Felicity exactly, but she had to admit, as annoying as Felicity was in real life, she had a certain something the camera and audiences were drawn to. Would Esme be able to capture something like that in her scruffy, cold kitchen?

She took a deep breath and shook out her arms and legs, like she did after a run, trying to unknot the kink in her neck. She switched on the camera and raced to the kitchen where she had everything prepared. Everything that is, except for a script.

On Friday night she had lain in bed after her earlier drink with Joe, thinking about what she would say. But every time she started, her brain got side-tracked thinking about Joe's eyes, or his smile, or his hair and how it would feel to run her hands through it. Whenever she did, she gave her head a good shake to dislodge the thoughts and rolled over to sleep. Now, standing in front of the camera, Esme wished she had prepared properly. She didn't know what she would say, but the one thing she did know was that she didn't want to be Felicity Fenchurch. No pouting at the camera, batting her eyelashes – not that she knew how to anyway – and no ridiculous alliteration.

Remembering the camera was now recording, she turned to

it and introduced the recipe, talking through everything she was doing as she did it.

'Thanks for joining me, folks. Tonight we're going to make a fabulous chocolate hazelnut cake. It's a great recipe for this time of year with all those pre-Christmas parties. It's super-easy to make too, so if you've got an office party or a school Christmas fair, you'll be able to whip this up in no time and impress the pants off everyone.' She swept her hair back from her face and cursed herself for not tying it up. 'The first thing you need to do is cream the butter and sugar together. If you've got an electric hand whisk, or a mixer, you can do it easily in there, but if you've just got a good bowl and a wooden spoon like me, you'll do just as well. It just takes a little bit more elbow grease.'

She beat them for a few moments till she had a light and fluffy mixture in the bowl.

'Next we're going to add in the eggs one at a time, making sure they're thoroughly mixed in. If the mixture starts to separate, you'll know because it'll go gloopy, so add a little of your measured flour and it'll help bring it back together. The next thing we need to do is sift, then mix the flour and cocoa. I'm not a snob, but I would recommend using a good cocoa powder. A rich one gives so much more flavour. If you can't get or afford a good one, use a cheapy and add a tiny bit of coffee. My grandma told me that tip because sometimes, when money was tight, that's what she'd do. Just a teaspoon or so of made-up black coffee brings out the chocolatiness, giving a nice depth.

'I love this recipe because it was one of my Grandma Pearl's and as we're called Grandma's Kitchen I thought it would be perfect for my first vlog. Plus, it's a really lovely Christmassy recipe. Sometimes, Grandma would use chestnuts that she'd boil and make into a paste herself. But, I mean, who can be bothered with that? Not me, though you can get chestnut puree these days. I've switched it up to hazelnut spread because it's my favourite. When I was little, I used to eat it from the jar with a spoon until

I felt sick. Don't do that, by the way, if you can help it. It gives you the absolute worst tummy ache. Or if you do, just don't eat the whole jar!'

She looked up at the camera again. It felt weird, but not as weird as she was expecting. Esme thought it would be a good idea to show the bowl to the camera and tipped it forward. The spoon dropped to the floor. She quickly bent down behind the counter to pick it up saying, 'Oh, shit, bollocks.' When she remembered she was on camera, she gave a silent apology and hoped the tiny microphone hadn't picked it up.

'Right, now we've got it all mixed, we need to divide the mixture between the two cake tins. And these tins have been greased and then floured so the cake will turn out nice and easily.' She spooned the mixture into the tins and ran it over the top for an even finish. When the cake was in the oven, she smiled at the camera. It was becoming more and more natural every time. 'Come back for part two later, when I assemble this bad boy.' She gave one last look and walked to switch it off. 'Bad boy?' she said out loud to herself. 'You've been on your own too long and gone mental.'

The baked cakes filled the kitchen with a deep, rich chocolate scent. Esme's mouth watered and she resisted the urge to pick a bit off the top to test the cake. The cooker might have been ancient and somewhat unsafe, but it cooked evenly, producing two light and airy sponges that sprang back as she tapped them to see if they were finished.

The cottage, now filled with the aroma of cocoa, felt warm and cosy from the heat of the oven and the roaring log fire. Esme turned the cakes out of the tins to let them cool on a wire rack and hummed while cleaning the worktops, preparing for the next segment. Once they were cold, she turned the camera on and went back into the kitchen.

'So, here we have our cold cakes and the first thing we're going to do is beat some cream to whip it up to a light and fluffy consistency.' She whipped the cream with a hand whisk. Her posh mixer was still in Mark's flat where he'd collected it from Leo – he hadn't managed to bring it down yet. She then pulled out her favourite cake stand. An old-fashioned rose patterned one she'd found at a car boot sale before moving to London.

'So first of all, put a dab of choccy spread on the cake stand to hold the bottom layer in place; that way it won't wobble around while you're working.' She wiggled it around to show what she meant, 'Wobble wobble.' But then instantly regretted it. 'Now add a layer of chocolate hazelnut spread. Next add a layer of whipped cream and then place the second cake layer on top. Now, add another layer of the spread to the top of the cake and a topping of whipped cream, then sprinkle with hazelnuts. And there you have it, a double-layer chocolate hazelnut cake. Enjoy!'

Esme showed off her cake to the camera and then ran back around to switch it off. She placed her hands on her hips admiring her perfect creation. There was just enough time for a cup of tea before Mark and Helena arrived.

At just after one, their car pulled up out front, and Esme ran to the door to meet them. 'I've done it.' she announced. 'I've recorded my first video. Yay me!' She clapped her hands together.

'Well done, sweetie,' replied Mark, engulfing her in a huge hug.

Helena grabbed their bags from the back seat. 'Good work, love. Does that mean we've got something scrumptious to eat?'

'Yep, there's a double-layer chocolate hazelnut cake. Come on, I'll slice us some.'

'Good,' said Mark. 'I am heartbroken, sweetie. Did they tell you? Gorgeous William from Payroll dumped me. My heart is shattered into a million pieces.'

Esme hugged him. 'I know. Isn't it awful being an unwanted cast-off, rejected by the one who loved you?'

A very faint blush appeared on Mark's gorgeous dark skin. 'I know you've had it worse, sweetie, I do. But I was convinced he was the one. Or at least, that it might turn into that.'

'You went out twice,' said Helena, laughing.

Helena was so ambitious no man had ever got close to derailing her career aspirations. Whoever did was going to have to be pretty special. Esme pulled a sad face and linked her arm through Mark's. She'd meant what she said. It was terrible being cast aside, but that had been the first time she'd actually laughed about it. Maybe her heart was mending a little, or maybe it was just the chocolate cake waiting for her. They walked into the house as grey clouds filled the sky, fading the light outside. Inside, the cottage was dim and Esme switched on the old-fashioned standing lamp with a pink fringed shade that stood in the corner of the living room. The bulb gave a crackle before starting up.

Mark looked around. 'That doesn't sound healthy. You need to get that checked out before the place burns down.'

'It's fine,' Esme replied. 'It only happens occasionally.' She went to the kitchen and began cutting the cake. 'One of you'll have to sleep on the sofa and the other can have the spare room. Which I have tidied and cleaned by the way. Unless you want to share the double bed?'

'Bagsy the spare room,' Helena and Mark said together, raising their hands like children in class.

'I pick Mark,' said Esme, smiling. 'As he's so heartbroken.' Helena crossed her arms over her chest and Mark gave her a playful shove.

Esme picked up her laptop and carried it over. 'Shall we watch it then? I'll just get the cake.'

'Wait,' shouted Mark, unpacking a bottle of wine from his bag. 'We need drinkies for this momentous occasion.'

'Glasses are in the cupboard next to the sink.'

Mark got up and went to the kitchen. He found them but grimaced as he examined the dirt and grime inside. The biggest problem with the old cottage was that everything seemed to get dirty and dusty no matter where you put it or how often you cleaned. He gave them a good wash and found a bottle opener, then carried everything back to the sofa to join Esme and Helena.

Esme sliced the cake and served it onto dainty tea plates. It stood proudly in all its chocolatey glory, waiting to be eaten.

As they began to watch, Mark kept tapping his feet.

'Do you need the toilet or something?' asked Esme.

'No. Um, do you realise that you can see straight down your top?'

Esme peered closer at the screen. She'd only been half-watching, too busy shovelling cake into her mouth. She slumped back then looked down at the pretty top she'd chosen to wear. It didn't look low-cut but she pulled it up a bit higher. 'I thought I'd set it up perfectly.' Her voice sounded out from the recording in front of them and she shuddered. 'Do I sound that squeaky in real life?'

'No,' said Mark. 'We all sound different on camera, just like on the phone.'

'What exactly are you doing there?' asked Helena pointing at the screen.

'I'm creaming the butter and sugar together till it's light and fluffy.'

'Your boobs look like they're having some kind of fight. You need a better bra before you go doing that again.' Esme yanked up her bra straps.

'When you turn I can't hear you at all,' said Mark. 'You'll have to remember to speak facing the front or get a better microphone.'

Then a few minutes later, a giggling Helena asked, 'Did you just say bollocks?'

Esme frowned. 'Might have done. I dropped the spoon.'

Helena gave her a hug. 'You need to look at the camera a bit more.'

'On a technical note,' said Mark, who as a lighting technician on Felicity's show so knew what he was talking about and was clearly trying to be tactful. 'It is quite dark. We can see down your top, but not much else. They look like whoppers by the way so you'd probably get some followers but maybe not the type you want.'

'It's a disaster,' said Esme, through a mouthful of chocolate cake, helping herself to another slice.

Mark patted her back. 'No, it's not, sweetie. You're amazing, honestly. We just need to get you some better lighting. I should've warned you you'd need a spotlight. I didn't think. That kitchen light looks like it's been there since 1973.'

'It has.'

'I quite like it. I think lit properly that kitchen will look fabulous on camera.'

'Can you steal some lights from work for me?'

'No, I most certainly cannot. They're too big to fit up my jumper or under my coat. But,' he said, putting the laptop on his knees and opening the browser, 'I'll help you find one online.'

Esme's face darkened. She'd had such high hopes but again things had come crashing down. It all felt like a total, utter disaster.

'I have to say,' said Helena. 'You have amazing presence on screen. You're bubbly and really likeable.'

'I wasn't like Felicity, was I?' Esme's eyes were wide with panic.

Helena shook her head. 'No, you were not.'

'No way,' said Mark. 'You were wonderful.'

'Well, that's one good thing.'

Helena, trying to be subtle, coughed to get Mark's attention then nodded in Esme's direction. Esme knew she was trying to get Mark to say something nice. 'What?' she demanded of Helena, who blushed furiously at being caught out.

'I'd definitely watch your stuff, Esme,' said Mark. 'You were great. From what we could hear, the instructions were well put and you're lively and fun. I think people will love it and love you. Just like we do.'

'You're just saying that,' said Esme.

'No, we're not,' assured Helena. 'I'd tell you if you were shit. You know that.'

'Okay,' said Esme, nodding to herself. It was true. Helena most definitely would. Esme took a deep breath. 'Okay, I can do this.'

Every setback was a learning opportunity if she chose to see it that way. She'd read that in a self-help book once. All she needed to do was prepare more and get some better equipment, but it was a step in the right direction. And being on camera hadn't felt as weird and unnatural as she'd expected. 'Come on then,' she said, sipping her wine. 'Let's get some lighting. But not too expensive, okay? I'm starting to seriously run out of money. Soon I'll be living off baked beans on toast.'

'I'm sure you could fantabulatise those as well,' said Mark.

'That's not even a word. But I like it. I might use it next time.'

'Can't you get any freelance work?' asked Helena, still eating her chocolate cake. She was one of life's nibblers, she didn't shovel food into her mouth at a rate of knots like the rest. 'There must be hundreds of other shows needing staff.'

Esme shrugged. 'I've been in touch with some agencies and some of the contacts I've made over the years. I'll just have to wait and see.'

'I'm sure it'll work out,' said Mark. 'Things always work out for the best.'

'I hope so,' Esme replied. She wanted to believe him, but without the routine of a normal job she felt adrift. Esme sighed, but she'd come too far now to quit. She studied the tiles behind the kitchen sink. They would look good when the lighting arrived, she reckoned. With pride, Esme thought of the cake she'd just made, of all the different ingredients and flavours there were to play with, and the cathartic act of cooking. She could make this work. No, she *would* make this work. 'More cake, everyone?' she said with a smile.

Chapter 16

London

Lying in his bed, next to Veronica's sleeping form, Leo stretched and placed his hands behind his head. Right before bed, Veronica had had a meltdown about the few odd items of Esme's that were still in the flat. Leo thought she was overreacting, and ruining what had been a nice Saturday night, but telling Veronica that wasn't an option. It was simpler to just agree to phone Esme and remind her the things still needed removing. It wasn't that much, just a large chest of drawers that had been too big for her weird friend Mark's hire car, and a couple of trinkets he'd found in a drawer in the kitchen. And seeing how quickly she'd moved out the rest of her stuff, which on reflection was very decent of her, he didn't feel he could keep nagging. To be fair, he'd just wanted Mark to get done and leave. He'd flounced around the flat giving Leo dirty looks, even though he hadn't actually done anything wrong. When Mark finally found someone for longer than two minutes, he'd realise that. Leo had never liked Mark, who was too exuberant and loud – it was off-putting.

Leo ran his hand over his chin, flung his legs out of bed and grabbed his dressing gown. He went into the living room and, checking his watch, thought about calling Esme now. It was almost one in the morning and even though it was late, Leo picked up the phone to dial, hoping she'd be asleep and wouldn't pick up. He'd tried to avoid speaking with her, not wanting to hear the heartbreak in her voice. She must have been destroyed by their break-up and he didn't want to have to deal with tears. He'd never been able to predict if she'd cry, laugh or get angry when they got into a fight thanks to her tempestuous nature. If only he'd mustered up the nerve to call before now. In his mind, he pictured Esme in her parents' awful poky little box room, devouring a tub of ice cream while she sobbed. For Esme's sake he hoped they were laying off the midnight activities. The last thing you need when you've just been dumped is to hear your parents getting it on. And she'd definitely have put on weight from all the comfort eating. If he phoned now though, it should click through to voicemail and he wouldn't have to actually speak to her.

'Hello?' came a harsh, wide awake voice from the other end.

Damn it. 'Oh, hi, Esme. It's Leo.' He could hear moving around, giggling and laughter in the background and his brow creased in confusion. Then he heard Mark's voice loud and clear.

'Is that that scumbag? What's he doing calling at . . . blimey, it's one in the morning. We're all asleep, Leo, you'll have to call back.'

Idiot. Taken aback, Leo forgot why he was calling. He hadn't expected her friends to be with her. Then Esme's voice cut into his thoughts.

'Leo? What the heck are you ringing me for? I can't imagine you've got anything to say to me and I definitely do not want to talk to you. Plus, it's the middle of the night. No one calls people in the middle of the night. What are you doing? Are you drunk?'

'Bog off, Leo,' he heard Helena shout. So she was there too. They couldn't all be at Carol and Stephen's. Esme must be staying somewhere else. But where? Confusion filled him and he suddenly felt adrift. Like he'd floated out to sea and his legs couldn't reach the bottom. It wasn't a sensation he was used to. Trying to find some control and regain his footing, he cleared his throat.

'Yeah, umm, sorry for ringing so late.' Leo ran a hand down his brilliant white T-shirt over striped pyjama bottoms and pulled his dressing gown tighter against the cold. 'I just wanted to say, that, you know, I'm sorry things didn't work out for us.'

'At one in the morning? Are you mad? And anyway, it's not that they didn't work out for us, Leo. You dumped me.'

'You tell him!' shouted Mark, before he began chanting 'Loser' over and over again.

Leo tutted at Mark's childishness. This wasn't the Esme he was used to. The Esme he was used to was much more . . . nurturing. He felt suddenly on the back foot. He did with Veronica some-times and it unnerved him. He'd never felt like that with Esme. 'Yes, but you'll find someone else, Esme. I know you will. You're an amazing girl.'

There was a pause. 'What's he saying?' asked Mark. 'Tell him if he calls you again I'll—'

'Sssshhhh!' Esme replied. 'What do you want, Leo?'

'I just wanted to ask if you could possibly come to get the last of your things? There isn't much. Just that old chest of drawers in the spare room and a few little ornaments. When Mark couldn't get it in the car he said he'd be back soon with a van but he hasn't. I didn't want to get rid of it because I know how much you love it.'

Silence.

'You've rung me at stupid o'clock in the morning to ask me to come and get my antique chest of drawers from the spare room?' He heard Mark and Helena in the background but couldn't make out what they were saying as their voices blended into one. It wouldn't be good though. 'Why is that, Leo? Are you moving in some other woman and you need the spare room clear for all her clothes and shoes and accessories?'

'Esme. I'm sorry, it's just Veronica—'

'Oh, yes, that's her name, isn't it?'

'Esme, please—'

'Don't worry, Leo. I'll get it sorted out tomorrow. Just don't be there when Mark shows up. For your sake.' She hung up and Leo tapped his phone against his chin, exhaling a long deep breath.

That had gone quite well considering her friends had been there. Wherever *there* was. The sound of Veronica's gentle snoring emerged from the bedroom and he debated whether to have a cup of tea before going back to bed.

Leo went to the kitchen and filled the kettle. Veronica would ease off a bit now. She required a lot more care and attention than Esme ever had. Veronica was great but it had to be said, she didn't look after him as well as Esme. They'd shared the house-work, and Esme had done all the cooking for them. He gave a scornful laugh; that had changed now. It was him who did all the cooking these days. And though Veronica was grateful, she didn't hesitate to tell him how he could improve next time. And she wanted to hire a cleaner. Esme had been messy when she first moved in, but she'd soon seen how important it was to be tidy and made an effort to clean up after herself. Veronica just wanted to hire someone to come in and clean up after her. Who would pay for that though? Financials were always a difficult subject in a new relationship, and it wasn't a conversation he particularly wanted to have yet. Still, things were going to work out fine with Veronica, he told himself as a familiar niggle gnawed at the back of his mind. Of course they were.

Chapter 17

Sandchester

A week later, Esme spent all Saturday morning waiting in for the lighting to arrive. By the time the courier knocked on the door just after lunchtime, she'd eaten an enormous sandwich and gulped down seven cups of tea but, excited, she didn't want to waste a second and called Mark to talk her through setting up the spotlight.

'Hello, sweetie. How's it going?' From his cheerful tone he must have got over his heartbreak already.

'Yeah, good,' Esme replied. Heavy metal clanged in the background. 'Are you working today or are you stalking local builders again?'

'Overtime, baby. They need everything set up for an early start on Monday so I volunteered. How's things with you?'

'Going okay, thanks. I've had a few visits to my blog and the lights have arrived. What do I do with them?'

'Right,' said Mark. 'Do exactly as I say.'

Esme followed Mark's instructions for setting it up in the right place to light the food and not her cleavage or the kitchen sink. She bustled around trying to do things with one hand, the other holding the phone. It was only at the difficult, two-handed parts, she put him on speaker. After half an hour she had a large overhead spotlight, similar to ones used on Felicity's show, in the corner of the kitchen, and the work bench was lit perfectly for her next attempt to vlog. She said goodbye to Mark and began readying the ingredients for another go.

Esme had decided on a Christmas recipe – after all, it was now December. It was also one of her grandma's favourites. When she was little it had been cooked every year, first by her great-grandma, then her grandma and now, Esme. Her mother had tried, but all she remembered from Carol's attempts was a lot of swearing and dancing to Christmas songs while things burnt on the stove. She smiled at the memory. Carol had been just as close to her mum as Esme, and the year she'd passed away had been difficult. Remembering times in the kitchen when it had been her grandma, Carol, and her and Alice made her smile.

Esme hurried over, turned on her laptop and camera, and grabbed the basic script she had written. She ran upstairs and changed into a high-neck top and tightened her bra straps to avoid anyone seeing her assets. She even added a little make-up for good measure. The world didn't need to see her without something on her face. They might think it was a horror movie and turn over. Soon she was back in the kitchen and ready to begin.

'Hi everyone. My name's Esme and welcome to my cooking vlog! This is Grandma's Kitchen.' She waved her hands around to show she was in a kitchen and instantly felt like an air stewardess demonstrating where the emergency exits were. She pulled her hands back to her sides. 'I thought today we'd record a brilliant make-ahead Christmas recipe. Trust me, this is super-impressive and super-easy. We're going to make sausage, chestnut and cranberry stuffing all ready for the big day, so when it arrives, all you have to do is shove it in the oven and crack open the bubbly. This is the stuffing we always have on Christmas Day in my family. It was originally my great-grandmother's recipe, but was taught

119

to me by my grandma. I always make it ahead and bring it with me on Christmas Eve when I come home.'

She paused, realising how different this year would be. 'Well, that's what I've done on previous years, but this year, I'm already home. So, anyway, we're going to begin by melting some butter and olive oil in a pan and sautéing some onions and leeks with a little bit of garlic. Let the leeks soften first because if you put in the garlic at the beginning, it'll burn and that'll give your dish a bitter taste.'

She remembered to look at the camera. Even when it felt uncomfortable and false, she made herself smile.

'Now we've got those all soft and translucent, put them to one side and brown your sausage meat.' She moved the meat around the pan. 'When it's just started to brown, add in the chestnuts and cranberries. If you're using frozen cranberries you can add them in straight from the freezer. They make such a great popping sound when they heat up and burst and all that juice trickles into the sausage meat making this all pinky and scrumptious. Now we just need to add the onion and leek back in and the breadcrumbs and you can throw in some extra herbs if you want to.' She grinned as a memory flashed into her brain. 'One year, when my sister and I were about 15 and my mum cooked this with us, she thought she'd do it whilst multi-tasking, waxing her top lip ready for a party.' She giggled at the memory. 'It didn't go well. Mum totally forgot about the cream on her top lip and we weren't paying much attention either, so by the time we actually remembered her top lip was free from hair, but it was also bright pink! Poor Mum was not impressed! Because my sister and I were teenagers we obviously found it hysterical. But my mum's a trooper and because it was a fancy-dress party, she decided to swap costumes with my dad and went as a policeman with a big false moustache to hide it and my poor dad had to go as a nun!"

Esme added in the chopped herbs and gave them a good stir around. Helena had reminded her to roll her shoulders back so she wasn't slumping and giving the world, or at least the three people who might be watching, a good eyeful. 'We're just going to add a little stock to bring it all together into a nice gooey mixture. If you're cooking this fresh on Christmas Day, then get it into the baking dish and add some stock to the top. It'll soak in and stop it drying out in the oven. If you're making ahead and freezing it, then stop here and add the rest on the day of cooking once it's thawed.'

She reached below the counter. 'Here's one I prepared earlier, so you can see what it looks like. This is a really tasty homemade stuffing for Christmas Day that's sure to impress your guests. I really, really, hope you enjoy it. Please let me know what you think by leaving me a comment on the blog, I'd love to get chatting to you all!' She really did; she was beginning to feel very lonely and isolated in the cottage when everyone else was at work, or busy with their own lives.

Esme turned off the camera and looked back at the kitchen. Pride at what she'd achieved bumped any negative emotions, and excitement and adrenaline welled inside as an overjoyed screech escaped her mouth. Esme congratulated herself on what a good job she'd done. She'd talked through every stage of the recipe without being pompous or patronising and the results were sure to be delicious.

She took a few deep breaths as the adrenaline subsided and made herself a cup of tea. As the heat of the oven died away and the kitchen became colder she had another go at lighting a fire and was pleased with the results. While the flames took hold, she ran upstairs to change into her warmest clothes: her fluffy pyjamas and two heavy jumpers. After all, she was her own boss and could do whatever she pleased.

Back in the kitchen she ate a spoonful of the cooked stuffing straight from the dish. The tang of cranberries popped on her tongue complimenting the savoury sausage meat. She made another cup of tea, then got comfy on the sofa while she edited the video and watched it back. It was much, much better and she posted it to her blog straight away. In the hours that followed, Esme kept checking the counter on her blog. It was slowly ticking up, which should have made her happy, but instead she felt like life was happening in slow motion. It was awful being reliant on the world to notice you and help make your fortune. For someone like Esme, naturally organised and pro-active, it was hard to give up that control.

As the afternoon wore on, and the day grew colder, Esme planned some more recipes and checked her emails. She wasn't checking them as regularly as she used to. There hadn't seemed much point. The rain tapped against the window pane and her neck stiffened. There were replies from two of the recruitment agencies and one of the contacts she'd made in the industry. She opened them in turn, and as she did, her face crumpled in disappointment, tears swelled in her eyes and though she tried to sniff them back, a couple escaped and ran down her cheeks. With trembling hands, she rang Lola.

'Lola, they've blacklisted me,' Esme cried, taking the phone from her ear and wiping away the tears with the back of her hand.

'What? Who?'

'Evil Felicity Fenchurch and I presume Dopey David. And Sasha, too, I expect. The agencies and people I contacted have said they've got nothing for me. One was kind enough to hint that they'd heard there'd been a problem on a previous show. You know what that means, don't you? It means that Felicity's been telling everyone not to employ me because I'm a liar. What am I going to do?'

'That's awful! Oh, Esme, poor you.'

'What am I going to do?' Esme repeated, sniffing.

Lola sighed. 'That Felicity is such a horrible woman. She's only doing this because she's scared of how talented you are.' Esme couldn't speak. 'Oh, Esme, honey. I wish there was something I could do.'

She wiped again at her wet cheeks. 'So do I. I just feel like jacking it all in. I'm trying so hard, Lola, but I'm not getting anywhere and I'm running out of money. It's a good job this place doesn't have central heating because I can't afford to put it on anyway.'

'Ezzy, please, don't get down.'

'I'm trying not to, but I feel like I'm going to end up begging on the streets.'

'Don't be ridiculous,' Lola chided.

'I'm not.'

'Yes, you are. Where's my normal positive Ezzy?'

Esme sniffed. 'She's buggered off to the sun for a holibobs. Oh, actually she hasn't because she can't bloody afford it.'

'Right,' said Lola, sounding like a teacher. 'Here's what you're going to do. You're going to get your trainers on and go for a big, long run. Who's been eating all this food you've been making?'

'Me,' Esme mumbled.

'Well, it'll do you good, then. Get up, get moving. And it always clears your head. Do you remember when you dragged me to the gym that time? When I was literally dying on the treadmill you told me to think about how strong and powerful I was. How strong my body was for working so hard and how strong my mind was for pushing me on when things got tough. You could definitely do with the endorphins right now.'

Esme blew a raspberry down the phone.

'That's very grown up.'

'Okay,' Esme conceded. 'I'll go for a run, but do I still carry on with the blog?'

'Yes, of course you do. You can't give up. Could you do private catering to get some money in?'

'Maybe. You know about PR—'

'Marketing, Esme, it's not the same thing.'

'It mostly is,' Esme teased. 'Can't you come up with some magic marketing thing that makes me uber-popular over night?'

'I wish I could, honey.' Lola's voice had returned to its normal kind, supportive tone. 'You just need to keep plugging away to increase your online presence and build a platform. Then, when you approach publishers, you'll be well-known already and they won't be able to say no. It's a shame we've got such a tight time-scale. You need to make a big splash now. What could we do?' she said to herself. Esme didn't speak, not wanting to interrupt her flow. 'How about a live broadcast?'

Esme lifted her head a little. 'How do I do that?'

'You just broadcast live. It's easy.' Esme sighed. 'No more huffing and puffing. Come on, chick, what do you have to lose?'

'Nothing, I suppose,' said Esme. 'Okay. I'll try that. Thanks for listening to me, Lola.'

'Always, sweetheart. Always.'

A second after hanging up from Lola, another call came through on Esme's mobile. It was Leo. She hesitated. Why was he calling her again? She couldn't imagine what he'd have to say to her after the last time. And she still didn't want to speak to him. That wasn't true – she wanted to shout at him. He'd caught her off guard last time, calling so late. This time she wanted to tell him what a bastard he was. What a lousy, rotten scumbag he'd become. When he'd called at 1 a.m. to ask her to get the chest of drawers shifted, she, Mark and Helena had stayed up even later going over the conversation. Helena was so livid Esme worried she wouldn't sleep at all, but eventually they'd all dozed off, curled up on the sofa together. Now she had time to think clearly, she wanted to say how she'd always hated it when he shaved and left weird little hairy shards in the sink, how she hated the way he talked all the way through TV programmes. A pinging noise told her she had a voicemail. *Poo!* She'd been ranting in her head so long she'd missed the chance to answer. Esme placed the phone to her ear and listened.

'Hi, Esme, it's Leo. Just wanted to say thanks for sending Mark to get the cabinet. I'm afraid he scratched the wall on his way out, but I don't want you worrying about that. I'll get the maintenance man to fix it, I'll even pay for it, as you've been through so much. Anyway, see you soon – well, I won't see you soon, but, you know, bye.'

Good for Mark scratching the wall and too right he could get the maintenance man to fix it! Esme felt the muscles tense in her arm as the urge to throw her phone against the wall took over. She knew it wouldn't help. She'd need to buy a new phone then and that was another thing she couldn't afford, but she needed to shout and destroy something. She stared at her phone and then threw it as hard as she could onto the sofa. Esme surveyed her new life. As pretty as the cottage was, and as comfortable as it felt, there was only one place she wanted to be right now.

Home.

*

Esme knocked on the door of her mum and dad's house but the lights were off and no one answered. She should have known. It was Saturday afternoon so they were, of course, in the pub. They preferred the old-fashioned decor of the Fox and Hound with its dark wooden tables and chairs, beer mats and friendly regulars. Esme pulled her coat tighter around her as she walked on into town. The rain had stopped and the cold wind brought a pinkness to her cheeks as a weak, watery sun shone in the pale sky. Though it was early December and the weather was no different to November, the prospect of Christmas made the air feel different. It was heavy with expectation but for Esme, it lacked the excitement she usually loved.

Yanking open the pub door against the wind, Esme edged inside. She hadn't been in here for a long time and memories of her and her friends, finally of age, drinking Malibu and thinking they were cool rushed back to her. Red tinsel lined the bar and was wrapped around the beer pumps, sparkling in the light. There was even a

Christmas tree. Esme was sure from its spindly fake branches that it was the same one from when she was a child. It was somehow comforting. The place was festive and jolly, and reminded her of Christmas Eve afternoons when Carol and Stephen had finished work early and took Alice and Esme to the pub where they spent a fortune on the jukebox. Esme saw her parents sat at a corner table and trudged over. The landlord had put on a CD of Rat Pack Christmas songs and as Dean Martin crooned away, Carol merrily sang too. She'd always been mad about Christmas – maybe that's where Esme had got it from – and started playing the songs as soon as the first of December rolled around.

'Hello, love,' said Carol. Then on seeing Esme's puffy red eyes she said, 'Oh, darling, what's wrong?' Esme collapsed into a chair and told them everything – the blacklisting, her failed attempts at blogging and the call from Leo. 'I've got half a mind to go to London, find Leo and his bit of stuff and – and—'

'Come on, love, calm down,' said her dad.

'Calm down? Stephen,' said Carol, rolling up the sleeves of her pale blue jumper as if readying for a fight. 'Drink for Esme, please.' Stephen stood up and nodded acceptance of the command.

'Right you are. Your mum's right. A good stiff drink will sort you out.' He patted Esme on the shoulder.

'Thanks, Dad. Can I have a white wine, please?' Her father strode away to the bar.

'Now,' continued Carol, 'about this stupid boy, Leo. What a callous idiot. If I lived near him I'd key his car and—'

'He doesn't own a car, Mum. No one does in London.'

'Well then, I'd put itching powder in his underpants and cut the arms and legs off all his suits.'

Esme suppressed a smile. 'Has Dad only stayed married to you all these years because he's too scared to leave?'

'Probably.' She sat back in her chair, relaxing a little and winked. 'But maybe Leo leaving that message is a good thing. Maybe he's shown his true colours. You've been home for three weeks now and it's about time you got the last of your stuff out and moved on.'

Her dad returned with the biggest glass of wine Esme had ever seen. The landlord must have bought his wine glasses at 'Tableware for Giants' or he'd found a vase and decided to use that instead. Over her shoulder Esme saw Joe at the bar and inhaled. 'Here you go, love. I told Fred all about it,' Stephen said, sitting down. 'And he said you needed a super-large glass of wine. So there you go. Enjoy. And he only charged me for a house white but he said you should have his best peanut gigolo.'

'Pinot Grigio,' corrected Esme.

'Aww, that was nice of him. Wasn't it, Esme?' said Carol as she swayed from side to side, clicking her fingers in time to the music. Esme nodded and took a sip of wine. The cold, velvet liquid slid down her throat. Then her brain caught up with what her dad had said.

'Wait, did you tell him everything I told you?' asked Esme. Her heart pounded and the red flame of embarrassment began to creep onto her cheeks. 'About Leo and the blacklisting and the blog?'

Stephen froze holding his pint glass. 'Umm . . . yes. Shouldn't I have?'

'No, Dad, you shouldn't!' Esme angrily tucked her hair behind her ear. 'Oh, great. Now everyone knows what a failure I am.'

'Nonsense,' replied Carol. 'Don't be so dramatic.'

Esme slumped down. 'For God's sake, I am not being dramatic.'

'You are being a little, dear,' said Carol, draining the last of her gin and bitter lemon. 'You used to say "For God's sake" all the time when you about 15.'

Stephen chuckled. 'From the age of 13 to 16 to be precise.'

'Precise,' repeated Carol. 'You were so funny. I think that's when you perfected your pout. Do you remember, Stephen?' Carol gave an impression of Esme pouting, which more resembled Mick Jagger. Especially when she put her hands on her hips and started wriggling. Stephen then joined her in homage

127

and before long, both her parents were doubled over laughing. Frank Sinatra's voice resonated in her ears and Esme sunk down in her chair.

'You two are so embarrassing.' She glanced over at the bar and saw Joe, who lifted his head and waved. 'Was Joe there when you told . . . who was it?'

'Fred?' asked Stephen. 'I think so.'

Esme gave a groan and grabbed her wine glass, taking a large gulp. The door opened again and Esme checked to see if Joe was leaving. He hadn't moved, but a tall, elegant young woman came in. The woman glanced around, saw Joe and waved, then nestled her way to the bar to stand beside him. She had long brown hair that hung straight down her back. It was glossy and thick, like chocolate when it was poured in those Dairy Milk commercials. Her figure was that of a toned salad-eating gym bunny. Esme could even see her eyelashes from where she sat in the corner. The woman stood so close to Joe their arms were touching and within seconds they were laughing and joking. Joe took her coat and hung it up for her.

Esme's stomach felt heavy and her heart shrivelled inside her chest. Seeing someone else happy was too much for her at the moment. She suddenly wished it was her with Joe but pushed the thought aside. As it all played out, she couldn't help checking over her shoulder while she and her parents drank their drinks.

'Right, here's twenty quid,' said Stephen. 'Your turn to get the drinks.' He put the note on the table in front of Esme. 'You know what we all have, don't you?'

Esme sunk down. 'Can't you go?'

'I went last time,' he replied. 'Why don't you want to go? You're not 15 anymore. You don't need fake ID.'

'Ha ha,' Esme replied sarcastically. 'I just don't want to go now they all know I'm a complete loser.'

Carol gave her daughter a stern look. 'Now stop that at once, you silly girl—'

'Silly? Thanks very much.'

'You are not a loser. You're just trying something different. And why shouldn't you? It's never too late to change career. And there's nothing wrong with doing things differently. Is there, Stephen? In fact, we've tried lots of new things in the bedr—'

'There isn't, my dear. Very true.' He strategically cut her off as Esme felt her eyes widening in shock. She'd need therapy by the end of the afternoon if she wasn't careful. Stephen tipped his head back for the dregs of his beer.

Her parents were indeed batshit crazy but she knew most people would kill to have parents like hers. Especially ones who were still in love and what's more, liked each other, after all these years. She knew Mark would. His parents had trouble believing their son was gay and, since he'd come out as a teenager, their relationship had been tense to say the least. Having such accepting parents was something Esme was eternally grateful for. How many parents would have been so supportive in her circumstances? How many would have encouraged her to follow her dream? The least she could do was go and get the next round of drinks. Even if it was embarrassing as hell. Esme grabbed the twenty pounds offered by her dad and walked to the bar. She stood at the opposite end to Joe, hoping he wouldn't see her and come over. For some reason, she didn't want to see him flirting and laughing with some gorgeous girl. It wasn't that she fancied Joe, she told herself. It was just that she was still sore from breaking up with Leo and seeing anyone flirting was too sickening.

Esme stood on tiptoes at the bar, leaning over, trying to catch the landlord's attention. She toyed with the tinsel in her finger-tips. She missed tinsel. Leo had banned it from the flat claiming it was tacky and cheap. Instead they had to have his weird glass ornamental modern take on a Christmas tree. It was ridiculously expensive from John Lewis and didn't look at all tree-like or give you that warm glow in your tummy proper Christmas trees did. After much wrangling, they'd agreed she could have a small fake tree in the bedroom but still no tinsel, only weird bead strings that tangled up into giant knots you could never undo. This year, in her cottage, she had tinsel everywhere. Yards and yards of it wrapped around the headboard of her bed, the banister, and any other surface she could find. An excitement tingled though her at the idea of Christmas. It was a time of year you couldn't fail to love. All the food, all the gifts, snuggling up under blankets to watch James Bond re-runs with full, fat bellies. Friends and family all together. Did Joe like tinsel, she wondered?

'Hello,' said Joe from beside her, and Esme started.

'Hello. How's it going?' She hated how much she wanted to ask who the other woman was and what was the exact nature of their relationship. Was she another one-night stand? Was she a girlfriend? He hadn't kissed her . . . yet.

'Good, thanks. You?'

'Yeah, fine.' Esme kept her eyes forwards. She looked a state. She'd been crying for almost an hour before she got here. She hadn't brushed her hair and her outfit couldn't be described as elegant. She had on the oldest, most comfortable pair of jeans she owned, and a large cable knit jumper. Esme glanced at the woman he was with. She was wearing skintight jeans over shapely legs, gorgeous knee-high boots and a fitted jumper, and was chatting happily to someone else while Joe was near Esme. She didn't seem in the slightest bit worried. Esme couldn't remember what it was like to have that much confidence. She'd been like that at one point, but these days her self-respect was clinging on by a thread and after Leo, she couldn't trust her own judgement. She lifted her head to speak to Joe, forgetting that she must look terrible. As she did, his face froze.

'Crikey, are you okay? You look upset. Have you been crying?' He reached out his hand and rested it gently on her shoulder. For a moment, Esme felt a tingle where it lay and as his eyes met hers, her breath caught. They were the most incredible pale green she'd ever seen. Then she shot her eyes to the confident woman, who glanced over at that moment, and Esme moved back, gently shrugging it off. Joe was clearly just a nice guy, only interested in being her friend. Esme chastised herself for the fluttering in her belly. Just because a man touched her, it didn't mean he wanted to leap into bed with her. She'd have to get some self-help books on flirting because she was clearly getting overexcited at the slightest thing and reading too much into it. 'Esme? Are you okay?' Joe repeated.

'Umm . . . yeah, I'm okay.' She rubbed at her eyes just to make sure there were no remnants of smudged mascara still lurking.

'Is it the break-up?' asked Joe, softly.

'Yes. Sort of. Is it? I don't know.' Esme shook her head in an attempt to rearrange her thoughts 'I might as well tell you, I guess. My dad told everyone in the general vicinity earlier so I'm surprised you haven't heard already. He might as well have put a poster up.' She took a deep breath. 'So, you know I told you I got sacked from my old job because the star of the show kept stealing my recipes and I wouldn't apologise? Well, normally I wouldn't mind, but this one was special.'

'Wait,' said Joe, holding up his hands. 'Star of the show?'

Esme paused. She forgot how much people loved a celebrity. 'I worked for Felicity Fenchurch. Well, on her TV show anyway.'

'Really? When you said before I'd just assumed it was a colleague you were talking about, not Felicity Fenchurch.'

'No, it was her.'

'What was she like?'

'Between you and me she was a giant bitch, but tell anyone and she'll track me down and sue me. Or kill me.'

'Can she do that?' he asked. His beautiful eyes sparkling as he spoke, a smile lighting his face.

Esme shrugged. 'I don't know. Probably. She's like MI5. She has spies everywhere.' Joe laughed and Esme's eyes were drawn to his lopsided grin. She could see how the women of Sandchester were lost after seeing one wide smile. 'So, anyway, because I called her out on it, I got sacked. Then my boyfriend, or should I say ex-boyfriend, dumped me and moved his new woman – his boss – in the next day. And now, Felicity "I can't stop pouting" Fenchurch has had me blacklisted so everyone thinks I'm trouble and I'll be lucky to get a job peeling potatoes in a prison kitchen.' He stared at her, unspeaking, but Esme couldn't stop the flow of words scrambling out of her mouth. 'My stupid friends convinced me I should write the recipe book I've always dreamed of writing and start a blog and do live video broadcasts too. The trouble is, I'm utterly shit at it and I feel like a complete idiot.'

Joe's mouth hung open, which wasn't quite the reaction Esme was hoping for, but to be fair it was a lot to take in. 'Right,' he said, slowly. 'Well, I'm sure everything will turn out all right in the end.'

Esme gave a weak smile and a small nod. Joe glimpsed up from under his long dark eyelashes. 'Sorry, that was pathetic wasn't it?'

'It's not the best pep talk I've ever heard.'

He scuffed his foot on the carpet. 'No, it isn't, is it? I'm not very good at this sort of thing.' He scratched the back of his head. 'All I can say is, I remember when me and Clara split up and I moved back, it took me over a year to even start talking to my friends again. I moved back here and I was virtually a recluse, spending all day in my dressing gown.' He glanced at her as he spoke, and the weight had returned to his eyes, even his strong shoulders had rounded a little. 'You're doing much better than I was.' Esme giggled, hoping he was exaggerating. 'And as far as work goes, you've always been really determined. I'm sure your blog will take off in time. What's it called?'

'Grandma's Kitchen,' she replied. 'After my grandma's cookbook I was given.'

'Joe?' called the brunette from across the bar. He turned and waved.

'Do you know what I think?' he said, turning back to Esme. 'I think you need a proper plan of action. Have you started writing your recipe book yet?'

'Not really. I've got random notes and ideas and stuff. I've been busy with the blog. Not that it's doing me any good.' She twisted the twenty-pound note in her hand and glanced over at her mum and dad. They were both watching her and when they caught her eye, gave her a big thumbs up and wide cheesy grins. Esme shook her head and turned back to Joe. He'd seen them too but thankfully was smiling.

'Why don't you start organising your time properly, giving so much to this task and so much to another? You might feel more in control that way. You know, be proper organised, like you would be in an office. Create a daily to-do list, that sort of thing.'

'That's great advice,' replied Esme and her heart felt a little lighter. 'I might come and talk to you more often.'

'You should,' said Joe and Esme glanced up. Was he blushing?

'Joe?' came the soft voice again from the other end of the bar. Her voice was low and sexy, not high and squeaky like Esme's was, or at least how she sounded in her recordings. Esme turned back to look for the barman.

'I'd better get back,' said Joe.

'Yeah, of course.' She studied the note in her hand. 'See you later.'

Esme watched him walk away admiring his broad shoulders and manly stride. When he reached his confident friend, he wrapped an arm around her waist and hugged her. The woman smiled at him, then turned to continue her conversation.

Esme realised she'd have to get better at reading the signs again now she was single. For a moment she'd thought he was flirting, or that there was more to the 'you should,' but there couldn't be. He clearly had a girlfriend and was just being friendly. He probably just sympathised with her heartache. For all she knew Joe still saw her as the gangly, clumsy ginger kid from school. Esme chewed her lip. The idea of getting back into the dating game was terrifying. She'd been with Leo so long she wouldn't know what to do if she ever went on a date again. Just then Fred, the barman, approached.

'Sorry to keep you waiting, love. What can I get you?'

'You know what my mum and dad have, don't you?' Esme asked, gesturing over her shoulder to Carol and Stephen.

He nodded and prepared the pint of bitter and gin and bitter lemon. 'And what can I get you?'

She glanced once more at Joe and the brunette in her chic outfit, then down to her own shabby clothes. 'You gave my dad a super-large glass of wine for me before.'

'Yes I did.' He laughed. 'Want another one?'

'Do you have anything bigger?'

*

Later that night, completely drunk and wearing a tinsel halo that Carol had stolen from the pub, Esme climbed out of the taxi her parents had deposited her into and unlocked the front door. The beautiful brunette and Joe had laughed and chatted together all evening but hadn't been all over each other the same way he had with the other woman. Joe was a muddle. After a couple of very large glasses of wine, Esme had relaxed and enjoyed her parents' company. She'd even crooned along with her mum to some of her favourite Christmas songs. Like Alice, they were perfectly content with their lives and Esme realised that was what she really craved.

Esme turned on the lights and paused, admiring the tatty old furniture, peeling walls and threadbare carpet covered in rugs she'd collected from friends and family. The cottage was shabby and still a bit grubby and her heart ached. She missed the view from the apartment. The twinkling lights of London, a constant reminder that the world was big and busy and full of opportunity. Every time she'd stared out she'd felt like it was exactly where she was meant to be and wished she felt that way about the cottage. She still felt like a lodger, like this was a temporary measure until her life got back on track, but she had no idea how that was going to happen now. As she stood by the sink, drinking a glass of water and looking out over the back garden, she remembered one of the first times she'd touched the window of the apartment, tracing the skyline of London with her finger. Leo had come and put his arm around her, then using his handkerchief had rubbed off the smudges her finger had left. Turning back from the window, and the memory, she wished now she'd never sold all her weird and wonderful furniture when they moved in together. But there hadn't been enough room for it. The only thing she'd been able to keep was the old-fashioned chest of drawers Mark had collected from Leo's flat that she'd bought from a second-hand store. At the time, she was sure she'd live in a period property one day and now she was. Sort of.

She flopped onto the ancient but comfortable sofa and sank into the seat. The springs were broken but it was far from uncomfortable, instead the sofa sucked you in like it was giving you a big hug. She pulled a blanket over her knees and another around her shoulders as she switched on her laptop. There were some nice comments on her blog complimenting her recipe choices and easy instructions and she even had a few more hits. But one comment from Penny85 caught her eye. It asked her what inspired her recipes and, excited to be interacting with someone, she began typing a response.

*

Grandma's Kitchen

Hi, Penny85. Thanks so much for your question. My inspiration comes from my grandma's recipe book. My mum has fond memories of her bustling around the kitchen and so do I. Mum doesn't like cooking quite so much, so the recipe book got passed on to me. I love that it hasn't changed, only added to over the years. My family aren't anything special, we're just normal, but it's our little piece of history. But I think cooking and baking is about more than just eating. Food should be delicious and nurturing, and I'm not talking about tiny organic salads. I'm talking about food that feeds the soul. Whether you need cheering up from a heartbreak – like me – or you're celebrating a promotion.

Tomorrow I'm going to cook myself an amazing chicken soup. They say it's good for the soul, and I could really use it at the moment. I hope it's good for my heart too. It doesn't seem to know where it is from one minute to the next. I love being here, back home, especially as it's Christmas, but I miss London — that's where I was before. And then there's this guy. I keep thinking about him, but the whole situation is so complex I don't know what to think. But never mind, anyway, back to cooking. Whatever you're making, cooking should be about being with the people you love, or loving the person you are. And sometimes loving yourself means eating homemade chicken soup or something healthy and nutritious, and other times it means eating an entire chocolate cake in one sitting. Cooking and baking is all about love. Plain and simple. So that's where I get my inspiration from!

*

Esme sat back and relaxed, some of her old confidence returning. She hit publish and placed the laptop back on the table, sleepy and tired. Going upstairs to bed seemed like far too much effort so she leaned to one side and curled up on the sofa. She woke in the dark but with the birds outside singing their cheerful songs. Her mouth felt fuzzy and Esme screwed up her face. She needed a glass of water. Braving the cold, she went to the sink and turned on the tap. It did nothing for a moment then the pipes rattled and came to life. She filled the glass and after a quick glance at the stairs went back to the sofa.

After some more sleep, Esme awoke to a bright sunny day. The pale grey sky was tinged with lilac and covered in soft white clouds. The wind blew hard into the trees, pushing their branches to and fro. She went upstairs, showered and changed and gave her teeth a good brush. Pulling her hair back into a ponytail Esme descended the stairs feeling brighter. Remembering Joe's advice, she decided it was time to get more organised and start treating this like a job. He'd mentioned his ex, Clara, yesterday. And Esme wondered if she'd ever find out what had happened there. It seemed there was something more going on than just a normal break-up. He was always so careful what he said and kept it to the bare minimum. As soon as he'd said her name his face had changed and his eyes lost their sparkle, becoming dull and heavy with pain.

Settling down with her laptop and a cup of tea, her eyes focused on the screen, then widened in disbelief. Her hit counter had trebled and there were so many comments on her blog posts and the sausage and cranberry stuffing vlog she had to scroll down to read them all. Penny85 had started several conversations with other commenters. She'd even asked a cheeky question about who the lucky guy was? Esme bit her lip. She'd have to be a bit more careful what she said in the future. But a wide grin spread across her face and her fingers tingled, resting on the keys. It wasn't a huge success but it was a vast improvement. A step in the right direction rather than a step backwards for a change.

She spent the next hour replying to all the comments and for the rest of the day, after planning a month's worth of blog posts, there was a spring in her step. She even danced around the kitchen listening to the radio and cleaning some of the darker corners she'd been trying to ignore. Things were coming together. It was still at a snail's pace, but she was finally moving forward. When she later sat back down with her laptop, flooded with confidence, Esme announced when her first live broadcast would be. She worked until the battery on her laptop ran down, then sat back and smiled. The date was set.

Chapter 18

Sandchester

The bright sunshine shone through Joe's bedroom window. He squinted and moaned in the light peeking through his curtains. He'd had an unusually good night's sleep last night but cursing now, he checked his alarm clock.

'Bugger,' he shouted, almost falling out of bed. It was Monday and already eight-thirty. He was due at work in half an hour. Joe scrabbled around getting dressed and brushing his teeth. There was no time for breakfast. Checking the diary on his phone, his first viewing wasn't until ten so he could at least grab a bacon butty from the sandwich shop next to his office.

As he left, he saw his camera bag in the corner and remembered his conversation with Esme about taking photos for her. Perhaps he could call her later, or text? A text might be better. She'd looked so sad when he'd seen her in the pub Saturday night and some protective instinct had kicked in. He wanted to make her feel better. Joe grabbed his watch from the top drawer of the bedside cabinet and put it on. 'Aargh.' It was 8.55 a.m. now. He hated being late. Mr Rigby was a sweet old man and wouldn't even mention it, but Joe disliked it nonetheless. It was disrespectful.

And he liked Mr Rigby. He'd never dream of taking advantage of him. Grabbing his wallet, keys and phone, he slammed the door shut behind him and ran to his car.

After a bacon sandwich and a successful viewing, Joe felt calmer. Back at his desk he took out his phone and texted Esme, asking if she wanted him to come over and take some photos. A bubble of nerves was bouncing around in his stomach. Joe placed the phone back on his desk and tried to concentrate on the admin he had to do but found his eyes wandering towards it every few seconds. He shook his head to stop himself and studied the computer screen.

When it beeped a few minutes later, he jumped. Esme asked if he was able to come over after work and do some today. She would even cook them dinner as a thank you. After everything he had heard about her cooking, and the amazing hot chocolate and biscuits she'd made, he couldn't wait. It would be a brilliant change from the terrible meals he made himself and that was when he could be bothered to even try cooking. Joe thought about waiting before responding. Would it make him look desperate and weird and stalkery if he answered straightaway? Joe gave himself a mental shake. He wasn't a kid anymore and that sort of attitude was childish and silly. Grabbing his phone, he texted back then and there.

The afternoon dragged by and the heavy rain outside only added to the gloom and dullness of the day. Joe tapped his pen against his notepad watching the office clock slowly tick by. When five o'clock rolled around and he could go, he was like a kid at the end of the school day. He'd turned everything off at two minutes to five and even had his coat on so he could be out of the door at exactly 5 p.m.

After a quick stop at home to grab his camera bag, he exited his car, pulling his collar up against the heavy rain that threatened to run down his neck. Esme had seen him arrive and held the door open for him and as he approached he could smell the sweet scents of cocoa and orange. 'Hi, Joe. Quick, come in!'

Joe stepped forward and undid his coat. The cottage was warm compared to outside, but seeing Esme's unusual outfit of a massive cardigan over a jumper and two pairs of fluffy socks, and seeing the dying embers of the fire, he knew it wouldn't last long. 'Are you still struggling with the fire?'

'The fire? No. Why?'He nodded to it. 'Oh, no, I was so busy cooking I forgot to add some more wood, that's all.'

Joe relaxed. 'No worries, I'll do it now if you like. Have you thought about getting central heating installed?' He threw his coat over the back of the sofa. 'I'm sure the owners wouldn't mind. They might even give you some money towards it.'

Esme frowned. 'I can't afford it at the moment. I'm not sure how long I'll even be here. Or be able to afford living here.'

'Really?' The thought of her moving away again so soon caused the muscles of his stomach to clench.

'Yeah, things aren't great.' But then, she suddenly brightened. 'But let's not talk about that now.'

'Okay – sure. So, I brought my camera.' He showed her the large camera bag and cringed inside. Why did he show her the bag? Of course she'd know it's a camera bag, it's not like he was going to move in. Why was he so nervous? But Esme, busy in the kitchen, hadn't seemed to notice.

'Brilliant. I've done some baking ready for the photos. They're all things I've mentioned on the blog. To be honest there's not much yet.'

'That's okay,' he replied. 'We can take some photos of the food and then add some other arty ones to bring your blog to life. It's better to have too many photos than not enough.' Esme smiled and Joe noticed a tendril of hair had fallen from her ponytail and framed her oval face. 'So, what have we got then?'

Esme showed him the Orange Tea Bread, Sausage and Cranberry Stuffing, Butter Bean Bruschetta and opened the fridge door for him to see the Double-Layer Chocolate Hazelnut Cake. Joe felt his mouth water. He'd never seen a cake look so appetising and was tempted to attack it before taking a single photo.

'This was from the dry run I did for the vlog,' Esme said, pointing to the cake. 'No one saw the video, but it's a good recipe and I don't want it to go to waste. I thought I might write it up and post it later if we get some nice shots. You'll have to take some of it home with you, I won't be able to eat it all. My waistband is getting tighter as it is.'

'Wow, thanks. It all looks amazing.' He wanted to say she did too, but worried he'd sound cheesy, and would a woman like her even be interested in someone like him? What did he have to offer except a damaged and ripped-apart heart? But as something within him fluttered like a baby bird trying to take flight, there was no denying that Esme was having an unexpected effect on him. He'd been able to mention Clara, and he found himself seeking Esme's company rather than shutting himself away. He'd even had a good night's sleep for once. Seeing her expectant face, he said, 'So, let's find some nice plates to pop them on. What sort of thing have you got?'

Esme took out different-sized plates from her cupboards, all with various patterns and laid them out. 'Some of these are mine, but quite a few were left here. They're real little treasures.'

Joe readied his camera and checked the screen, seeing how they'd appear in a photo. 'How about these ones?' He pointed out a couple of vintage-looking ones. 'They'd be great for the butter bean thing and the cake.'

'I've got this beautiful cake stand for the chocolate cake,' she replied, taking it from the other side of the kitchen. 'I bought it years ago at a car boot sale, before I moved to London. The cake is chilling in the fridge at the moment. I'll take it out for the photos but it's warm in here for once, so I don't want to take it out too soon or it'll get too hot.'

'You really know your stuff, don't you?' he asked.

'Yes, I do,' Esme nodded, pleased, and placing her hands on her hips. 'When food is photographed, it's not always as it appears. Once I had to spray-paint a chicken to get it the perfect colour bronze.'

'You did not.'

Esme smiled at him and he noticed the strange burnt gold of her eyes, sparkling in the evening light. 'I did. But I'm not doing anything like that to my food. I want to eat it afterwards and I think for the blog, it should look real. Right, let's do this.'

They began taking the photos, Joe angling around the plate, sometimes using the little stool she had for reaching the top shelf of the pantry to get a better angle. They even used the spotlight and some tin foil as a reflector. Once all the food was done, he took some photos of the recipe book and the quirky cottage. He was just photographing an odd, lopsided bookshelf from the living-room alcove when Esme brought over some tea and cake.

'Shall we have some pudding?' she asked, sitting down on the sofa.

Joe joined her. 'That bruschetta thing was amazing.'

Esme sliced the cake. 'Thank you. I like creating new recipes.'

'You made that one up yourself?'

'Yes. It's based on Welsh Rarebit, but I wanted to make it a bit more substantial, so added the butter beans underneath.'

'Wow. You've got quite a talent.' She was incredibly impressive.

'Thanks.' Esme went quiet for a moment. 'Joe? Do you mind if I ask you something?' He shook his head, his mouth full of the amazing chocolate cake. 'How are you doing since your break-up?'

A crumb caught at the back of his throat and he coughed. He hadn't expected that. People simply didn't ask him anymore. Those who knew him well just accepted he still struggled and that he would come out of it at some point in the future. To strangers he was just normal, if a little sullen. It was nice to be asked, but what could he say? He shrugged and put his plate down. 'It's complicated.'

'Sorry, I didn't mean to pry.' Esme fussed with the cushions and Joe felt bad for sounding so dramatic.

'It's not that, I know you're not. It's just . . .' He took a deep breath. Would he at last tell someone the whole truth? Esme met his gaze, her eyes gentle and kind. He could see she wasn't going to push and for the first time he actually wanted to tell someone. 'She . . . Clara, my ex . . .' He shook his head. 'It was all a mess.' He ran a hand through his hair and scrunched it into a tight fist.

Esme didn't speak.

'We were going out for a long time. We met at university. She was from Australia and after we graduated, she wanted to move back there, so I went with her and we were happy, for a while at least. It wasn't anyone's fault.' In his lap, he linked his fingers together, tensing them so hard they were turning white.

'You don't have to talk about it if you don't want to,' Esme said, and her lack of pressure was reassuring.

Joe smiled. It felt kind of good to talk. It had been the most he'd talked for a long time. But as he got closer to having to say it, he felt the guilt, the shame and the anger at the unfairness of it all, rise in him. He tried to keep going. 'It's okay. I was miserable being so far away from home. I didn't think I would be, but that physical distance from everyone you love is hard. We split up after about five years out there and I moved back here.' He tried to carry on and finish the story but then his throat closed over, and a queasiness rose within him. He took a deep breath and tried to open his mouth to speak but couldn't as the sharp pains pierced is chest, running into his heart. He so desperately wanted to fill the noiseless space between them and finally open up to someone, but he couldn't. And before long, the silence had wrapped itself around him, closing in like a thick, invisible wall.

'I'm sorry,' Esme said, sipping her tea. 'It sounds like you've had it much worse than me.'

Joe met her gaze. 'I think with all your work troubles as well, we're pretty much even.'

Esme's hair was illuminated by the dreadful Seventies lamp and cast an aura around her. He wanted to reach out and touch her face. To run his thumb over her full, pink lips, then kiss them. Her steady gaze examined his soul and his heart was suddenly awoken. After all this time of locking the pieces of his broken heart away, was he was ready to let someone else in? Was she? As he couldn't even tell her everything about his break-up with Clara, he didn't think so and at that thought, a heavy weight like a wrecking ball hit his chest, making him shrink backwards.

'So,' said Joe, feigning cheerfulness. 'I'll put all these pictures on a memory stick and then you can upload them to your blog whenever you like.'

'Thank you,' Esme replied, but Joe knew it was like a curtain had suddenly been drawn between them, that she felt brushed off, but he couldn't help it. Joe glanced at his watch.

'I'd better be going.'

'It's quite late isn't it? Thank you again, Joe. I'm sure the photos will make a real difference to the blog.' He walked around the sofa towards the door and picked up his coat. She followed and got ready to open it for him. 'I'm sure I'll see you around, but, if I don't . . .' She paused, considering her words. 'If you ever need to talk, I'm here, you know?'

Joe's breath paused and he didn't know what to say. 'With food like that on offer, you may find me here more often than you'd like. Goodnight, Esme Kendrick.'

'Goodnight, Joe Holloway.'

The teachers had always read out their full names when reading the register. He had no idea why they were doing it now, but it made him smile. It was like there was a special connection between them. He heard the door close behind him and climbed into his car. Joe took a breath. It felt like the first time in years he'd been able to take anything resembling a deep breath. He hadn't been able to tell her everything, but he'd told her a lot more than most other people. The weight on his shoulders felt a little lighter. Not by much, but by enough that he could roll them back and stand a little straighter.

Glancing back at the cottage he realised that he hadn't seen any Christmas decorations. No tree. No nothing. Though he hadn't bothered with Christmas decorations for the last few years, he didn't want Esme to feel the desolation he did at Christmas time when everyone else was celebrating the season and he'd go home to an empty, undecorated house. Then an idea occurred to him and he placed the key in the ignition. Taking a quick look up at the stars sparkling in the sky, he turned the key and drove home.

Chapter 19

Sandchester

Recipe books sat open and Esme poured through them all deciding what type of recipe to cook for her first live show, narrowing down the choices to two or three she loved the most. Sat on the living-room floor with her legs crossed, her jeans and jumper covered in flour and smudges of butter from the baking she'd been doing all day, she turned the pages back and forth.

It was mid-afternoon and her thoughts flew back to Joe. He'd told her about the break-up but it still seemed like there was more to it. When he'd suddenly shut down, his eyes losing their sparkle again, she'd assumed she'd overstepped the mark. She couldn't get over how different he was to what she'd expected. Not only was he all grown up but the break-up had clearly affected him deeply. She couldn't help but wonder if he really had dealt with it. As he was happy spending the night with other people, Esme supposed he must have. She looked again at the piles of books around her. She had to concentrate. All her previous recipes and blogs had been about flashy food. The type of thing you'd cook for dinner parties or special times of year. She wanted to do something simple, but tasty. It needed to be thick and comforting and perfect for long winter nights.

They were edging slowly towards Christmas now and the time of year felt so different. The rain beat down almost every day and the wind was cold and strong. Some of the windows in the cottage leaked and she had taken to rolling up towels and stuffing them along the windowsills. It stopped some of the draughts and soaked up the rain, but they did get a bit smelly if she didn't change them regularly.

She'd thought at first of making a stew. A chicken stew like her grandma used to make. Esme smiled as she remembered the terrifying pressure cooker that whistled and steamed in the kitchen every Monday, after they'd had roast chicken the day before. Grandma would use the leftovers, throw in vegetables and pearl barley, and it would cook for hours, finishing just as she got home from school. The stew made her think of autumn and returning to school amidst the red and golden leaves falling from the trees, and the smell of her new leather satchel. The start of a new school year had always brought some bullying by some of the kids, teasing her for her ginger hair. It would eventually die down, but those comforting Monday nights had helped her get through the week.

Esme thought back to the days when she had entered the kitchen at home; the strong smell of cooked chicken made her mouth water but the terrifying contraption sounded like it would explode any moment. She remembered edging round the wall, opposite the cooker, scared it would blow up in her face while Grandma tutted and told her not to be a wimp. Then her mum and dad would come home from work and with Alice, they'd all gather round the table. Then there were the dumplings. Grandma made the best dumplings. Soft fluffy clouds, sometimes with fresh thyme, which floated in the top of the thick stew and fell apart as you ladled them out.

147

As wonderful as that recipe was, she wanted something a little more modern. She'd thought then of a cassoulet, or a chicken chasseur, but this needed to be more of a midweek supper. Something you could cook from the ingredients in your fridge or a quick stop-off at the local shop, not something that required hours upon hours of preparation.

It was then she decided on a risotto. A lot of people were afraid of cooking risotto. The thought of standing over a pan of simmering stock, continually stirring, made people think it was hard work, but actually, it was easy. You could stand there for twenty minutes or so, thinking about the day you'd had, planning the day to come, or just listening to the radio while you stirred. It was a great midweek dish to help you relax and you ended up with a delicious meal at the end of it. A pea and pancetta risotto would be perfect. The sweet peas – frozen was fine – dotted throughout, all green and shiny, were the perfect contrast to the smoky, salty pancetta. When it was mixed in with the velvety rice that had been flavoured with a chicken stock (made from a stock pot or cube, she wasn't a sadist), it was perfect for this time of year.

Esme listed the ingredients she would need, checked what she had in the cupboards and noted the things she needed to buy. It wasn't much, which reassured her she'd made the right choice. The wind howled through the cottage and she huddled closer to her open fire roaring with heat. Holding up her hands, she warmed them as her body shivered. A timer in the kitchen pinged and she got up to remove the delicious pie she'd made for her dinner. The best thing about her new life was that she could eat when she was hungry; she didn't have to eat at particular times. Esme pulled open the oven and smelt the golden pastry, the dark red wine gravy bubbling and oozing from the sides, and the tender chunks of beef mixed with dense earthy mushrooms. Dishes liked this always brought out her nurturing side. Comfort food was great for bringing people together. She checked her phone for a message from someone – one of her friends. Joe, maybe? Seeing nothing, she felt a pang of disappointment. Since she'd overstepped the mark the other night, Joe hadn't been in contact at all and it made her feel both concerned and guilty. She cut the pie and placed a large slice on a plate along with peas and carrots she'd steamed on the hob. Taking it to the sofa, Esme sat down and grabbed a book from the pile waiting to be read on the coffee table.

Just as she'd finished, she heard a knock at the door and went to answer it, glancing at the time as she went. It was almost three. As she opened the door her mouth dropped open a little. She hadn't expected to see Joe stood there, looking shy and anxious. Esme worried he was embarrassed about their discussion last night and thought it best to just ignore it and pretend it hadn't happened. 'Hi, Joe. What's up?'

He scratched the back of his head, reaching his fingers into his dark hair. She kind of wanted to do the same but stopped herself and focused on the conversation 'Hey, umm, I wondered if you fancied coming for a drive?'

'A drive?' Esme knew she was scrunching up her face unattractively but it was a very odd suggestion. It was something her dad used to suggest on a Sunday afternoon and she and Alice would moan and try and make the best of it by listening to the Top 40 and singing along. She didn't think people did that sort of thing nowadays.

'Yeah.' A blush crept into his cheeks. He took a step back. 'If you don't want to, that's fine.'

'No, I would. I do,' she replied, annoyed at herself for being so ungrateful. 'Let me just get my coat and stuff.' She left Joe on the doorstep for a moment as she scrabbled around grabbing her things and putting the fire out. Slinging her bag on her shoulder she found the key and locked the door behind her. Once they were in the car she asked, 'So where are we going?'

'I've got somewhere I want to show you. It's not far'

'Okay.' Esme didn't know what was happening but was happy to trust herself to it and to Joe. 'Can we have the radio on?' she asked and shared her memory of the family drives when she was little.

'My dad used to do the same thing too.' Joe smiled at her and whizzed the car down the country lanes.

The dark brown of the hedgerows, bereft of leaves and the bright greenery she loved, mixed with the dull verdigris of the privet, guided their path. The sky was overcast with thick grey cloud and the trees swayed heavily in the wind. She had no idea where they were going until eventually Joe pulled down a lane and that was when she saw it – a nursery in the middle of nowhere with row upon row of Christmas trees.

Esme felt the smile light up her face, just as it lit her heart. She'd wanted a Christmas tree but couldn't convince herself to spend the money on a real one. She had to hold onto every penny and it felt self-indulgent to spend it on something that would only be up for a few weeks then gone. But she loved the piney scent that a real Christmas tree gave and at the thought of getting one now, of Joe bringing her here to get one, excitement rose like she was a kid again. She turned to him and beamed a great, wide grin. 'Are we getting a Christmas tree?'

'We are,' he nodded. Esme squealed and jumped on the spot. Joe laughed then led them towards the stacks of trees. 'How big should it be?'

'Six foot, of course!'

'Esme, the ceiling of the cottage is only just over that. I have to bend to get through some of the doors.'

'Oh, okay,' she conceded. 'Five then.'

'I think four might be better.' She sharpened her eyes in fake annoyance and Joe held up his hands in surrender. 'All right then, we'll look at the five-foot ones first.'

They walked to the trees lined up under a hand-painted sign. The smell alone made Esme's tummy flutter with excitement. She tucked her scarf inside the neckline of her coat but couldn't have cared less about the wind. Joe grabbed a tree and grappled with it until it was ready for Esme to appraise. She pulled a face.

'What?' Joe asked, eyeing the tree, clearly unable to see anything wrong with it.

'It's all lopsided. Look.' She pointed to where one side was all squished and bent, some of the branches broken.

'Fair enough. What about this one?' He pulled out another one.

'Better, but it's a bit skinny. I like quite a wide one.' Joe eyed her to remind her of the size of the cottage. 'Oh, yeah, tiny living room. Okay, well, let's try a four-foot one. I'd rather have a smaller wide one than a tall skinny one.'

A lady who worked at the nursery came over carrying two takeaway cups. 'Would you two like a hot chocolate. They're free.'

'Oh, yes, please,' said Esme. 'Thank you.' Joe thanked the lady and took his. As they walked on to find the four-foot trees, they sipped. It wasn't as nice as the one Esme made, this one was quite sugary and sweet, but it was still nice, plus she hadn't had to make it herself. The steam warmed her face against the cold wind and what could be better than looking for a Christmas tree with a cup of hot chocolate. Esme's heart pounded with anticipation as they walked through muddy tracks, the tinny, faint sound of Christmas songs coming from the main shop. The sky was growing dark, warning everyone to get back inside, safe and warm for the night.

This was one of the most special moments of her life. Much more special than anything Leo had ever done and something within told her to commit every sight, sound and smell to memory. A family walked past, the children dancing and running to and fro full of excitement. They'd clearly come straight from school and Esme remembered being little and getting the tree every year with her mum and dad, and Alice. It was always such a special day.

Esme and Joe found the four-foot trees and Esme held his hot chocolate as he began pulling ones out for her to choose from. These were much better, much more fitting for the cottage. They'd look amazing next to the fire. She'd have to move some bits around, and possibly chop the back of the tree down a little bit, but it would look gorgeous, and no one would know when it was pushed into the corner. It would look splendid, even if she didn't have any baubles for it.

After a few that weren't quite right, Joe pulled out a tree and as the branches fell down into place and he twizzled it around, Esme gasped. It was perfect. Just the right size, evenly spaced and it smelt great. She moved closer, placed the hot chocolates on the floor and grabbed it, her fingers locking with Joe's. Even in gloves it was like their fingers were meant to be together, and when he looked into her eyes, her heart pulsed. His eyes, wide open and searching, met her gaze. She really wanted to kiss him and hoped he wanted to kiss her too. As if fate was controlling her body, her head moved towards his, each dropping sideways, hopeful of a kiss. She could feel her heart throb in her body overtaking all other senses and silencing her brain.

'Ezzy, what are you doing here?'

What the hell? She and Joe pulled away from each other, and the cold air made the heat of her cheeks burn hotter. It was her mum. Her mum! What the heck were her mum and dad doing here? And how did her mum manage to have the worst timing in history? A few drops of rain landed on Esme's face waking her up to the cold harsh reality that her crazy parents had seen her and Joe nearly kiss. 'Mum? Dad? What are you doing here?'

Carol gazed around at the trees surrounding them. 'I thought I'd buy a new bathroom suite. What about you? What do you think we're doing here, you doughnut? We're buying a Christmas tree. Joe Holloway? What are you doing here?'

'Afternoon, Mrs Kendrick. Mr Kendrick.' He nodded then dropped his eyes to the ground, looking more like the 15-year-old boy Esme had known at school than ever before. She stifled a giggle at his nervous expression.

'Hello, Joe,' said her dad. 'How's business?'

'Good thanks.' Joe shuffled. 'I just thought I'd bring Esme to get a tree.'

'That's kind of you. Isn't it, Carol?'

'It is,' Carol replied, smiling like a lunatic and nudging Esme, then nodding towards Joe. Esme cringed and retrieved their hot chocolates from the ground.

'Mum, stop it,' she whispered. Her mum ignored her.

'What? I'm not doing anything. Am I doing anything, Stephen?'

'Well, we'll leave you to it,' said Stephen, rolling his eyes and taking Carol's arm, pulling her away. 'See you later, Ezzy.' Esme didn't think she'd ever loved her dad more than at that moment as he dragged Carol off, smirking and craning her neck to see over her shoulder. Poor Joe looked like he'd just seen the headmaster and had to go home and tell his mum. The look on his face should have made Esme embarrassed but instead it just made her laugh and before she could help it, a great big chortle escaped. Within seconds it had consumed her, and Joe too. 'My parents are the absolute worst,' she said in between giggles.

'No, they're not. They've always been amazing,' said Joe. 'I remember that parents' evening you ran into the girl who'd been bullying you, and your mum threatened to punch the mum's lights out if her daughter came near you again—'

'Oh, don't remind me.'

'It was bloody brilliant.'

'I'm glad you think so,' she said, brushing the hair from her face. The laughter died down and Joe inspected the tree again. 'Is this the one?' Esme nodded. 'We'd better go and buy it then.'

Esme followed as Joe asked one of the guys to wrap it and went to pay but her brain kept replaying his words. *'Is this the one?'* She knew he meant the tree, and at only a month after her break-up it could just be a rebound thing, but her brain didn't want to let that sentence go. And even after he'd helped get the tree inside the cottage and into a bucket, the words remained.

Lying in bed that night she had to force herself to think of something else. But in the darkness of her room, 'Is this the one?' played over and over again relentlessly and wouldn't leave her alone. And didn't he have a girlfriend? Joe was more than confusing — she couldn't make him out at all. He had so many different sides to his character, it was scary. But the scariest thing of all was the feeling his words had created in her heart.

Chapter 20

Sandchester

The nerves in Esme's stomach danced around. Her hands trembled and she couldn't stop checking the clock. It was Friday night and time for the live broadcast.

She'd made sure the lighting was set up and the kitchen gleamed and sparkled like something from a real cooking show. The spotlight illuminated the kitchen counter and she had arranged some rustic earthenware bowls, found in one of the dusty cupboards, on the countertop. One contained fruit, the other fresh sprigs of rosemary she'd collected from a bush in the garden. Esme had spent the last hour preparing all the ingredients. The parmesan had been grated and placed in a pretty pink dish, the peas sat proudly in a white bowl, their verdant green a fresh pop of colour, and the pancetta had been cubed and piled in another. The risotto rice she would pour straight from the packet and the herbs were in a small mason jar of water waiting to be chopped. On the hob in a large saucepan sat a simmering pan of chicken stock.

Everything was ready.

Esme sipped her tea, hoping it would help calm her down, but after two mouthfuls she felt nauseous. She cast her eyes around and focused on the Christmas tree in the corner of the living room. Even in its bare, undecorated state it was still beautiful. Slowly the clock ticked down and finally, it was time to start the broadcast.

She switched on the camera and took up her place. As the cooker was on the end wall of the kitchen, at a right angle to the camera, she was going to have to be really careful and make sure she spoke over her right shoulder while she stirred. Esme cursed herself for not thinking that aspect of it through, but it was too late now.

'Hi everyone, and welcome to Grandma's Kitchen for my first live video broadcast. I hope you've all had a great day but if you haven't, the dish we're going to cook tonight will be a real pick-me-up. It always works for me after I've had a bad day. Tonight, we're going to make a gorgeous pea and pancetta risotto and believe me, it's like a giant hug on a cold, rainy winter's day.'

Her nerves calmed a little, but Esme still felt queasy, more used to being on the other side of the camera.

'Most people think risottos are difficult to make, but they're actually very simple. They just take a little time. I love this recipe for an everyday meal, but it is so delicious it even works well for a Christmas Eve supper with friends. Just imagine everyone chatting while you stir the pot, glass of wine in hand. Or it's great for a comforting New Year's Day dinner when you've maybe had a bit too much to drink the night before. The first thing I'm going to do is fry the pancetta. Pancetta is fantastic but you can just use bacon instead. Or if you're a veggie, just leave it out altogether.'

She began sautéing the pancetta, then once it was crispy took it out, placing it back in the dish. In the pot, she added the onions, leeks, a little butter and a splash of stock. 'You don't want the onions to colour, so I always add a little stock. It helps get all those flavoursome gnarly bits off the bottom too, and stops the onions frying and going brown, which is fab in a burger, but not what we want for our elegant risotto.'

Esme's heart slowed to a normal pace and the sickness subsided as the delicious and comforting smell of cooked onion wafted up. She took the tea towel from her shoulder and tossed it into the corner of the worktop. Things were going well. She remembered to look at the camera more, not in a pouty Felicity Fenchurch kind of way, but like a proper TV presenter.

'Now, add the risotto rice and mix it around, making sure it gets coated in the oil. This'll help give it a great flavour. So all you have to do, for about twenty minutes or so, is add a ladle full of stock and stir it until it's disappeared. The way you tell is to drag your spoon across the bottom of the pan and the risotto should part but there won't be lots of liquid left. If there is, just stir a bit more until it's absorbed then try again.' The repetitive motion of adding stock then stirring, made her shoulders relax. 'Some people think making risotto is way too time-consuming for a weekday supper and while there are quicker meals you can make, this one doesn't take that long and I adore this part. It helps me process the day – all the good things and bad things – and put it behind me.'

An odd smell reached her nostrils and she checked she wasn't burning anything in the pan. Everything was fine. Esme realised she'd been silent for almost a minute, which was a long time in TV-land so she began to speak, trying to remember her script.

'This wasn't one of grandma's recipes. To be honest, I don't think she ever had risotto in her life, but I'm pretty sure she would have liked it. I learned to make this when I was at university, living with one of my best friends—'

The strange smell hit her again. It was like something burning. She checked the underneath of the pan wondering if something was stuck to the bottom. Nothing there. Out of the corner of her eye a flash of yellow and orange drew her attention and her heart rate shot up. She spun around and saw the very end of the tea towel she had thrown to one side was on fire. It must have caught light from the low heat underneath the saucepan of stock.

'Oh shit,' Esme shouted, running towards it. She searched for her tongs, grabbed them from the utensil jar and picked up the other end of the tea towel then threw it into the old butler's sink where it was thankfully out of sight and extinguished by the water left in the bottom. 'Shit, shit, shit, shit, shit,' she said, without thinking.

Esme turned to the camera and remembered this was all being broadcast live, to the entire world. Her chin trembled and she felt clammy. She was sure they wouldn't be watching anything more after that. Esme's face froze and her brain kept screaming 'fire!'. She bit her lip. *What would a real TV presenter do?* After a deep breath, Esme lifted her chin and smiled at the camera. 'Umm . . . sorry about that. But it just goes to show that sometimes accidents happen in the kitchen and the key thing is not to panic.' She shrugged but her hands were shaking as she said, 'I might have panicked a little, but, you know, never mind. Disaster was still averted.

'So now we just need to add the peas. Frozen ones are fine, you don't need to buy fresh ones and pod them. God knows life's hard enough, isn't it? We don't need to put more pressure on ourselves. And also, I should tell you, this stock is from a stock pot. I could make my own and I do sometimes, for very special occasions, but who can be arsed unless like, the Queen's coming round, or your mother-in-law or something?'

Leo's mum was a very nice lady, but she was so proud of Leo, he could do no wrong, and she was very particular. That was probably where Leo got it from. But Boxing Days spent with Leo's family were nowhere near as fun as the Christmas Days spent with her own, crazy tribe. Esme cooked the peas in with the risotto, added the parmesan, then chopped and added the parsley, and the result was a delicious-smelling risotto. 'So, there you go. Pea and pancetta risotto. I wish you could smell this. It really does smell delicious. It's even masking the smell of burnt tea towel!'

She served it into a basic white pasta bowl as she wanted to show off the beautiful colours of the peas and crispy pancetta. Her hands were still quivering as she sprinkled on a little parsley and grated parmesan, then cleaned the rim of the bowl with a piece of kitchen roll. She would have used a tea towel, but her mind was such a confused mess she didn't think she'd be able to find another one. *'Bon appetit* everyone. Give it a try and let me know what you think on the blog.'

She waved as she walked out of the kitchen to the camera to turn it off. As soon as she had replaced the lens cap, she poured herself a large glass of wine and called Mark.

'Well done, sweetie. You did great! Apart from setting that tea towel on fire, of course.'

'Of course.' Esme took a large gulp of wine and sat down on the sofa to check her blog and see what the reaction was.

Comments were coming in already, which was great – it meant people had been watching along. Some were nice and kind about the recipe, others commented on how funny she was which, considering Esme hadn't intended to be, wasn't necessarily a compliment, but at least they enjoyed it. Then the angry ones started.

'What's the matter?' asked Mark. 'What's that noise?'

Esme sniffed then found a piece of kitchen roll in the pocket of her jeans and blew her nose. 'I can't do anything right.'

'What? Why do you say that? Sweetie, it was great.'

'Some woman has just posted a comment saying she was watching it with her 3-year-old daughter and now she's running around the house shouting, "shit". She says I'm a disgrace and I should have put a parental advisory notice up or something.'

'Well, she needs to chill the fuck out. You were fab and we all do things like that from time to time. I bet she's sworn in front of her kid before. Anyway, it's eight o'clock, don't little humans go to bed before now? I think her child should have been asleep, she shouldn't be shouting at you.'

'You're talking nonsense,' said Esme. 'You're rambling, trying to make me feel better.'

159

'I am. Sorry. Is it working?' She could hear the smile in his voice. 'A bit.'

'But honestly, darling you were really, really good and that risotto looked so delicious my mouth is watering. I only had my dinner an hour ago, but it's made me hungry again.' There was silence for a moment. 'And the lighting was spectacular,' he continued. 'That's something to be glad about. We nailed the lighting and your kitchen looked like something from a fairy tale.' Another tear fell down her cheek and she sniffed. 'Right,' said Mark. 'Ready the beds. I'm gathering everyone and we're coming down first thing for damage limitation.'

'Really?' asked Esme, her heart lifting. She still felt desperately lonely being so far away from her friends.

'Of course,' Mark replied. 'I'll hire a van and bring your chest of drawers while I'm at it. I had to plonk it in our hallway and you know how small that is. Helena had to mount it to get her scarf yesterday.'

Esme giggled. 'You guys are the best.'

'I know, sweetie. Make some of your delicious choccy pancakes, won't you? We'll be there for breakfast.'

'Okay,' she replied, wiping her nose with the scrunched-up kitchen roll. Knowing Mark would be on the phone to Lola as soon as she'd hung up, and that they'd be with her for the whole day tomorrow, made her heart lighten. But before Mark could hang up, Esme quickly shouted, 'Bring wine!' because judging by the latest comment that had popped up, they were going to need it.

*

Joe sat back at the end of the vlog and puffed out his cheeks. That was quite a show.

Somehow he'd expected something practised and polished — a toned-down, subdued version of Esme, rather than the real thing. Instead, it had been the best cookery show he'd ever seen.

It actually made him want to try and cook the recipe. It made him want to get up and cook something for himself instead of relying on the greasy takeaway down the road or meals that came in plastic trays with depressing little sections. There was something so alive about Esme when she cooked. A sparkle came to her eyes when she was happy and doing what she loved; the burnt golden flecks suddenly glittered. Was it wrong to wish he could be the one to make that happen?

Having never seen a future with anyone except for Clara, Joe had thought he would never love again. But he could picture them together in that little cottage, her teasing him while she taught him to make something delicious. Joe smiled to himself and took a sip of his beer. Maybe they'd get a dog and go walking in the woods together, wrapped up against the cold. Then they'd return home to an amazing roast with all the trimmings.

Esme had dealt with the fire thing well. She just shrugged it off. She didn't panic or screech or need anyone else to save her. She just handled it. And she could laugh at herself about it, even when it was live for all the world to see. Clara was always a little more highly strung. At first she'd seemed like a laid-back Australian. A cliché but it was true. But as things had worn on she'd become dependent on him, which made the break-up even more difficult. Joe felt guilty for that too. He shouldn't have let it happen. All the times he begrudgingly agreed to organise stuff because she didn't want to – plumbers, car insurance, you name it – he now realised made the situation worse not better. Familiar guilt gurgled in him. Why did everything end up with him thinking of Clara?

After half an hour of staring at a blank computer screen, Joe scanned his messy little flat. Clothes lay strewn on the floor, dishes were piled in the sink and there were no pictures or personal items on display. They were all still boxed up and piled in the corner of the living room. He'd been in the flat for over two years now. It was shocking he hadn't done anything. Esme's cottage looked exactly that – Esme's. She'd somehow put her stamp on it already, like she was meant to be there. With a sickening embarrassment he realised how much he'd kept himself locked away from everyone, not letting himself believe this was really his home. Why? he wondered, but he already knew the answer. Because accepting that this *was* really his home meant accepting the actual truth about Clara, and somehow that felt like a betrayal. Perhaps he should be braver, like Esme. Perhaps he should call Clara's parents and apologise. It might be something they had waited to hear, that he was sorry. Maybe they were sorry as well. Maybe they understood how he felt, just as he understood how they felt. It must have been even more devastating for them. If only he could explain.

Melbourne was eleven hours ahead. It was now quarter past ten in the UK, so it would be quarter past nine in the morning there. Early for a phone call, granted, but he'd never come this close to actually doing it and couldn't risk stopping now. He took another swig of his beer and picked up his mobile phone, finding the number of Clara's parents, glad now he hadn't deleted it. He'd come close so many times, determined that he would let his past life go and move on, but anytime his fingers hovered over the keys, it felt disloyal and cowardly, and the number had remained.

Joe drummed his fingers while it rang. His heart beat hard against his chest and he felt a fierce heat at the back of his neck. His shoulders tensed and he tapped his heels against the floor.

'Hello?' a groggy voice answered.

In a surge of nerves, his windpipe felt like it had been punched. 'Umm, hi? Is that Siobhan?'

'Yeah, who's this?'

'It's, umm, it's Joe Holloway.'

He heard Siobhan shift around. 'Joe? Clara's Joe?'

'Yes, I—'

'I have nothing to say to you.'

The line went dead. She'd hung up.

Joe rested his head in his hands. Why? Why had he bothered? He should have known what response he'd get. He shouldn't have tried to be brave. To be something he so clearly wasn't. Joe lifted his head, gasping for air as tears fell. He wasn't too manly to cry. He'd cried so many times, alone in his flat. He leaned forward and cupped his hands around his head again, trying to block out all thought and feeling. For a moment Joe couldn't move, trapped in this terrible moment. Angrily he wiped at his eyes and stood up, taking a deep breath to try and calm his racing heart but it didn't work. Doubled over, with his hands on his knees, he forced himself to take long slow breaths. This was all Esme's fault. If she hadn't come back, if she hadn't walked into his life making him feel things again, he'd be fine right now. She'd made him think about a future, made him realise he couldn't keep just existing in the present. She'd ruined everything. He knew he should be grateful to her, but right now a dark mist had descended again, soaking into his soul.

Joe walked to the kitchen, grabbed a bottle of Jack Daniels and a glass, and poured himself a hefty measure. Some people just weren't meant to be brave.

Chapter 21

Sandchester

The gang arrived early the next morning as promised, in a small white van. Esme hadn't slept for worrying about her sweary debut, so getting up before dawn and making pancakes was a welcome distraction from tossing and turning in bed. She'd gone into overdrive trying to keep her mind occupied and made enough pancakes to feed the town, and some sausage breakfast muffins too. She saw the van pull into the drive and added some fresh whipped cream on top of the hot chocolates, then unlatched the front door. Helena, Mark and Lola came in one after another as Esme walked back to the kitchen, untying her apron.

'Yoo-hoo?' called Mark, walking in first. Lola came out from behind Helena and ran over to hug Esme.

'Right,' Helena said, in her usual professional manner. 'Let's eat, then we'll see what the damage is.' She gave Esme a kiss on the cheek just as Lola let go.

'How are you, honey?' asked Lola. 'I thought you were fantastic, by the way.'

Esme tried to smile. 'Did you bring wine?' she asked Mark.

Mark stared at her and tutted. 'You can't drink wine at nine o'clock in the morning. That would make you a lush and tell me you have a problem.'

'So you didn't?' asked Esme, giving her most pathetically sad look and sticking out her bottom lip.

'I said you can't drink wine at this time of the morning – I brought Buck's Fizz. Much more respectable.'

Esme grinned. 'Well done. I'll get some glasses.' She was beginning to feel better already. 'I did make some hot chocolates too if you want them, but if not, don't worry.'

'Is it your special one?' asked Lola. 'With a bit of cinnamon and chilli like you used to make at uni?'

'Yep, with whipped cream on top.'

'Then give me one now!' Lola turned to Mark and Helena. 'This is the only thing that got me through my exams.'

'We'll take one too, please,' replied Mark, his eyes searching the kitchen for them. Esme placed them on the countertop and they tucked in. Mark sat back with cream on his top lip. 'Yours are the best hot chocolates I've ever tasted.'

'Better than sex,' agreed Helena.

'For you, maybe,' teased Mark, and Helena scowled.

They went to the sofa and Esme brought over a huge platter full of pancakes, a bowl of fresh strawberries and two jugs – one with white chocolate sauce, the other with homemade caramel.

'Load up the beast then, and we'll see what we're facing,' said Lola, already tucking into chocolate pancakes covered in caramel sauce. For a tiny, petite human being, she could certainly tuck a good plate of food away. Esme turned on her laptop while everyone settled with plates on their knees. She opened her blog and turned the screen to face them.

'Gosh, some of these are quite fierce,' said Helena, helping herself to some of Esme's delicious white chocolate sauce.

'I know,' Esme replied. She hadn't felt like eating anything before, but now everyone was here she felt calmer and helped herself to a small stack of pancakes, adding some strawberries to offset the rich chocolate.

'This woman needs to get a life,' said Helena. 'She's called you "the devil incarnate", which is a bit extreme. I think if we were going to compare you to the devil you'd be like . . . his understudy or something.'

Mark giggled. 'Assistant Manager, maybe?'

Esme eyed them and sarcastically replied, 'Thank you very much, you two. I knew there was a reason I invited you down.'

Helena pointed at the screen with her fork. 'There's a nice one from Penny85 though.'

'She's commented before,' said Esme. 'She asked me where I got my inspiration from and she's started lots of conversations.'

'She said it was great to see someone normal, doing normal things, while cooking something amazing. That's nice.'

'I wouldn't call you normal,' said Lola, a smear of caramel sauce on her chin.

'That's because you're mean,' Esme replied. 'Buck's Fizz?'

Everyone nodded with mouths full. She popped open the bottle and poured. 'You're my marketing guru, Lola, what do I do? By the way, you've got caramel on your chin.'

Lola wiped it away with her fingers. 'Ooh, look, Penny85 got stuck into this person. She told them to calm down and said if she'd set a tea towel on fire she'd have said a lot more than just shit. I like Penny85.'

'Me too,' said Mark.

'I think you should just keep going, Esme. Maybe in your next blog post say you're sorry you swore and you'll put the time back a bit for the next broadcast. That would be safer. You do get a little bit sweary sometimes—'

'I do not,' replied Esme.

'Yes you do. When we went out last Christmas and you twisted your ankle in those three-inch heels I warned you not to buy, you said more swear words in thirty seconds than I've ever heard in my entire life. Plus, I've never heard anyone call a pair of shoes "bastard foot prisons" before.'

'All right, thank you.' Esme found herself smiling again. Her friends always had that effect on her, even though they teased her mercilessly.

'Anyway,' continued Lola, 'say you're sorry and move on. Most of the comments are nice. You can't quit because a few people got a bit grumpy.' Esme thought about it as Mark nodded in agreement.

Then Helena leaned forwards and said, 'On the plus side, your numbers have massively increased.'

Esme read the hit counter. At least a hundred more people had checked out her blog, even if they hadn't left a comment. Some had even signed up to her mailing list.

'Before you do another broadcast,' said Mark, snatching the last pancake with his fork, while Helena glared at him open-mouthed, 'you need to get some Christmas decorations up and make it all sparkly and Christmassy. It's all about staging you know. I can't believe you haven't done it already. Normally you're the first one to have decorated. It's only a week till Christmas. How come you've got a bare tree and no other deccies?'

Esme felt her cheeks burn the same red as her hair. 'Umm, Joe got it for me.'

'Joe?' screeched Lola. 'Joe Holloway?' Everyone else was smirking at her.

'Yes, but it was just to help me settle in. He's been through a bad break-up too and I think he sympathises. I didn't have the heart to tell him I wasn't going to put any decorations up this year,' said Esme, avoiding everyone's horrified gaze. 'I can't really afford any and I don't want to ask Mum and Dad for some of theirs. They'll start worrying. Plus, asking my parents for their cast-offs is just depressing at my age.'

'It'll be more depressing without any decorations,' said Mark. 'And won't they notice when they come round?'

'They won't. I don't invite them. They came in once and

it was so cold Mum cried. After that, I felt so bad knowing she'd be worrying about me I've done everything I can to keep them away.'

'Okay,' said Mark, hesitantly. 'When do we get to meet this Joe?'

Esme ignored their glancing at each other. 'You can't. Maybe I can get a string of fairy lights for the kitchen though, so it looks good on camera.'

They nodded and Helena reached forward. 'How are you finding being home, honey?'

'Some bits are great,' Esme said. 'I went to watch Daniel's nativity play at his nursery the other afternoon. It was lovely. But sometimes I just feel so lost.' Helena squeezed her hand.

'Come on, don't let this knock you. Time to pick yourself up again, love.' She gave her arm a squeeze. 'You've had a rough time, but that's life. You're made of sterner stuff. And this really isn't that big a deal.'

'But try not to set anything on fire next time,' said Mark. 'If you can possibly help it.'

Esme picked up her glass. 'I promise I'll try.'

It was just after lunchtime when they had finished assessing the damage from the vlog and moving in Esme's chest of drawers. It was now squeezed into the far corner of her bedroom so she had to stand on the bed to get round to the window but she didn't care. The dark mahogany had travelled with her when she and Lola rented their first flat and she'd negotiated keeping it when she'd moved in with Leo. Leo would have had the maintenance man destroy it if he'd had half a chance. But it was safely back with her now, and whether it fitted in her new cosy cottage or not, she wasn't going to let it go. After that was done, Mark, Helena and Lola wandered into town while Esme penned a heartfelt apology to her readers. She didn't want to go with them and risk running into Joe. Her friends were an intimidating bunch. And she was sorry. Not for setting the tea towel alight – these things happened in the kitchen, even professional ones – but for swearing in front of children (even if she hadn't realised they were watching).

*

Grandma's Kitchen

To all my lovely followers, please know I am so sorry for setting a tea towel on fire and swearing like a trooper during my first live vlog. I have a nephew and I'd be mortified if I turned on a programme and the presenter started swearing in front of him. To the lady whose child copied me, I am so terribly sorry that your baby saw me swear. I know it didn't seem very professional and I'll try not to in the future, but I think it's important that my vlogs aren't all perfect and flawless. As much as I want them to be about the food, I want them to be about connecting with people too – connecting with you – and I don't want to pretend to be something I'm not. I'm quite clumsy and always have been, so sometimes things might go wrong and I might make mistakes.

My lovely friends who have joined me today have said that I do get a bit sweary sometimes, so I will try not to cuss in the future. But as I can't promise, I thought I could move my live broadcasts back a bit. Maybe to nine o'clock? Then there shouldn't be any little ears around if the odd naughty word pops out when things inevitably go wrong again.

If it's any consolation, the tea towel that was murderously set upon by the gas hob was a bit old and manky anyway. Nevertheless, it's had a proper burial in the back garden. I hope you'll accept my apology and join me for my first Christmassy broadcast, on Monday, at the new and safer time of nine o'clock!

*

Esme imagined her readers smiling as they read her words, and found she was smiling too. Hopefully they would feel the sincerity of her words. She closed the laptop and made a cup of tea to warm up. Was it just her or was the cottage even colder than usual today? She lit a fire and enjoyed the warmth as it permeated through the kitchen and living room.

After a while, as the afternoon sky became dense and the first signs of impending darkness appeared, she heard her friends arriving, laughing and giggling as they walked up the path. She'd worried they'd got lost they'd been so long, but as she went to the window she saw them carrying cardboard boxes, gasping for air and laughing so hard they couldn't walk in a straight line. Esme went to the front door and opened it to see Mark and Helena bent double, giggling and trying not to drop their half of the large cardboard box. 'What on earth have you lot been up to?' asked Esme, smiling at the contented looks on her friends' faces.

'We brought you some Christmas decorations,' announced Mark. He straightened and wiped a thin sheen of sweat from his forehead. 'And they are gorgeous. Your cottage is going to look amazing by the time we've finished.'

Esme ran out and hugged them one after another. 'You guys are amazing. Thank you.' The wide grin hurt her cheeks. 'Come on, let's get inside – it's absolutely freezing.' She took a box from Lola. 'Where did you get these from, Lola? They look just like Mum and Dad's old ones.'

'They are,' she answered nonchalantly, as Esme walked back inside, nudging the door closed with her hip.

Esme narrowed her eyes. 'Did you take everyone to Mum and Dad's?'

'Yes. Your parents are amazing and Mark hadn't met them yet.'

'You were right,' offered Mark, and Esme turned to him, confused. 'Your mum is completely mental. Now I know where you get it from. Oh, and thanks for telling your mum I'm single again, she's now trying to set me up with every gay man in

Sandchester.' He chuckled. 'She even started asking Lola if she thought so and so might be gay, just in case.'

Lola smiled and began taking decorations from the box. They were just plain baubles, but Esme knew there'd be some of the precious glass ones in there somewhere. Her mum didn't use them anymore with Daniel being so young, but Esme knew if Carol had had a hand in this, she'd have popped them in there, knowing how much Esme had always loved them.

'Your mum loved Mark,' said Lola. 'She wants to adopt him.'

'She's welcome to,' Esme replied.

'Though in between setting him up with the neighbours, she did say it was a shame he was gay because he'd be perfect for you.'

'What?' Esme shouted. 'God, they are so embarrassing. Mark, I'm so sorry. They're not homophobic. They're just idiots.'

'Don't worry,' Mark replied. 'I know what she meant, I wasn't in the last bit offended. Who could be with your mum and dad? She said that if there was no chance of me changing my mind, she knew this very nice young man she could set me up with when I next come down! Believe me, your parents are fabulous.'

Relieved, they all set to decorating. Esme unpacked the baubles from the box, examining each one in turn, remembering it from her childhood. Helena cranked up the radio while Mark danced around with tinsel on his shoulders like a feather boa. Lola watched them, crafting a makeshift wreath for the front door from greenery she'd collected on their walk.

'Look,' said Mark, hanging a bunch up in the kitchen.

'What's that?' asked Esme.

'Mistletoe!'

'Mistletoe? I don't need mistletoe in the kitchen. I need it strategically placed throughout the house, leading to the bedroom in case any fit strangers stop by.' She had a sudden image of her and Joe kissing and studied the bauble in her hands in case her cheeks betrayed her embarrassment. 'I should have made some mulled wine and mince pies.'

'Could you do it now?' asked Lola. 'I can grab the booze from the van.'

'I thought you only brought Buck's Fizz?' asked Esme, looking at Mark.

'Only for this morning,' he replied, with a mischievous glint in his eye. 'There's about six bottles of wine out there.'

Esme grinned and walked to the kitchen to check the ingredients for mince pies. She didn't buy mincemeat, normally making her own. Not from her family cookbook but from her tried and trusted Delia Smith one. No one else's recipe measured up to good old Delia's. But with everything going on she hadn't done it yet. She did, however, have nuts, dried fruit and some brandy. She could definitely create something with that, and she always had butter, flour and sugar in abundance. Esme grabbed her apron and got to work.

Mark opened a bottle of red wine while Helena draped every available surface in fairy lights and before long Esme's mince pies were baking in the oven and a saucepan full of mulled wine simmered on the hob. The aroma made them giddy, as only Christmas smells of cinnamon and all-spice do, and the cottage looked glorious. The fire gave everything a warming orange glow, and the twinkling fairy lights made Esme feel like she was in a make-believe world all of her own. And the tree, nestled in the corner next to the fire, was beautiful. White lights glittered and made the mix of old wooden and glass decorations shine. Esme's heart was full. She was just thinking of the flaky pastry and warm, tangy filling, when there was a knock at the door. Mark, Helena and Lola turned to Esme who shrugged, not knowing who it could be. She pulled the heavy wooden door open. It was Joe, looking handsome in a long navy pea coat with his dark hair ruffling in the wind.

'Hello,' said Esme, using the door to shield him from her friends prying eyes. She wasn't sure he was ready for all of them at once. She hadn't introduced Leo to them for over a year, and even then, he'd seemed quite shell-shocked afterwards.

'Hi. I thought I'd stop by and see how you're doing.' He looked down at the floor and shuffled as if he didn't think really think he should be there.

Mark edged his way over to the window to peer out and Esme glanced in his direction and scowled. From the corner of her eye she saw Mark turn back from the window and mouth the words, 'He is gorgeous.' Esme tried to ignore him.

'I'm fine, thanks,' she replied, turning back to Joe. 'Thanks for stopping by, but really I'm fine.' She began slowly closing the door. 'See you later.'

'Oh, right,' said Joe and Esme's heart lurched at his bereft expression. Before Esme could do anything more, Mark leapt over the back of the sofa to join her at the door, pulling it wide open.

'Hello. I'm Mark. One of Esme's friends.'

Joe paused then gave a polite smile and in a quiet voice said, 'Hi, I'm Joe.'

'Don't worry, sweetie,' said Mark. 'I'm as gay as can be. I won't be swiping Esme away from you.' Esme cringed. Sometimes he was worse than her mother. When Mark normally turned up with one of his beautiful female friends, their would-be boyfriends became discouraged, thinking he'd bagged them first. So Mark had taken to just blurting out that he was gay, believing that if they were man enough to stay after that, then they were a bit closer to being good enough for his friends. If they flinched, they were out. It was a technique that had worked surprisingly well in the past. 'Come in, come in!' he continued.

'Oh, okay. Excellent.'

Mark shoved Esme out of the way and welcomed him inside.

Excellent? thought Esme. *What did he mean by excellent?* Joe walked into the living room and removed his coat, introducing himself to Helena and reminiscing with Lola, who he remembered well from school.

Mark leaned in towards Esme. 'Where have you been hiding him, you sneaky little minx? He's gorgeous.'

'He's just my estate agent. I knew him at school.'

'Estate agents and old school friends don't buy you Christmas trees unless they want to get in your knickers.'

'It's not like that.'

Mark raised an eyebrow. 'Mm-hmm.'

'It's really not,' whispered Esme. 'I'm not ready.'

'You better get ready then, sweetie. He's too good to let go.'

Esme shook her head. 'I think he has a girlfriend.'

'This isn't the behaviour of a man who has a girlfriend.'

'But I saw her. I saw them in the pub.'

'Well, maybe they split up? Maybe it wasn't serious. Do you think he checks on all his clients in the evenings?' Mark went off and poured Joe a glass of mulled wine.

'Thanks,' said Joe, taking it from him. His gaze went around the room and rested on Esme. She dropped her eyes to her old floral apron and pulled her hair behind her ear.

'Do you want to sit down?'

'Sure,' he replied, making himself comfortable on the sofa. Mark moved faster than Esme had ever seen him move before and nestled in beside him. Poor Joe, this was going to be a baptism of fire!

*

Joe felt decidedly uncomfortable. Not because Esme's gay friend was sitting very, very close to him – Mark seemed like a really nice guy. It was that he was horribly outnumbered by Esme's friends, people who knew her so much better than he did, and he wanted to impress them. He wanted them to know he was worthy of being friends with her too.

The previous night he'd drunk half a bottle of whisky after trying to call Siobhan and apologise. His hangover this morning had been horrendous but as the day had worn on his head had cleared and any residual anger at Esme had faded. He knew he couldn't just leave her alone. He wanted to help her build her new life, even if he couldn't be a part of it. Looking up, he saw everyone staring at him.

'So how are you, Joe?' asked Lola.

He nodded. 'Not too bad, thanks.' Lola hadn't aged. She hadn't grown much either. She'd always been petite but her unlined face was the same. Her hair was as blonde as he remembered and her small features formed a kind and caring expression. 'Are you enjoying London? You've been up there a long time, haven't you?'

'Yes, I love it there.'

'That's great. So, Helena, you're a food technologist, like Esme?'

'Not nearly as good though,' said Helena, she was perched on the armchair with Lola. She seemed a lot more formidable than Lola, with a sharp brown bob and a general air of authority. Esme went to the kitchen to retrieve something from the oven.

'That smells amazing,' said Joe, taking a sip of his wine.

'They're mince pies,' Esme replied. 'Well, kind of. They're not technically mince pies as I made them with some nuts and dried cranberries. I guess I need to think of a name for them. They're just Christmas pies.' She put them on a rack to cool.

'So you know Esme from school, do you?' asked Mark.

'Yeah, she was the major success story of our year. Her and Lola, of course. Those two were thick as thieves.'

'I'm surprised you even remember us,' said Esme, joining them on the sofa, snuggling in at the end next to Mark. She'd opened another bottle of wine and brought it with her.

'Of course I do. You guys were so close. It was always just the two of you. No one else could even speak to you.'

'How do you know?' asked Lola, teasingly. 'You never tried.'

'Yes, I did,' Joe replied and he felt his cheeks growing hot as Esme's head shot up. 'So, do you all live in London?'

Helena and Mark nodded in agreement. 'We're down here as moral support for Ezzy,' said Helena. 'There were some mean comments after her live vlog.'

'I saw.' Joe turned to Esme. 'Some of them are ridiculous. That women moaning about her kid? I'd have thought he – she – it – should've been in bed by then.'

'That's what I said,' said Mark excitedly.

'I wouldn't pay much attention to them. You're doing amazing. I thought it was a brilliant show.' Esme glanced at the floor. She always looked away when she was paid a compliment. Joe caught Mark and Helena glancing at each other and smiling. En masse they were a bit intimidating, but anyone could see how close they all were. Another piece of ice surrounding his heart fell away and he couldn't deny it anymore. There was something there in the pieces for Esme. If only he had the courage to try and put and it back together.

*

As the evening wore on, Esme felt almost as at ease in Joe's company as she did her friends. Unlike Leo, they had warmed to Joe immediately and laughed like they'd known each other forever. Leo had never fitted in that well with Esme's friends. He thought them flighty and silly and she thought his too serious. How she and Leo had lasted as long as they did, she had no idea. They seemed so different from each other now. She remembered her mum asking her if she'd go back to him if he asked and though it took a little longer to answer the question, she was still verging on yes, if she could go back to the way things had been before he'd become distant. She missed being able to see her friends every day of the week. She missed being able to go to the theatre on the off-chance of cheap tickets. She missed the bars and the clubs, the dancing and the noise. And she missed the man she'd fallen in love with originally.

'I'd better get going,' said Joe, standing up. Esme checked her watch and was surprised to find it was almost ten o'clock. 'Shall I get you a taxi?'

'No, it's fine. I'll walk.'

'But it's pitch-black out there.'

'It's fine, honest,' said Joe. 'I know the area well. I won't get lost. And I've got a torch.'

Esme wanted to ask him to stay, just for one more drink, but she couldn't bring herself to. She wasn't ready to put herself out there, not even a little bit. Plus the brunette in the pub had clearly got in there already and she wasn't a cheat. She knew how badly that felt. Mark was wrong, Joe just wanted to be her friend, she was sure of that. She handed him his coat and showed him to the door. 'Are you sure you don't want me to call a taxi?'

'No, it's fine. I'm happy to walk.' He glanced up at the clear night sky and pulled out a torch. The wind had died away and the stars shone brightly, illuminating the vast expanse of black. 'It's a nice night.'

'It is, isn't it?'Esme took a deep breath of the cold night air.

'I had a great time tonight. Your friends are very funny. Especially Mark. He's got a wicked sense of humour.'

'They are pretty special,' she replied, smiling. 'I'm very lucky.'

'You are, but you deserve it.'

Esme's eyes lifted from the ground to examine his face. His eyes were the colour of rain-soaked grass, but there was still a glint of the school bad boy behind them. What was he doing here spending time with her and her friends? Buying her Christmas trees? Joe was like a jigsaw puzzle she was trying to solve, only she didn't have the picture to go by. Was he was just being friendly? Yet she couldn't help but feel he was searching for something. There was clearly more to his break-up with Clara. Had it been particularly nasty? Was Clara still on the scene somehow, causing trouble? Though Joe seemed kind and caring when he was with her, there was an impenetrable sadness about him, a weight he carried, and she wondered if it would ever lift.

Joe pulled his coat collar close. 'I guess I'll see you around then.'

'Maybe I could let you know when this lot are coming down again?'

'That'd be nice,' he replied, smiling, and switched on his torch before strolling away into the darkness, turning one last time, he shouted, 'Goodnight, Esme Kendrick,' forcing a grin onto her face.

'Goodnight, Joe Holloway.'

'Tell your friends goodnight,' he said, shining his torch at the front window. She followed its beam to see the gang grinning at him, waving like idiots. Esme laughed and as she closed the door slowly behind her, she leaned against it biting her lip to calm the pounding in her chest.

Chapter 22

London

Leo wasn't going to put up with this anymore. For a month now he'd lived with it but he could feel his limits being tested to breaking point. Not only had Veronica moved in all her things and taken over the entire wardrobe, including his half, and all the space in the bathroom cabinets, but she'd even taken over the spare room with all her extra stuff. Then last night, when she'd come in at God knows what time after another Saturday night out with her friends and fallen into bed, she mumbled something about *him* needing to change. *Him?* How could he be the one needing to change? He was the most sorted person he knew. According to her, he needed to be more ambitious and stop making plans for his life in five and ten years' time and actually start achieving things now. She didn't want him to be left behind when her career hit the next level, which apparently, was just around the corner. Then this morning when she'd woken up and gone off to the gym, she'd grabbed his last protein shake from the fridge. The fridge that contained all the food he'd bought because she was always too busy to take her turn in doing the shopping.

Lying in bed, Leo angrily wrestled with the pillows and sat

up. His gut had told him it was all happening too fast. Thinking back now, he may have made the wrong decision. The months of sneaking around had culminated in a monster tantrum with Veronica demanding it was time to move in or move on. *Damn it*. He shouldn't have caved. He didn't normally. He'd never caved with Esme. He'd always felt that he'd been the one in charge of their relationship, but now he was the weaker one. And what was even worse was that, after watching Esme's live broadcast the other night, home alone as Veronica was out, Esme seemed to be moving on. He wasn't quite sure how he felt about that. The broadcast hadn't gone perfectly, but he'd seen the Esme he'd fallen in love with. The flaming red hair, the wild, carefree nature. She'd never have treated him the way Veronica did.

Today's latest message had been downright patronising. She had texted him saying they were going to have an 'open and honest discussion' when she got home from the gym and her brunch with her friends. And they would brainstorm ways for him to become more successful at work, like her. Well, he didn't need this shit. Leo knew exactly where his life was going and it dawned on him: he didn't want Veronica in it. He wanted someone like Esme. No, not someone like Esme. He wanted Esme. Esme who listened to him and didn't ignore him because she was too busy putting her needs above his.

A smile spread across his face as he remembered all the nights he and Esme had gone out together, enjoying London and everything it had to offer. And even better, all their nights in, when they curled up on the sofa and watched TV box sets or movies. She'd prepare popcorn herself rather than buying it at the shops, covering it in that toffee sauce she made. It was so good you never wanted to eat any other snack. But most of all he remembered her smile, her laugh and the way her glorious red curls could never be tamed. So often they would lie in bed, her head on his shoulder and he would wind them around his finger.

Leo picked up his phone to call Esme, then paused. Perhaps he should text. His thumb hovered over the keypad but he couldn't think what to say. As Leo watched Felicity Fenchurch gaze out at him from under her long, false eyelashes, his mind cleared. He wanted Esme back. And no doubt she'd want to come back. She'd loved his flat and loved being in London. Plus she'd never get a decent job out in the sticks. By taking her back he'd be helping her career get on track again. With the prospect of his old life returning, Leo smiled. He could easily find out where she was. Carol and her friends wouldn't tell her, but she'd clearly rented a place or Esme would have told him about that cottage before now. A quick search of the internet would sort that out.

He began to write a new text message. This time to Veronica. But he'd have to brace himself for the fallout. He wouldn't get away with a tactical retreat to the bathroom this time.

Chapter 23

Sandchester

After her friends had left on Sunday afternoon, Esme had felt lifted and joyous for the first time in ages. The week passed quickly and even though it was a boring normal Thursday for most people, Esme buzzed around the kitchen, excited about the day to come. Not only had snow been forecast, but last night she'd had an amazing idea while staring at her Christmas tree.

Though it was now decorated, it was missing a star, and she'd invited Alice and Daniel over to make some decorations with her. Daniel had just finished nursery for the Christmas holidays and Alice had finished work too. One of the things Esme remembered most about Christmas was making salt dough decorations with her grandma. Alice had agreed Esme could film them and put it on her vlog and Esme hoped it would go some way to showing her angry fans that she didn't always have a mouth like a sewer. The camera was ready to go, and she'd placed the little stool she used for reaching the top shelf behind the counter for Daniel; without it the only thing you'd see would be the top of his cute little head bobbing about.

When there was a knock at the door, Esme knew who it was

and could hear Daniel's excited voice. She'd lit the fire so the place would be warm and toasty for him, and had pulled the coffee table in front of the hearth so Daniel couldn't get too near. As Esme opened the door her eyes widened in shock. Alice, who when she wasn't working at the local supermarket spent her days in jeans and baggy jumpers with no make-up on and hair scrunched up into a simple ponytail, was reminiscent of her wedding day. The only thing she was missing was an actual wedding dress. Her make-up was flawless, her skin perfect and glowing and her hair head been curled and fixed up in a messy bun. She looked incredible. Esme thought about her unbrushed tied back hair and her stained apron. She was going to have to tart herself up before she turned on that camera.

'Aunty Ezzy!' shouted Daniel, grabbing hold of her legs.

Ezzy scooped him up into a hug and kissed his cheek. 'Hey, little man. How are you? Have you been a good boy for Mummy?' He nodded and once she put him down, he darted past her into the house. Esme watched him go and turned back to her sister, giving her a hug. 'You look nice.'

'Don't.'

'What?' Esme giggled as they walked into the cottage. 'You look great.'

'Don't,' she said again, but a hint of a smile was creeping out from under her blushes. 'Mum insisted.' With the tips of her fingers, Alice gently touched the bun. 'She said I can't go on TV looking like I normally do.'

'She has a way with words, doesn't she? Come on, let's get this show on the road. But I've got to re-do my make-up first.'

'Stop it!'

'Seriously, you look hot and I look like a mess. Not even a hot mess.' Esme glanced up at the sky. A sheet of low cloud covered the sun, casting a strange eerie light all around. Esme's tummy fizzed with excitement at the prospect of snow. It was bitterly cold but the air was strangely still. Hurrying to close the door,

Esme said, 'Give me five minutes to sort out my do and shove some foundation on.'

She quickly applied some more make-up and even tweezed her eyebrows while Alice put the kettle on. Once she was done and they'd swallowed a cup of tea, they moved to the kitchen. 'You ready, little man? I've got you a stool to stand on so you can see everything.' Daniel nodded, his whole body bobbing up and down in excitement. 'Here we go then.' She switched the camera on and started her introduction.

'Hi everyone, I thought I'd do a special video today with this little guy here, my gorgeous nephew, Daniel.' She gave him a scratch on the head as he waved at the camera. 'And this is my lovely sister, Alice.' Alice gave a shy quick smile towards the camera.

'I finished nursery yesterday!' Daniel shouted and Esme laughed.

'That's just what I was going to say, little man! Hi-five!' Daniel hi-fived his aunty. 'So as this little guy finished nursery yesterday and I'm sure your little ones are finishing soon too, I thought I'd show you a great recipe for salt dough decorations. When Alice and I were little, our mum and grandma used to make this recipe, and every year we'd make new decorations for the tree. Alice's were always better than mine because she's much more artistic than me.' Alice rolled her eyes. 'But we absolutely loved making them. So here goes. Daniel—'

'Hi everyone!' he shouted at the top of his voice into the camera.

'You don't need to shout, sweetheart,' said Alice. 'There's a special microphone that picks up what you're saying.'

'Oh. Hello everyone,' he said again, quieter this time.

'Daniel,' Esme continued, a wide grin lifting her heart, she was enjoying herself already, 'could you put that flour into the mixing bowl and this huge amount of salt. Don't taste it, it's gross.' Daniel, of course tasted it, and pulled a face which made Alice laugh. 'Alice, could you fill this jug with water, please?' Alice obliged and as she turned back Esme noticed she was keeping her eyes focused on

184

Daniel so she didn't have to look directly at the camera. Esme marvelled at how much she enjoyed filming now. Even though her last attempt hadn't gone exactly according to plan. Esme took the jug. 'Thanks, sis. Now just add the water slowly until you get a thick dough. If you put in too much water, just add more flour.'

Esme added the water slowly while Daniel was mixing with a wooden spoon that looked far too big for his little hands. Settling, Alice said, 'Do you remember that Christmas Mum and Dad had to work Christmas Eve so we were with Grandma all day?' Esme paused. She'd forgotten about that memory, lost somewhere in the depths of her mind, kept down by all the grown-up stuff she had to deal with. Their mum and dad had been unable to get the day off so Grandma had looked after them and even though they'd already spent the day making salt dough decorations, Grandma decided they should make a giant star to be tied to the top of the tree. Esme smiled. That must be where her idea had come from, though she hadn't realised it.

'Grandma didn't have any cutters, did she?' said Esme. 'So we had to cut it by hand and ended up with that lopsided monster of a star. It was more like a circle with odd strange pointy bits.'

Alice nodded. 'That's on our tree now.'

'Is it?'

Esme felt embarrassed she didn't know that. For the last few years, she and Leo had only come down on Christmas Eve and gone straight to her mum and dad's house. They'd be there for Christmas Day then away on Boxing Day morning to see Leo's family. She hadn't actually been to her sister's house for ages. As shame bit her throat, Esme realised that she'd been caught up in her London life. And with only fleeting visits home to be told how clever she was by her old school friends, and so absorbed in her life with Leo, she'd become distant from her actual family and especially her sister. She was pleased the star was now there for Daniel, just as it should be.

'It wasn't exactly star-shaped in the first place,' said Alice. 'It's pretty much falling apart now.'

'Then let's make another one, hey?' Esme said, gently holding Daniel's shoulder. He turned to her and gave a great toothy grin. 'And you can make one for me.'

Once the dough was made and rolled out, Esme handed Daniel the template she'd made as she couldn't find cutters big enough. He held it in place and Alice cut round it to make the topper for his tree but when it came to doing another he said, 'Aunty Ezzy, can I make you an angel, please?'

Esme felt a stinging in her eyes. She'd missed out on so many special moments with her family, missed so many moments of Daniel growing up. To be here now, making a special memory with him, just as her grandma had with her, meant more to Esme than she ever imagined it could. 'Of course you can, little man. Let's make a big one, shall we? I can show our lovely viewers how to make a template.' Esme found the cardboard she'd used to make the star template and asked Alice to draw a much bigger outline they could cut out and use. Remembering she was actually filming, Esme added, 'Now you just need to bake them and when they're cooled, we can paint them.'

'Yay!' shouted Daniel again, and Esme went to turn off the camera.

'I'll turn it on again when we're ready to paint, then I'll edit it all together later.'

'Okay,' Alice replied. She was looking a little flushed now and Esme wasn't sure if it was the heat from the oven or her nerves. 'Can Daniel play outside?'

'Of course. There's loads of space. If he plays out front we can watch him from the living room. Fancy a hot choccy?'

Alice nodded and got Daniel wrapped up in his hat, scarf and gloves, which he only agreed to wear after Esme promised him a biscuit and extra whipped cream on his hot chocolate. As Esme pottered about making the drinks, Alice said, 'So how are you, sis, really?'

Esme concentrated on whisking the milk. 'To be honest, I don't really know how I am. Sometimes I'm absolutely fine. At other times I really miss Leo. My Leo. The one I knew before we moved in together.' She took a deep breath. 'And I miss being in London and being near my friends.' Alice nodded. 'But you know what?'

'What?'

'When you were saying about Grandma just now, I realised how much I've missed seeing you and Daniel, and everyone else, all the time. I've missed out on so much with that little guy already. When I think of all the nativity plays I've missed, all the special days out – I loved seeing him the other afternoon.'

'When you've seen one, you've seen them all,' said Alice, smiling. But Esme knew how much she loved them.

'All those times we could have been making special memories baking together and I was just too busy.' Esme poured the hot chocolates and brought them over to the coffee table, plonking down next to Alice.

'We never minded. We're all so proud of you. And you were a long way away. We understood you couldn't pop down every weekend.'

'Well, I'm proud of you,' Esme said in return. 'You're raising a fabulous little human there.' She pointed out of the window to where Daniel was using a stick to beat up a bush. 'A part of me really wants to stay here. But I always thought once I got back on my feet, I'd go back to London.' She shrugged and let out a big sigh. 'Oh, I don't know.'

'We love having you here,' said Alice, giving Esme's hand a squeeze. 'But we'll be there for you whatever you decide. If you wanted to go back to London, we'd just have to make sure we get more family time. Especially without Lousy Leo.'

Esme gawped. 'Don't tell me you didn't like him either?'

Alice scrunched up her nose. 'Not especially. But he was your choice so we supported you.' Esme tutted. If she'd known her family's opinion before, would things have been different? Would they have ended quicker and with less heartbreak? She didn't know, but her family's point of view was something to think about. Had they seen the real him while she was looking through rose-tinted glasses? 'So, Joe Holloway's been making sure you're all settled in then?'

Esme eyed her. 'He's just called in a few times, that's all. There's nothing going on. He has a girlfriend.'

'Does he?' Alice sounded surprised. 'I thought he was all about the one-night stands.'

Esme remembered the first woman in the pub and then the brunette. Who knew what he was up to? 'He said he had quite a bad break-up. Do you know anything about that?'

Alice nodded. 'Only the local gossip. I remember when he came back he was a bit of a mess. I don't know what happened after that. Once, his mum talked to our mum and said he was in a really bad way, hiding in his flat like a teenager. She said he was really sad.'

'That doesn't sound like sad to me, that sounds like depressed.' Maybe he had been. She remembered him saying about hiding in his dressing gown for a year. At the time she'd thought he was joking but when she thought over the way he'd talked about it, about the sadness in his eyes, and the way he'd closed down when she got too close, there was definitely something more going on. Was that why he'd clicked with her? A kindred spirit? Was it only the fact that she was going through something similar that made him seek out her friendship? She didn't know, but even though the thought made her heart unusually heavy, she'd help him if she could.

The timer pinged and Esme went to retrieve the salt dough decorations from the oven. They were perfect. Suddenly, Daniel burst through the front door that they'd left slightly open for him.

'It's snowing, it's snowing!'

Esme and Alice ran to the doorway and peered out. A few tiny flakes were beginning to fall, drifting lazily on the air. Grabbing coats and boots they ran outside too, jumping about and dancing around. Esme smiled, feeling like a kid again. There wasn't enough snow for a snowman yet, but they still had fun spinning around with their mouths open, trying to catch the flakes on their tongues. When it got a little heavier they headed inside for warm drinks and homemade chocolate biscuits.

Once the salt dough decorations had cooled, Esme switched the camera on for the painting session. She didn't remember talking to the camera much during this bit as she was too busy laughing. Laughing with Daniel as he painted her angel strange colours, giving it a green face and decorating the wings with Spiderman webs. Somehow paint ended up everywhere, even on the camera lens. As she wiped it off, saying goodbye to her viewers, and thanking her sister and nephew for joining her, her cheeks hurt from the pure joy of it all. A feeling of warmth consumed her. A feeling that, this time, had nothing to do with the roaring log fire in the living room.

Chapter 24

Sandchester

The night of the next live video arrived far quicker than Esme had hoped for. Even though the video with Daniel had gone down really well, winning over the anti-swearing lady, Esme couldn't help noticing the horrible sense of pressure tensing her body.

Despite all her planning, she was even more nervous than the first time, and poured herself a glass of wine to steady her nerves. As she prepared all the ingredients for a special Christmas recipe, she took a sip and gazed around. Since Joe had bought her the tree, the cottage had smelt of pine and she'd come down every morning smiling as soon as she saw it. The decorations brought a life to the cottage she hadn't imagined it could have when she first moved in. It was brighter, more comforting and homely. And now her crazy salt dough angel sat on top, tied on with ribbon.

The thin covering of snow had disappeared just as quickly as it had come, but it had been fun while it lasted. As it was only four days to Christmas, she'd decided to make some old-fashioned Christmas staples of sausage rolls and cheese scones, but with a twist. The sausage rolls would have a spicy chilli ketchup added under the pastry and the cheese scones would be made with a fantastic cheddar that had garlic and herbs added in.

Esme sipped some more wine as she chopped the onion to add to the sausage meat and grated the cheese for the scones. Before long, her glass was empty. She checked the time; it was still only eight-fifteen. Forty-five minutes till she went live. Esme topped up her glass once more and checked the camera was in the right place. When she viewed the screen, the kitchen sparkled with the fairy lights. She had even bought some sweet red tea-light holders, dotting them over the countertop, and the flame inside flickered gently. Esme had found three large glass jars in the pantry cupboard and filled them with pine cones collected on her walks. They sat by the butler's sink, finishing it off. It looked as good as any Christmas cookery show, better even, as it was lived in, not a sterile set designed by boring men in an office.

While she weighed out the flour and butter she needed for the scones, the negative comments posted on her blog, and the blacklisting from the industry she loved, jostled in her brain. She tried to ignore it all but before long, a nausea was rising in her stomach and she was chewing the inside of her cheek. What if this one went wrong as well? What would she do then? People would hate her. At some point she'd have to give up and find a new career. She grabbed the wine from the fridge and topped up her glass. It somehow felt worse to be hated by someone you didn't know. At least if they got to know you first and didn't like you after that, you'd had a chance to put your best foot forward. Being rude online was just mean. She was grateful for Penny85, though, who always seemed to be fighting her corner, commenting almost daily. Esme pictured a kind old lady similar to her grandma. Wherever Penny85 was, she was sure she was a nice woman.

When the clock showed five minutes to nine, Esme took a final swig of wine and switched on the camera to begin. She focused on her notes but the writing seemed more squiggly than normal;

191

she'd have to type it up next time. She took a deep breath and began.

'Hi again, everyone. Thanks for joining me tonight. If you haven't had a chance to watch the salt dough video, then please check that one out. It's great if you have little ones to keep occupied. Also, you might not have noticed but Grandma's Kitchen has been Christmasified! Do you like my fairy lights? About time, isn't it?' Esme gestured around her. 'Tonight we're going to make two fantastic snacks that you *have* to have at Christmas. Well, in my family you do. We're going to make sausage rolls and cheese scones. But never fear, these aren't normal, boring sausage rolls or bland, forgettable cheese scones. We're making spicy ketchup sausage rolls and ramped up cheesy cheese scones.'

Esme's mouth felt dry. She looked for a glass of water but hadn't got herself one before filming. Another rookie error. She saw her wine and took a sip. 'So, we'll begin with the sausage rolls, but these ones have a little surprise in them — a nice kick of chilli ketchup.'

A voice in her head said, '*You're going to screw this up,*' and she swallowed hard.

'To begin, we need to flavour our sausage meat. You can use good sausage meat from a butcher if you can get it, but if you can't, just use good-quality sausages from the supermarket and take the meat out of the skins . . .' As she went on to talk about herbs, her brain said, '*Don't forget anything, you idiot.*' She cleaned her hands and took another swig of wine.

'So now, for the chilli ketchup. You can make this yourself if you like and I've put a recipe on my blog for those who want to. But if you haven't made some already, you can make a cheat's version now using normal ketchup.' She added a big squeeze to a bowl. 'Now some paprika, cayenne, onion powder and garlic powder.' She mixed in each of the spices. 'You can even add some Worcestershire sauce if you like, or hot sauce. It really depends on your taste buds. Just try it and see what you prefer.' *What the hell do you think you're doing? No one's going to watch this rubbish!* Esme gave herself a mental shake. 'This recipe came about completely by accident one year. I was making normal sausage rolls with a ketchup-type dip, so I had a bowl of ketchup out on the side that I was going to doctor up afterwards, then I tripped over my shoelace and knocked it over onto the pastry. I decided to carry on and it kind of went from there. I love making these because they're my dad's favourite Christmas snack now.'

She took the puff pastry out of the fridge and decided to take out the wine as well, as the doubts were beginning to fade, she topped up her glass. 'Now, roll the pastry out into a sheet. You can buy ready-made puff pastry, which is a great cheat. Making proper puff pastry takes like, a gazillion years, and to be honest, you'd never know the difference. Paint on a nice thick layer of chilli ketchup, leaving a one-inch margin on all sides. Now, roll out the sausage meat into a long, well . . . sausage, and place it about an inch from the top. Egg-wash around the side and fold over the pastry.'

She assembled the sausage roll, which took an inordinate amount of concentration. 'Now, cut it into about nine pieces, egg-wash the top and let's get it in the oven. 'She picked up the tray to move it to the oven and knocked over a knife. 'Oops.' She picked it up and placed it on the worktop, silently congratulating herself for not swearing, and slid the tray in the oven. Her head popped up from behind the counter.

'Boo!' she shouted, then giggled to herself. 'Now onto the cheese scones.'

Esme sautéed some onion, 'Just until it's soft and translucent, you don't want it coloured, otherwise it'll look like flecks of poo in your scone.' She giggled to herself again. 'Sorry, just made myself laugh. Now, once that's cooled we can mix all the ingredients together.' She put that bowl to one side and grabbed another. 'While they're cooling, in this bowl I've got some flour, butter and two different cheeses. I've got this lovely Cheddar with garlic and herbs in it and a Red Leicester. I love the colour Red Leicester gives to scones as well as the taste. And the garlic cheese is amazing. It's like the garlic has been slow-roasted, so it's really sweet. I've also included a little parsley and some chives.'

She threw everything into the bowl and mixed it with her fingers. 'Once it's formed into a ball, flatten it out to about an inch thick and cut them with a one-inch cutter.' As she started to cut them out, she wanted to make sure they were cut all the way through so started shouting 'bang' every time she pressed down extra hard. 'Bang, bang, bang, bang, bang.' Once they were done, she placed them on the baking tray and added those to the oven.

Picking up her wine glass, Esme leaned on the counter, relaxed and happy. Everything had gone well for once. She took a sip.

'The best advice I can give is to use a timer. Don't assume that you'll remember when you put the bits in the oven. I know professional cooks who've put something in, then forgotten about it or the phone's rung and before you know it, poof! The scones are burnt and the house is full of smoke.' She turned on the timer and placed it on the countertop so the viewers could see it too.

She took another sip of wine. 'The other thing people forget is the egg wash.' She saw it on the counter and giggled again. 'Which I've done too.' She sipped the last of her wine and waved her hand dismissively. 'Never mind, but, if you can remember, I'd definitely recommend brushing on some egg wash. It gives them a nice golden colour on top. Never fear though, they will be fine without should you forget. Oh, my glass is empty.' Esme topped it up and leaned on the counter to continue chatting with her viewers.

'So, how are you lot today? Having a good day? I hope so.' She brandished her glass around in the air as she spoke. 'I'm doing okay at the moment. It's been a rough few weeks though, I can tell you. I won't go into details, I'd probably get sued if I did, but this is my new job.' She motioned around her kitchen. 'Doing this blog — vlog — video thing. It's quite hard changing direction, especially in your thirties when you're supposed to have your life all figured out, but my friends keep saying it'll all be worth it in the end. Have you ever done that? Changed direction? Let me know, especially if you have some good advice. I could use it. I can't talk about it though, so ssshhhh!' She signed, zipping up her lips and throwing away the key. 'My poor heart.' She pressed a hand to her chest then leant back on the countertop, leaning in conspiratorially. 'Let me ask you a question, have you guys ever liked a guy but then people keep saying things about them so you don't know what to do? Do you follow your gut, even though your gut seems quite confused, or do you use your head? Or do you do nothing?' She shrugged. Thankfully though, this was all going well and she felt relaxed for once. All those people who'd made negative comments could naff off. She was good at this.

'I know I should make a load of these in advance, so that I can whip them out and be like, "Here's some I made earlier, aren't they perfect and golden brown and shiny," but it's much more fun to have a chat, isn't it?' She took her wine glass and checked the timer. The numbers seemed to be upside down. She picked it up and turned it back the right way, but the numbers were still wrong. Her feet felt a little wobbly and all the muscles in her legs were wiggling about of their own accord.

Esme realised with a sudden sinking in her stomach that she was drunk. She took a deep breath and tried to calm down. The timer would sound when it was ready, but that was assuming she'd set it right in the first place. *See, I knew you'd screw it up*, her brain said. 'Oh, shut up!' Esme shouted. Then realising she'd said it out loud, she added, 'Oh, sorry, there was a bird.' *Shit.* She had to stay on top of this, she couldn't let it all go wrong. People would never watch her again.

'I'm just going to check the sausage rolls.' She placed her oven gloves on and bent down to the oven. Her head swam and it took all her concentration to keep her eyes focused. She opened the oven and the sausage rolls were golden on top. The scones needed a few more minutes, but were rising. 'Here we go,' she said taking out the tray of sausage rolls and placing it on the side. As relief steadied her a little, she moved her wine glass away. 'Don't they look delicious?'

They did. The golden pastry smelt buttery and the chilli ketchup was oozing out a little from under the sausage meat. 'We just need to wait a few more minutes for the cheese scones but they're turning a beautiful golden brown.' Esme leaned on the counter again and glanced at the camera then back down. 'I wish we could have a proper conversation. It feels weird talking to myself. And a bit lonely. When I was little, I used to pretend I was filming a cookery show all the time. Did you guys ever do that?'

She picked up her wine glass again and took another sip. *Sod it.* She was already way past tipsy and on her way to legless, she might as well enjoy it. There was no point in drinking water now. She'd never be sober before the end of the show and the wine was nice. 'Write on the blog, won't you, and let me know if you ever played cookery shows when you were little. And let me know what you made.'

The timer sounded and she removed the cheese scones. 'I wish you could smell these guys,' she said, placing the hot tray on the countertop. 'They smell so delicious. You can almost taste the onion and garlic without taking a bite and the cheese has melted going all gooey.'

Esme placed them down one side of a Victorian platter, next to the sausage rolls and showed them to the camera. 'So here you are, these are the staples in our house at Christmas. No matter what else we eat, we always need sausage rolls and cheese scones.'

She lifted up her wine glass to the camera. 'And the best thing is, they are so easy you can even make them drunk. Cheers, everyone!' She took a final gulp of wine and tottered unsteadily to turn the camera off.

*

196

Joe switched on his laptop, laid back on the sofa with a beer in one hand, the other propping up his head and readied himself to be swept up in Esme's magic. After seeing the first video she'd made, he'd worried that something else might catch alight. But as he watched Esme getting more and more drunk as time wore on, his head sunk further and further down, like a turtle hiding in its shell. He couldn't decide if this was better or much, much worse. She hadn't set her kitchen or anything else on fire, but here she was slurring and waving a wine glass around when she was in charge of an oven. An oven that had fire in it.

He sighed, but as he watched on, a smile began to creep over his face until he felt it in his cheeks and the endorphins filled his body. She was incredibly endearing, even when drunk. Her cheeks were growing pinker with the booze and the heat of the oven. The way she was leaning on the counter and chatting, like you were there in the kitchen with her, was new and different to all those static TV shows where it was more like a lesson at school than being in a friend's home. This could really take off if she kept going. If only those people on the blog would stop making mean comments.

He grabbed a handful of peanuts. The last time he'd watched her blog he'd made the mistake of calling Siobhan to try and make amends. Just when he felt his heart was cold and dead, it had taken another knock and one he thought he'd never recover from. But each new day had come and with it the possibility of running into Esme, or the thought of watching one of her videos, and it had got him out of bed every morning. The strangest thing was that she didn't seem to have any idea of the effect she had on those around her. She was completely clueless to the positivity and love she radiated. Watching her now, Joe felt the overwhelming urge to ask her out for a drink the next time he saw her. He hadn't felt like that about anyone in such a long time that it felt strange, but not as scary as he'd expected.

Esme was leaning on the counter, chatting. He hoped people

loved this vlog as much as he did. She needed the boost right now. But who was this guy she was talking about? The ex? He really hoped she wasn't thinking of going back to him. If people were mean about the blog, would she go back if he asked? The idea filled him with dread. She deserved so much more and a flicker of hope started in the back of his mind. If only he could get himself together, could he be the man for her?

*

'She's knocking back that Pinot a bit quick,' said Mark, leaning back and rubbing his chocolate-covered fingers onto his old sweatpants. He and Helena were huddled together on the sofa with an enormous bag of Maltesers, watching Esme on Helena's laptop.

'She's doing well so far,' Helena replied. 'Her personality shines through much better than a lot of the boring people we've worked for.'

They watched as she took the tray full of sausage rolls from the countertop and knocked over a knife. Helena grabbed Mark's arm and he placed his hand over hers. They waited for the swearing, or for blood to start pouring from her stabbed foot, but it didn't. Mark sat back and exhaled.

'That was close,' said Helena, just as Esme popped her head up and shouted boo. 'What the hell is she doing now?' They exchanged worried glances. 'At least she hasn't set anything on fire this time.'

Mark narrowed his eyes at the screen. 'I'm really not happy with the number of glasses of wine she's had.'

'No, me neither.'

'Drink some water!' Mark shouted. 'You're in a kitchen, woman, just turn around, get a glass and fill it.' They grinned at each other and Mark raised his eyebrows.

'There's nothing we can do about it now,' Helena replied. 'If we ring or text we're just going to disturb the broadcast and that

198

would completely throw her off. Just cross everything you have.' She sipped her own glass of wine and popped a Malteser in her mouth.

They watched on as Esme prepared the cheese scone mix.

'Did she just talk about poo?' asked Mark, giggling. Helena nodded. 'Oh God, I love that girl.'

Helena giggled too. 'It feels like we're all there with her. Can you feel the atmosphere she's creating? It's more like she's preparing for a party and there's that excitement in the air. Do you know what I mean?'

'I do.' A few minutes later, Mark paused, his glass of wine untouched he was so absorbed in Esme's monologue. 'Christ on a bike, she's completely pissed. She only ever gets this chatty when she's pissed.'

Esme's voice rang out in front of them. 'I won't go into details. I'd probably get sued if I did.'

'Not probably!' shouted Helena. 'Definitely. You will definitely get sued! Esme, don't you dare mention Felicity's name.' She picked up her phone ready to interrupt the video if required. She didn't want Esme to land herself in more trouble.

'Wait, wait,' said Mark. 'It's okay, she's changing topic.' He leaned back against the soft sofa cushions. 'I nearly had kittens then. That would've been a mess even we couldn't clean up.'

'She would totally have got sued,' repeated Helena.

'Let's hope she doesn't start on about Leo. It's one thing for us to listen to it, but another for the general public.' Mark rubbed his forehead. 'She is, isn't she? She's talking about Leo now. Bloody hell. What was that? Is she thinking of going back to him? She never said.'

'No, she didn't, did she. She wouldn't though, I suppose. He's such a knob sometimes I really hope she doesn't. I was hoping she might get together with that Joe. He seemed really nice.'

'And he was gorgeous with a capital G.'

Helena nodded in agreement. 'She's going to have a raging hangover tomorrow.'

'Who's she shouting at? Did someone come to the door or something?'

'She said it was a bird.'

Mark shook his head. 'That's it, she's officially lost it.'

Esme signed off and said goodnight, and Mark and Helena both let out a deep breath.

'Pass the vino, love,' said Mark. 'I need a top up after that, I'm exhausted.' Helena passed the wine and he topped up their glasses. 'She is bloody brilliant though, isn't she?'

Helena smiled. 'She certainly is.'

Chapter 25

Sandchester

Esme awoke the next day with someone banging a drum inside her head and rolled over to look at the clock. The numbers kept moving about as her eyes tried to focus. In the darkness, she reached out her hand and pushed the clock over then went back to sleep. When she next woke, the morning light shone in through her thin curtains and hurt her eyes. Esme shielded them and turned back the other way. Her stomach rolled with her and her head hurt. Groaning, she screwed up her face, took a deep breath and lay very, very still until her phone started ringing. 'Urgh. Hello?'

'Hello to you too, sweetie,' teased Mark. 'Is that anyway to greet a friend? Too early for proper sentences, is it?'

'Mark, I'm feeling a little bit unwell today.' She rubbed her tired, gritty eyes. 'Can I call you back later?'

'It wouldn't have anything to do with the insane amount of wine you consumed last night would it?'

'Urgh?'

'Don't you remember anything from your latest amazing broadcast?'

Esme sat bolt upright and for a second stared wildly, trying to remember everything she'd done the night before. Her head spun as she remembered how much wine she'd consumed and her stomach somersaulted, trying to climb out of her throat. *Oh no*, she'd probably lost what few remaining viewers she had now. Esme slowly lowered herself back down and placed her hand over her forehead. She could taste the stale wine on her fuzzy teeth.

'Personally, I thought you were amazing,' said Mark. 'It was the best cookery show I've ever seen.'

Esme heard the hustle and bustle of the TV set in the background and her heart twinged, longing to be there. For a life where things were familiar and assured. 'Oh, shut up, Mark. People are going to think I'm an idiot. At least, those who didn't think that already.'

'You can't please everyone, sweetie. What do the comments say?'

A deep thudding in Esme's chest made her wince. 'I haven't read them yet. Look, can I call you back, I think I need some more sleep before I can deal with this one.'

'All right, sweetie,' he replied. 'I'll ring you later.'

Esme closed her eyes and tried to sleep the hangover off, but it was no good. She was so worried about the blog and what people were saying that her mind was racing. Knowing her luck, they thought she was an alcoholic, or worse, an amateur. Oh God, what if Felicity Fenchurch had seen it? Felicity had lackeys who kept an eye on all the cookery blogs, looking out for the next sensation she could imitate. All right, Esme's wasn't well-known yet, but that woman would relish something like this and Esme didn't think she could take anymore ridicule right now. But try as she might, she couldn't sleep. She needed to know for sure what people were saying. And she needed to know now. Sliding out of bed, shivering, she ran downstairs to get her laptop. By the time she got back into bed she felt so ill she thought she'd contracted some terrible disease rather than just having a hangover. Her head throbbed and every muscle in her body hurt. She pulled the covers and blankets up around her and loaded up her blog.

At first it didn't seem real. The hit counter had quadrupled. Nearly five hundred people were now watching her blog and there were so many comments she didn't think she'd be able to read them all. Glancing through them, they were overwhelmingly positive. Okay, there were one or two saying she was a disgrace and sending the wrong message, but she didn't care about those. Again, Penny85 had responded telling them to lighten up. Esme smiled. That was so nice of her.

The message Esme wanted to convey to the world was that cooking could be easy and fun and she'd certainly proved that. She took a sip of water, stretched her arms above her head, and began replying to the comments, her hangover fading. Esme sat typing until an email popped up on screen and she paused. Her fingers trembled over the keys. The title said, 'URGENT: Unprofessional Conduct.'

She took a big breath and clicked on the email. It was from one of the agencies she had applied to as a freelance food technologist. Her heart sank deeper into her chest and tears pricked her eyes. Grabbing a handful of duvet, covered with three blankets, she pulled it up around her chin. The agency had seen the two live videos and thought her conduct was unprofessional to say the least. She was a liability rather than an asset in the kitchen, and they didn't feel they could put her on their books. Sat alone in her bed, Esme nodded at the screen as if agreeing with the email and then closed her laptop, placing it to one side. She sank down and felt a coldness in her bones that emanated from inside. A part of her wanted to pretend it wasn't happening. She was sick of picking herself up after every failure. Sick of trying to carry on and shake it off. Without any energy to move, or face the cold light of day, she hid under the duvet and tried not to cry.

A few hours later Mark called again. 'Do you resemble anything near human now, sweetie?'

'Not really,' Esme replied, burying her face into the pillow.

'Have you got a cold or have you just been sick? What's going on?' Mark's voice was panicked. 'What's the matter?' Esme sobbed. 'Sweetie? I've read your blog and most of the comments are nice. There are a few from some crazy Puritans, but you don't need to think about those. You did great, you were amaz—'

'It's not that,' Esme replied. Through short gasps she told him about the email. 'Even the possibility of going back to my old life is gone now. I've ruined it.'

'OMG,' Mark replied. 'OMFG. That is so bloody ridiculous.' Mark's movements always became more flamboyant the more outraged he got; Esme could picture him flailing his arms around.

'I don't want to be all self-pitying, Mark, but I just don't think I deserve all this.'

'You don't, sweetie. Of course you don't. You're amazing and the world has decided to be a giant evil bitch to you at the moment. But it will get better, I promise.' Esme didn't answer, just sniffed and snuggled down further into bed. 'But look at it this way, the comments on your blog are positive and fabulous. People are loving you and your madcap cookery show. The world *is* beginning to notice—'

'They just think I'm a joke. *I* think I'm a joke. No one can take me seriously now. I've made myself a laughing stock.'

'Don't you dare think like that, Missy. You are amazing and people love you. Just re-read the comments. Maybe this is where your future lies and not back in the industry?'

'It looks like there's no going back now anyway, doesn't it? What will I do for money though?' she said, sniffing back the tears again. 'I've been really careful but my bank balance is dwindling and at the moment there's no chance of topping it up. I've been putting off buying Christmas presents because I have no idea how I'm going to afford that and next month's rent.' Esme shivered.

'There are other agencies you haven't applied to yet. Or can you get advertising on the blog? Sponsorship, maybe? Do you want us to come down?' asked Mark.

'No, it's fine. I think I'd prefer to be on my own anyway.'

'Okay,' he said softly. 'But we're here if you need us. You know that?'

'I know.' Esme hung up, her head throbbing even more than it had before and her stomach swirling. Completely demoralised, her body relented and somehow as tense, knotted muscles gave way, she fell back to sleep.

It was late afternoon and getting dark when she awoke again and made it out of bed. The make-up she had put on for the video was still streaked on the pillow and it was slightly damp from the tears spilled. She kicked some clothes out of the way. Life was a large dark hole that she was falling deeper and deeper into, and at the moment there didn't seem to be a bottom, or a way back to the top. She was just tumbling endlessly downwards. Esme glanced in the mirror propped up in the corner of her room and saw her frizzy hair larger than any Eighties rock god. There was no way she was going to get a brush through that with her head pounding.

On the bedside table, Esme's phone vibrated with a message. As Daniel was staying with Sean's parents for the evening, Alice was inviting her to the pub. The major effects of the hangover had gone but she still felt delicate, like she was made of glass and would break if someone knocked her over. Esme texted back to decline and within minutes received another text from Alice saying too late, she was already on her way, so Esme had better get ready. Huffing, and feeling too lost to argue, Esme picked up the clothes from the floor, decided they would do and went to brush her teeth. She removed the remnants of last night's make-up with a wet wipe and applied some powder to stop her face from shining – apart from that she didn't really care right now.

Esme made it downstairs just as Alice and her husband, Sean, pulled up outside. She waved from the window, then locked the door behind her and climbed into the car.

'What's up with you?' asked Alice when she saw Esme's pale face and puffy eyes. Esme told her about the blog. 'I thought you were great.' Alice giggled. 'I wish all cookery shows were like that. I couldn't stop giggling.'

Tears stung her eyes again and she stared out of the window, willing them not to escape. 'Can you please not laugh at me right now? I know I'm a laughing stock, but still.'

'You're not a laughing stock,' reassured Alice, her tone softening and losing its teasing edge. 'Honestly, all my friends love your blog. They think you're the best thing since Nigella Lawson. They all said they love how you're so normal.'

'I find that hard to believe. 'Esme looked down at the jeans and jumper she had changed into. The jumper had bits of dried pastry hanging off it and her jeans were smudged with what appeared to be chocolate. She hoped it was chocolate, but living in the country, you couldn't take that for granted and decided against wiping it off with her thumb.

'It's true,' Alice replied.

'The trouble is, even if that's true, it doesn't pay the rent and I think I'm going to miss next month's payment.'

'Is it really that bad?' asked Alice, turning from the front seat to see her sister.

Esme rubbed her tired eyes. 'It is. I can just about make this month, but with Christmas presents to sort out, if I don't get some cash in, next month might be it and then I'll have to leave.'

'You don't need to get us Christmas presents,' Alice replied. 'I might know some mums who want birthday cakes if that'll help?'

She gave a half smile. 'I'll take anything at the moment.'

'Blimey, honey. Come on, let's get you a drink. Hair of the dog and all that.'

At the pub, Alice and Esme found a table while Sean went to the bar and bought them all a drink, though Esme refused to be swayed with anything other than water.

'Is that Joe Holloway over there?' asked Alice.

Esme peered over. 'Yeah, it is.' She gave a wave and turned back to Alice. 'What?'

'Nothing,' replied Alice, smiling.

'What?'

Alice giggled. 'You do know he fancies the pants off you, don't you?'

'Don't be silly. He's just being nice because I'm clearly a saddo who has no life.' Esme played with her fingernails.

'I don't think that look in his eye means, "I'll befriend a pathetic saddo", I think that look means, "Mmm, I'd quite like to party in her pants."' She'd deepened her voice to sound like a man and Esme couldn't help but laugh.

'I'm sure it doesn't.' Esme waited until Alice was talking to Sean and glanced over her shoulder at Joe. A soft golden light shone down and as it caught his face, it cast a gentle shadow under his sharp cheekbones. Esme's eyes were drawn to his lips and she imagined kissing them. A sudden urge to speak to him and hear his name out loud made her say, 'I'd better go and tell Joe about the rent.' And taking her water, she headed over. In the background, the familiar sounds of Christmassy bells intertwined with cheesy lyrics sounded out from the stereo.

The lady with the long dark hair wasn't around this time and Esme hoped Mark was right, that they'd split up. 'Hi, Joe.' She placed her water down on the bar next to his drink.

He spun round. 'Esme, hi. Nice show last night.' His smile was wide and there was a twinkle in his green eyes. Esme felt herself blush.

'You saw it?'

'Yeah, I saw it. I thought it was great. Were you drunk or just play-acting?'

'Nope, I was drunk,' replied Esme, pointing to her water. She tried not to smile but couldn't stop it.

'Well, it was very funny – in a good way. And I loved the recipes. I'm going to have a go tomorrow, ready for Christmas Day.'

'Yeah? That's amazing.' Though Joe wouldn't know it, that was some of the best praise she could have received. It was her whole purpose in doing the blog in the first place.

Then nervously, Joe stared down into his pint. She couldn't quite figure him out. At times, he was so flirty, kind and genuine, but then there was his reputation and the dark-haired beauty from the other night, not to mention all he'd told her about Clara. Which was the real Joe? Seeing him relax, Esme didn't want to tell him about the rent. She didn't want to remove the smile that, for once, had reached his eyes, lifting his face so all his worries vanished. But she had to. And for her, it had already been a terrible day, so she might as well get it over with now. She was just going to have to come straight out and say it. 'Umm, Joe, listen, I don't think I'm going to be able to afford next month's rent. With Christmas presents to buy and stuff, I don't know how I'm going to do it all.'

'Oh, all right,' replied Joe. 'Well, your rent's not due for a while, so if after Christmas you still think that's the case, I'll tell the landlord.'

'Will he be okay about it?'

Joe's brow crinkled in concern. 'I don't know. But he owes me one so I'll do my best for you.'

'If I can pick up some freelance jobs it won't be so bad and I could make a few smaller part payments. Alice mentioned some cake-making which should bring in a bit.' She took a sip of her drink.

Joe nodded. 'The landlord's pretty easy-going. I'm sure he'll be fine as long as you don't miss another one.'

Relief flooded through Esme. It wasn't much of a break, but it was still a break. Catching Joe's eye, she held it. 'Thank you.' Esme noticed the thin layer of stubble on his cheeks. He hadn't shaved for a day or so and it made him even more handsome. Joe dipped his eyes to his shoes like a shy schoolboy.

'Listen, you will keep going with the blog and the videos and stuff, won't you?' he said, suddenly looking at her very seriously. 'You're talented and you always look so happy when you're on camera. You shouldn't give up.'

Esme's head shot up, taken aback by his kind words. His opinion mattered more than anyone else's. 'Do you think so?'

'I do.' He looked her straight in the eye and neither one wanted to look away. The air between them was suddenly tangible and Esme was horribly aware of every movement of her body. 'Can I get you a drink?'

'No, thanks. I'm sticking to water today and for the foreseeable future.'

'That sounds . . . sensible,' replied Joe, laughing. 'Boring, but sensible. I don't blame you, I should probably do the same. Maybe in the New Year.'

Esme hesitated, unsure whether to ask the question that had been burning in her mind or not, but she'd been thinking about it a lot over the last week. Joe seemed so keen to help her she wanted to return the favour.

'Joe,' Esme began tentatively. 'Have you ever thought about seeing someone to talk about Clara?'

'Why?' he asked quickly. 'What have you heard?'

'Nothing. I was just thinking about some of the things you've said and I wondered if it would help. I got really down when my grandma died, and I know a break-up isn't quite the same thing but, if you were feeling low, sometimes it can really help to talk about it. You can always talk to me, if you like.'

Leo had suggested counselling when a few months after her grandma's death she was still crying pretty much every day. It had helped a lot. But now she thought back to it, with Leo it seemed more because he hadn't been able to cope with Esme's emotions rather than for her benefit.

Joe's eyes focused on Esme's, wounded, scared even, and she shrank back wondering what he was thinking now. Did he hate her for prying? With her heart pounding, she waited for him to speak.

*

209

Under Esme's kind eyes, Joe felt the slow stranglehold of guilt and fear tighten its fingers around his throat. His mother had suggested therapy. He'd attended a couple of sessions but hadn't felt that he was making progress, or if he had, the progress had been too slow. He'd wanted a magic pill, or to attend one session and suddenly feel better, but grief, fear, loss, they didn't fade like that. They were more like a shadow that faded slowly, only his never had. How could he tell her it wasn't exactly the break-up that had ripped apart his heart? It was so much more than that, so much worse.

He cleared his throat and, locked in her gaze, felt himself opening up, a shard of light piercing the dark cocoon he'd wrapped himself in. 'Clara was great,' he began slowly. 'We just sort of grew apart. We were young at university – all about having fun. We didn't have any responsibilities, nothing to worry about. But when real life hits, you start changing and . . . you turn into different people. I guess you have to learn to grow together or grow apart and I don't think we made enough effort to grow together.' He swallowed hard, trying to push down the pain in his heart. For the first time he wanted to carry on talking. Who knew what might happen if he bottled it all up again? And Esme wasn't pushing like others did. She was letting him speak at his own pace, her brow knitted in concern.

'She, umm – there was a car crash about six months after I came back. She died.'

Esme's eyes were suddenly wider and Joe could see the concern in her face, her genuine caring nature. It was like his own pain was reflected back at him, she understood so clearly.

On a normal Saturday morning his life had changed beyond recognition. Joe had been back for about six months and had just started working at the estate agent's. He had a rare Saturday off and had slept in until his phone started ringing. When he picked it up, he'd thought it was Mr Rigby asking him to come in and cover for someone, but it wasn't. It was Clara's mother, distant and sobbing. He leapt out of bed knowing something was wrong and paced his room. There'd been a crash. A terrible car crash on the highway in Melbourne and Clara was dead. Joe's hand had shaken just holding the phone to his ear. The trembling travelled through his arm, down his body and into his legs, and before long he'd had to grab the door frame for support. She'd been cut from the wreckage and taken to hospital, but there was nothing they could do to save her. She had internal bleeding and though the paramedics had arrived on the scene within minutes and done everything possible, she was dead when they arrived at the emergency department.

Clara's mother had rung off in a flood of tears and uncontrolled weeping, and he'd paced his bedroom, which was still lined with boxes he hadn't unpacked. It had taken everything he had to force himself to breath until, unable to contain it any longer, the tears he'd been holding back escaped and he collapsed on the bedroom floor, still clutching his phone. Thinking back on it now, tears welled in his eyes again and he dropped them away from Esme's, studying the dark swirling pattern of the carpet. The noise of the pub disappeared into the background and silence swallowed him up.

'Oh, Joe,' Esme said, softly. 'Joe, I'm so, so sorry.'

He gripped his pint glass tightly. It had been three years since the accident, three years of carrying around the heavy weight of guilt in his heart. 'I just can't help thinking that things could have been different if only I'd . . .' His voice trailed off and he rallied. He'd come so far this time. 'If I could've hacked being out there instead of coming home – if we'd stayed together – she might not have been on the motorway at that exact time. If I'd stayed, her future might have been different – *our* future might have been different. She might not have been on the highway at that time and would still be alive now – we might have worked through the rough patch and been happy. Mum says I shouldn't blame myself, but I do. Every day.'

There. He'd done it. He'd told someone. Finally spoken the

211

words and let some of the pain release. His chest physically hurt from the effort and he felt almost woozy.

'You can't think like that, Joe.' Esme edged nearer to him, resting her hand on his forearm. 'There are so many things that could have been different that are nothing to do with you. What if she'd lost her keys and left ten minutes later? What if she'd got the flu and not got out of bed that day? A million things could've happened. It isn't your fault.'

People always said that, but there was something about Esme that made it seem real and not just platitudes. 'I just wish I'd made the funeral.'

'You didn't go?' He'd heard the question before but it was normally said in incredulous or scornful tones. Esme's voice was clear and there was no judgement in it.

Joe shook his head. 'No. I tried, but I didn't think her parents would want me there.'

'Did they say that? That's so cruel.'

'We didn't speak before the funeral, apart from the call to tell me what had happened. But they must have thought it best I stayed away. Who'd want the ex-boyfriend who'd broken up with their daughter standing at the graveside? And I couldn't afford the flight. That's what I told myself anyway.' He scratched the back of his head; he couldn't believe he was saying all this after bottling it up for so long. 'The truth is I couldn't face their grief on top of my own guilt.' His parents had offered to pay for the flight, thinking he should go, but the thought of turning up and making things worse had terrified him. The result, he realised, was that he'd never said goodbye to Clara. Not properly. And he'd been a coward. Siobhan and Jackson, Clara's parents, must think him a coward too and the weight of that shame had been dragging him further down.

'How long has it been since it happened?'

'Almost three years.'

Esme placed her hand over his. 'You should call them and make your peace.'

Fear crept up his spine like an icy cold hand. He wasn't brave enough to try again and couldn't admit to how badly it had gone on his recent attempt. 'No. I'm sure they hate me.'

Esme's voice was loaded with emotion as she spoke. 'When I lost Gran I saw someone to talk about my grief and it really helped. I think that's why I love using her recipe book so much. It still feels like I'm connecting with her, and when I add a recipe, it's like we're still talking to each other. If you want to apologise to Clara's parents, if you think it'll help, then you should try.'

Joe studied her face. 'We're all in this crazy world together,' she said, with a small sweet smile, 'bashing into each other, causing things and dealing with consequences of other people's actions. You can't blame yourself for the break-up. Relationships fail all the time. And you definitely can't blame yourself for Clara's death. It was an accident.'

Joe remembered the therapist he'd seen telling him to write an apology to Clara, just to get the words out of his head and onto paper, hoping it would help rid him of them. He'd never done it, perhaps he could try now? Or could he try one more time to speak to Siobhan? The thought terrified him, and yet, with Esme in front of him it didn't feel insurmountable. Joe wanted to reach out and take her hand, and just as his arm was lifting, almost of its own accord, Alice came over and offered Esme me a drink.

'I'd better get back to my crazy family,' Esme said with a smile. 'But you know where I am if you need me.'

'Yeah. Thanks.' He stood back, taking a big deep breath. The rest of the weight that had been pressing down on his chest had lifted, and the release sent a rush of energy through him. Smiling, he turned back to the bar and his friends, ignoring the glances of one of his previous one-night stands hoping for a re-run. Somehow, he didn't feel the need anymore.

*

When Joe left the pub that night, long after Esme had escaped with Alice, it was a clear, cold night and the sky was littered with stars. As he walked to a bench and sat down, the path ahead glistened with the start of a frost. The town was silent and the strings of Christmas lights that littered the streets hung from corner to corner, shining above him. Esme had been amazing. Patient, kind and understanding. A small voice inside him said he deserved someone like her, but what if he ruined her life, just like he'd ruined Clara's? Before he could even think about a life with Esme, there was something he had to do.

He took his phone from his pocket, strengthened again by the courage Esme had instilled in him. But at finding Siobhan's number, Joe hesitated. Could he do it? Should he try again? Back then he'd been unable to give counselling a fair try but the advice had remained with him. Esme had stuck with it and it had worked for her. His fingers shook with the impulse sent from his brain. Or maybe it was his heart this time. It would be early morning there now but before he could make an excuse and convince himself not to, he dialled.

'Hello?'

'Hi Siobhan, it's Joe.' He felt a hand grip his heart and tighten around it.

The other line was silent for a moment and Joe worried she'd hung up again. 'Hi. Umm, how are you?'

'I'm o – okay,' he stuttered. This was a slightly better start than last time. Siobhan was still hesitating.

'You tried to call the other day?'

'Yeah, I—'

'It was kind of weird hearing from you after all this time.'

Joe lifted his eyes to the skies once more. A bright star shone above and he thought of Clara up there shining down on him. 'I just wanted to speak to you and you know, say I'm sorry.' He felt tears sting his eyes and his voice wavered. 'I'm sorry for everything. I'm sorry I couldn't make it back for the funeral.'

Siobhan didn't speak but he could hear her heavy breathing and a loud sniff. Was she fighting back tears too? After what felt like a long, long time, she said, 'I thought that might be it.' He kicked a can on the ground. 'Joe, we never blamed you for what happened to Clara. It wasn't your fault. It was just . . . ' She sniffed again. 'It was just one of those horrible accidents. Our life was torn apart but it wasn't your fault. I'm sure your life was torn apart too.'

As tears fell from Joe's eyes, years of pain and self-hatred were released in a wave of emotion so strong his whole body shook. 'I'm so sorry I never made it back for the funeral,' he cried. His words came thick and fast between loud sobs. He didn't care if anyone could see him. 'I didn't have enough money and I knew I could have borrowed some, but I didn't want to turn up and you hate me even more than I hated myself and—'

'No, Joe, I'm sorry.' Siobhan was so calm, and the voice in Joe's head, so used to beating him up, told him he didn't deserve it, but she carried on. 'We should have known you'd be hurting too and made contact before then, to let you know that you were welcome. But when you didn't come to the funeral, I assumed it was because you'd moved on and it seemed to come so easily that . . .' She took a deep breath. 'I'm sorry, Joe. I shouldn't have made assumptions about you.'

Joe sat on a bench in the town centre wiping his eyes and searching for a tissue. He settled on the sleeve of his coat. 'I should have called you and asked if I could come. With everything you were dealing with, it was unfair of me to expect you to call and say it was all right. I should have been braver.' They sat in silence for a moment, Joe crying tears he had kept locked away for so long and Siobhan, he suspected, doing the same. 'I did love her, you know. I loved her so much for such a long time. It just didn't work out for us in the end.'

'Oh, honey, I know that. She was fond of you, even after the break-up. She wished you could have made it work too, but some things just aren't meant to be. She didn't hate you. She wasn't angry with you.'

Joe sat on a bench and, underneath the stars, he cried his heart out.

'There now, Joe, come on,' Siobhan said after a few minutes. 'She wouldn't have wanted you beating yourself up about this. Not after all this time.'

'I know,' he replied, again wiping his cheek on his already damp sleeve. 'I know.'

'She'd have wanted you to be happy. And Jackson and I do too.'

'Thank you, Siobhan. Thank you.' Joe tried to gain control of his erratic breathing. 'You were always kind. It's where Clara got it from.'

'She did.' He heard the amusement in her voice. 'I'm guessing this conversation means you haven't found anyone yet?'

'No. No, I haven't. Not yet.'

'Then you'd better get out there, sweetheart. Life's too short. As we both know.'

'I know,' he replied, nodding. 'Siobhan?'

'Yeah?'

'Thank you.'

She paused. 'Merry Christmas, Joe.'

He stared up at the stars trying to stem his tears and focused on the one shining brightly, the one he hoped was Clara. As his heart lightened, he finally replied. 'Merry Christmas, Siobhan.'

Chapter 26

London

At half past eleven in the morning, Juanita sat with her feet up on the antique suitcase coffee table wiggling her toes in the little white socks Felicity made her wear. Laying back on the large comfortable sofa, she examined the ridiculous maid outfit, like something from a costume drama. She'd only worn it because Felicity sometimes sent people to check on her when she was away. But they only ever came to the door, enquired after Felicity and left, pretending they hadn't known she wasn't there.

She wiggled her toes again, smiled and picked up a handful of crisps from the giant bowl on her lap and threw them into her mouth. By now Juanita was expected to have cleaned the living room, kitchen, downstairs bathroom and be making her way up the stairs, polishing the large wooden staircase and vacuuming the carpet with the latest handheld device that made her feel like an astronaut ascending into space. Instead though, she was just finishing watching an action movie on the fifty-two-inch telly. It had a very handsome man in the lead and she was enjoying herself thoroughly. If she didn't work so hard the rest of the time, she'd feel guilty about not working today, but the beautiful house was spotless. A couple of days without a clean wouldn't hurt. Juanita munched on another crisp.

Felicity had run off to the Maldives, or as she put it, was having a 'well-deserved break'. Her energy levels were zapped, apparently, and her manic schedule was causing her chakras to misalign. Juanita giggled to herself at how stupid Felicity thought she was. Juanita knew perfectly well that the show's producer was called Sasha, and Sasha had been furious when a triple-layer chocolate chestnut cake had been a disaster. Felicity had been sulking ever since that day's shooting had gone so wrong. Then, a couple of days after the call to the solicitor, Juanita had overheard Felicity on the phone to her sister sobbing about how everyone was laughing at her and how she thought someone called Esme was out to get her. Felicity told her sister that she'd simply borrowed the recipe from this girl, but now she thought the girl had told her the wrong thing as a trap to set her up for failure. And if there was one thing Felicity Fenchurch couldn't stand, it was feeling a failure, or worse, looking like one.

The impromptu holiday to the Maldives was definitely a case of running away while the fire died down. And, as she was away until the New Year, it couldn't have come at a better time for Juanita, who had been on the verge of resigning and finding something else. How could one person be expected to act as a live-in maid, cook, cleaner and housekeeper in such a large house? She was even expected to clean the door knocker every day until it shone, just in case any paparazzi should call. Felicity didn't want them snapping a photo of a dirty knocker.

As Juanita popped another handful of crisps into her mouth, a few fell down her front and landed on the floor amidst the others that hadn't quite hit their mark. She smirked at the gathering pile. *Never mind*, she thought with a grin. It was the day before Christmas Eve and she deserved a break. She'd simply clean it up later when she could be bothered.

Flicking channels after the movie ended, Juanita found a re-run of Felicity's last television series. Seeing her pouting and flicking her hair while looking lustfully at the camera, Juanita felt that familiar tingle down her spine. She recalled the draft pages of Felicity's new recipe book were still on her desk and a heavy dread threatened to derail her good mood. Her recipe book still lay at the bottom of the box in her room with the nail varnish stain dirtying its pages.

After a quick sip of her mojito, made from a secret recipe, Juanita went to the study. Sitting in Felicity's ergonomic chair, she pulled the large pages of *Felicity Fenchurch's Fabulous Fiestas* in front of her and began reading through the recipes. She'd always found Felicity's sudden interest in Spanish food strange but had put it down to her following a sudden fad. As Juanita read on, she found, with mounting anger, special recipes from her own family cookbook, the one kept in *her* bedroom in *her* flat.

Felicity's version of her Spanish empanadas was an insult to her culture and her upbringing. Not to mention an insult to Juanita's mother, who had taught her the recipe and how to make the pastry herself. Felicity's version used low-fat cottage cheese and a high-protein filling. They were a disgrace. Where was the avocado mixed with chilli and lime juice? Where was the salsa made by hand with fresh tomatoes, shallots, cilantro and jalapenos? Where was the sour cream to cool it down as it hit your mouth? She'd tried to make it different enough to be a different recipe, but Juanita knew it was based on hers. Some things were the same. The recipe for the pastry was exactly the same, as was the technique to make it. It had to be. Felicity wasn't skilled enough to figure out a different way.

Juanita felt the strong muscles in her arms tighten. How could she prove that Felicity had stolen her recipes? Who would believe her if she showed them her own messy notebook? She knew very well what Felicity was like. She would pretend it was all a coincidence, or an out-and-out lie – that Juanita had told her the recipes but couldn't remember doing it. A heavy stone of disappointment settled in her stomach. Who would believe a mere cleaner?

But then there'd been that telephone call between Felicity and her slimy lawyer. And in the call to her sister she'd said the girl's name – a girl she was clearly stealing recipes from too – the same as she was doing to Juanita. Perhaps she could be exposed without Juanita having to actually say anything and risk losing her job? She'd leave as soon as she got another though. There was no way she was staying here now.

Searching Felicity's desk for some information on this girl, Juanita moved the papers and flicked through other assorted letters. The drawers were locked, but she knew where Felicity kept the key. It was always under the old-fashioned ink well in which Felicity used to stub out her cheeky cigarettes. But after opening the drawers and searching, Juanita found nothing and exasperated, she pushed the chair and stood with her hands on her hips.

Felicity loved her study but she would often print out emails and read them in bed, drafting replies in pen while she sat propped up against the pillows. Many times Juanita had cleaned up scraps of paper thrown on the ground, with Felicity being too lazy to put them in the bin. She went to the rubbish bins. Luckily, they weren't due to be collected for another day – there might be something still there. Searching through the rubbish wasn't a pleasant job, but she'd dealt with worse. Like the time Felicity had suffered from thrush again and refused to see the doctor, knowing he would tell her off. Juanita was told to buy large tubs of natural yoghurt which Felicity then smeared all over her nether regions and Juanita had the pleasure of picking up and washing her smelly, yoghurt-coated knickers. What she was doing now paled in comparison, but Juanita still shuddered at the memory.

At last, Juanita found some papers. She read them and discovered the one she was hoping for – an email from Sasha Crawford. A name she'd heard cursed often enough. The email asked her to confirm that Esme Kendrick was mistaken regarding the recipe for a chocolate cake. The response was there too, drafted in pen in Felicity's scribbly hand. Felicity denied it. Categorically and wholeheartedly. She had not stolen that recipe. And reading on, Juanita saw that the poor girl had been fired for it.

A grin edged its way onto Juanita's face. Though it would still be her word against Felicity's and she may not be able to prove that she'd had stolen her recipes or this girl Esme's, as Felicity often said, mud sticks. She made her way back to Felicity's desk. Felicity was terrible with technology and insisted her PA copy all the contacts from her mobile phone to a handwritten address book at least once a month, just in case. Juanita read through and found the details for one of the food critics Felicity sometimes used for spreading rumours about the new, up-and-coming presenters. Anything to try and maintain her position at the top.

Sitting down in Felicity's chair, Juanita spun herself around before turning on the computer and entering the password Felicity kept noted down on a piece of paper. Slowly, Juanita created a new email account using a pseudonym and wrote a message to the critic. She sat back with a warm glow of contentment and spun once more in the chair, lifting her legs and whizzing around with childlike glee. Perhaps another mojito was in order.

Chapter 27

Sandchester

Esme had spent the day making Christmas presents for her friends and family, trying to save money. She'd bought something for Daniel – a drum kit – which Alice would hate, but it would make them all laugh, and Esme had made foodie gifts for the rest of them. She loved making presents like that. It felt so much more personal than grabbing something off a shelf along with ten other people. You could really tailor things to an individual's tastes. If they liked something sweet you could make them chocolates, if they liked savoury things you could make them chilli-fried nuts. Or you could make booze, which was always a hit with Mark.

Hunching forwards and wrapping presents was beginning to give her a crick in her neck, so Esme stood and stretched before making lunch. Settling down again, holding a hot bowl of soup in a tea towel, she snuggled down on the sofa to reply to the comments on her blog. Most were asking for alternative ingredients and there were more kind things from Penny85. She'd even started some great conversations with the rest of the commenters. Her little blog was beginning to build a community, and a lot of it was down to Penny85. Looking back, Penny85 had commented on every post and every video. Always in an encouraging and friendly way. This time she was asking where she could get harissa paste from.

Esme spooned the homemade vegetable soup into her mouth, trying not to dribble it over her keyboard and responded, saying which aisle it was usually in at the supermarket. Her own local supermarket didn't have it so she suggested some alternatives. Within seconds Penny85 had responded again. She'd scoured her local store but couldn't find it. She asked if a wholefoods shop like Pepperson's would have it?

Esme went to type but something Penny had said caused her to hesitate. Pepperson's was a specialist shop in town, not a chain store found on every high street. There weren't any more of them as far as Esme was aware. After a quick search online her suspicions were confirmed – there weren't any other shops with the same name. It must mean that Penny was local. Esme chewed the inside of her cheek. Could she ask her or would that be prying? Esme sat back and tapped her lip with her spoon. Something in Penny's posts made Esme want to know her better. She'd always been so supportive and kind and if she was local, Esme would love to meet her. Perhaps if she was local, she already knew Esme or her family?

Esme decided to risk it and ask, and typed the question before she could change her mind. For a while there was no answer and Esme worried she'd gone too far or that Penny would think it weird and creepy and Esme had scared her off. Had she crossed some invisible line? Some law of internet etiquette she didn't know about? Esme replied to some of the other comments to keep herself occupied but kept glancing back to Penny's.

An hour later, Penny replied confirming that she was from the same town. As soon as the reply popped up, Esme read and scoured her mind for anyone she knew called Penny. She had no idea how old Penny was and had presumed the 85 was her age. If it was the year she was born, she could be a friend from school. Regardless, Esme still wanted to meet her and thank her for being so supportive. Penny may not realise it, but she meant a lot to Esme.

Esme swallowed down her nerves and asked the question, reading aloud as she typed. 'Penny85, thank you so much for all the support you've given me on the blog. As we're from the same town, would you like to meet up after Christmas? I'd love to buy you a coffee and a cake!' She waited for a reply but yet again the response didn't come straight away. Keeping herself busy, Esme tried to keep her eyes from the screen until after another hour the answer came that she'd love to.

It was a short response and less effusive than her other posts. When nothing more was added, Esme worried that Penny had felt pressured into meeting. Whether she did or she didn't, there wasn't anything Esme could do about it now. But Esme planned to take her to the new café at the old end of the high street, the one with all the books and homemade chocolate brownies. It would be her treat.

Just as she cleared away her lunch and returned to wrapping gifts, listening to Christmas songs on her laptop, a knock at the door made her start. After their meeting in the pub yesterday, she hadn't expected to see Joe. Normally when a bloke had an emotional moment they disappeared for a while – that's what Leo had always done. 'Hey,' Esme said with a smile, glad he was there.

'Hi. I . . . umm.' He scratched the back of his head, then thrust both hands into his jeans pockets. 'I just wanted to ask if you fancied coming to a Christmas Eve party with me tomorrow night?'

'With you?' repeated Esme, wanting to check she'd heard right. She hadn't planned on going out but here Joe was, asking her, and he looked so nervous and vulnerable, her heart gave a double beat. She wanted to say yes but was she ready to? Was he? His jaw was covered in thin, dark stubble but there was something different about him this afternoon. His face seemed younger and less worn down. And when he followed his question with a shy lopsided grin, her muscles pulsed. There couldn't be any harm, could there? She hadn't seen the brunette the last time they were at the pub and he hadn't mentioned her at all. They must have finished. She liked Joe's company and as she'd said to herself many times before, if she could help him, she would. Maybe he just didn't want to be on his own and was asking her as a friend, or to stop her being lonely. 'That sounds fun,' she said at last. 'Where's the party?'

Joe's terrified face relaxed. 'It's a friend of mine. He owns a new wine bar in town. It's only just opened. It'll be fun. And besides, no one should be on their own on Christmas Eve.'

Ah, there it was, she thought. with a slight sinking feeling she tried to ignore. Just as friends. 'That sounds great,' she replied, remaining cheerful but disappointment bit at her.

Joe smiled and nodded. 'Okay. I'll pick you up at seven then, if that's all right?'

'Yeah, okay.' Slowly, he edged away, still grinning and Esme closed the door behind him. She felt 15 again. Joe, the school bad boy who all the girls fancied, had asked her out, like she'd imagined so many times when she was younger. Okay, so this wasn't exactly a date, and maybe it was only so neither one of them would be on their own, but still, she went back to wrapping presents with a grin pulling at her face.

Esme spent the next day dancing around her cottage. She couldn't help it; she was excited to go out with Joe. They'd got on so well when he came to take the pictures, and that night he had met her friends. Every time they'd been together it had felt so easy and natural but special somehow. She couldn't deny it anymore, she fancied him. Not in the teenage crush way she had at school. Well, not totally. He was still completely gorgeous. But knowing now how much he'd been hurting just made her want to ease that pain.

Then Esme started to panic. Her mind still ran back to thoughts of Leo at every available opportunity. Playing over all the times they'd been happy and in love. It was hard to let that go. And what if she made a fool of herself? She hadn't been out with anyone new who hadn't seen her at her worst – drunk, hungover, ill and grumpy – for such a long time. What if she couldn't make conversation? What if she had something in her teeth from dinner? What if the zipper on her dress broke halfway through the night? Everything was fitting a bit more snugly than it had before. Joe was very handsome – what if someone turned up who was prettier than her, cleverer than her, more successful than her? It wouldn't be hard to achieve those things, thought Esme dismally and, in an instant, her excitable mood faded to a dreary dullness where nothing was right. Esme gave herself a mental shake. Mark always said, 'Fake it till you make it' and that was exactly what she'd do. Though she wasn't feeling confident, she'd pretend to.

As the afternoon light became watery and pale, she poured a glass of wine and went upstairs for a long hot bath. Before long she was dressed in her favourite little black dress, tights and black heeled boots. She added a deep red purse and pink lipgloss. With a flick of eyeliner and two coats of mascara she was ready to go, her curls tamed, elegant and chic.

When Esme opened the door to Joe half an hour later, she couldn't believe her eyes. He looked sharp in a black suit, bright white shirt and long, thin black tie. She felt her cheeks lift as she smiled, unable to contain it. Joe's eyes glanced over her body, probably surprised to see in her something other than dirty jeans and baggy jumpers, and with unbrushed hair. She hoped he liked what he saw. 'Wow. You look amazing.'

'Thanks.' Her confidence lifted a little. 'I was worried it'd be a bit much.'

'No. No. You look great.' They stood in silence for a second until he pointed at his car. 'Shall we make a move?'

Esme nodded and climbed in quickly, shivering in the cold. Having grown used to multiple layers of clothes on all parts of her body, her elegant jacket and scarf didn't offer much protection against the chill of the night. Joe turned up the heater and began the drive into town.

'Are you looking forward to Christmas?' Esme asked. It wasn't the most exciting question to start the evening, but she couldn't exactly begin with, 'Have you got over your dead ex-girlfriend and total heartbreak yet?'

'I kind of am this year.' They fell back into a moment's silence as Joe concentrated on the road. He glanced at her from time to time and Esme pulled down her skirt, nervous it was too short. 'Are you enjoying being in the cottage?' he asked as they left the pitch-black winding country lanes behind and drove along the streets of Sandchester lit by streetlamps and houses.

Esme brightened. 'Definitely. I do like it there. It's scruffy, and sweet, and crazy. Bloody cold, even with the fire, but I like it.' She had grown to like it in its mad way but whether this was her future or just a stepping stone to something else, she still wasn't sure. Since being blacklisted by a couple of agencies, she'd been researching other career options that still used her food tech skills; at night, when that eerie silence descended, London still called to her. She still missed the hustle and bustle of the city, and of course, her friends.

Joe pulled up in the car park and ran to open the door for Esme, like a gentleman. They walked down the steep high street to the wine bar chatting about Joe's work and some of the new houses that were coming onto the market. Esme spoke of her recipes and how the blog was beginning to flourish a little. It was already busy when they entered the bar, but it was a pleasant change from the pub, especially as there was far less chance of her parents being there. Esme could only imagine what Carol would say at seeing her a) tarted up for a change and b) there with Joe. After the whole Christmas tree episode, it didn't bear thinking about. A bright full moon shone in through the large glass windows on one side and a glitzy bar ran along the other.

Subtle lighting gave an elegant feel and groups chatted merrily to each other.

Joe met his friend with a firm handshake and introduced Esme. Then the owner showed them to their table where a bottle of champagne in a cooler full of ice waited for them. Joe poured, his hand shaking a little. Esme hoped everything was okay and that it wasn't anything to do with memories of Clara. 'So, the blog's going well?' he asked, passing her a glass.

'Yeah, really good, I think. Some people think I'm a bit unprofessional, but others like it. I've had some sweet messages from someone called Penny85. She's been really supportive right from the start and I found out she's local. I'm going to meet her to say thank you.'

Joe's face flickered with concern and Esme worried he thought it was a bad idea, but then he said. 'You're not unprofessional, you're just not boring, like most TV presenters.'

'Thank you,' she replied. 'How are things with you?'

Joe lifted his eyes and met her gaze. 'Do you know, for the first time in a long while, things are going okay.' He shook his head as if not believing his own words. 'I took your advice and called Clara's mum. I'd tried before but she didn't want to speak to me. But then this time we had a great chat and cleared the air. I apologised for not making it to the funeral, and she apologised for not asking me, and she let me know they didn't blame me.' He took a sip of his drink like his mouth was dry, the words zapping him of his energy. 'Not that it was an apology they needed to make, but it meant a lot. I'll never forget Clara, but ringing her parents, speaking to them and knowing they don't blame me, like I blamed myself, I feel like a giant weight's been lifted. I can't remember the last time Christmas felt exciting. I'm not dreading it, which is great.'

'That's fantastic.' Esme smiled. Did that mean he was ready to move on? Maybe with her? She shook the thought away. She wasn't even sure that was what she wanted right now. And her future might still lie in London, not here. 'That was really brave of you.'

A gentle blush touched his cheeks as he grinned. 'Shall we get some food to soak up this booze? I've got a feeling there could be a lot of drinks tonight. It seems we both have things to celebrate.'

*

Though it wasn't really a date, it was turning out to be one the best nights of her life. They talked endlessly during dinner with no uncomfortable silences and afterwards, Joe asked her to dance to the cheesy Christmas songs playing. There was hardly enough room for all the people shifting and moving on the dance floor, and more than once Esme bumped into someone, turning to apologise to be met with a huge grin. Joe was a pretty good dancer and when his hand went to the small of her back Esme had a sudden flashback to Leo and the night she'd called Sasha. The night she'd changed her future forever. But the gentle pressure of Joe's strong hand sent a tingle down her spine. The air was heavy with the smell of perfume and alcohol, and carried the buzz of excitement that work was finished and Christmas nearly here. The couples surrounding them laughed and kissed, and she turned to Joe.

Her heart had been a broken clock and now something had clicked and the cogs had started working again. Had Alice been right that everything happened for a reason? Was this going to be the best thing that had ever happened to her? Being in Joe's arms felt right. Was this the man she was supposed to be with? As they swayed in time to the music, their bodies coming closer together, she could feel his torso press against hers and her heart began to pound. If she looked up at him, would he kiss her? Did he want it as much as she did right now? Risking a look, she tilted her head upwards, and his dipped. His mouth was coming closer to hers and she shut her eyes, her body tingling with anticipation. Then a voice called his name and Esme looked up to see Joe's raised head watching as the dark-haired woman he'd been with in the pub ran up to him. Esme backed away, and Joe's hand fell from the small of her back as the other woman flung her arms over his shoulders.

'Joe! Where've you been? You've been ignoring me.' She kissed him on the cheek then turned to Esme who, startled by how pretty she was close up, studied her shoes. 'What are you doing here? You're not being naughty, are you? Anyway, I need to see you. Can you meet me after Christmas?'

All at once Esme's confidence, not to mention her belief in Joe, was cut down. He hadn't changed. Lola was right, some men never grew up. She'd been taken in by the vulnerability of a man she had imagined. Joe's eyes darted from Esme to the brunette and back again, his cheeks red with embarrassment at being caught out and, Esme hoped, shame.

'Esme, this is—'

'Excuse me,' Esme said as she clenched her jaw and rushed to the door. Did he think he could use her then cast her off, just like Leo had? Like he did with his one-night stands? Well, she wasn't going to stand for this. She wasn't going to stand there and be humiliated.

Over her shoulder she heard Joe say, 'Just wait there a second, angel.'

What? He was calling her his 'angel' when Esme hadn't even left the building? She was only a few yards away! The palms of her hands were sweaty as, outraged, she made her way to the front door and out into the street. The cold night air hit her face, taking her breath away. Stupidly, she'd left her jacket and scarf back at the bar. Never mind. She hadn't liked them much anyway and wouldn't want to wear them again after tonight. A taxi sat ready and waiting in the taxi rank a few metres away.

'Esme? Esme, wait.' Joe's voice carried on the wind but she didn't look back, just ran on towards a taxi. Pulling open the door and jumping in, she tried hard to fight back the tears that were threatening to spill down her face. She'd thought her heart was beginning to rebuild itself again. That slowly, piece by piece it was mending and her with it. She'd allowed Joe to inch his way inside and now, instead of helping her heal, like she'd helped him, he'd battered it, tearing it in half again.

Chapter 28

Sandchester

As Christmas Eve had ended so badly, Esme was grateful to spend Christmas Day with her parents. The noise and hubbub of their celebrations would stop her thinking about Joe and there was no way she could cope with being in the cottage all on her own.

Dressed in a tacky Christmas jumper she'd found in a charity shop, decorated with a snowman whose large woollen carrot nose stuck out, Esme climbed into her dad's waiting car. He wore something similar: a jumper with an Christmas elf on it. Stephen's thin face and weak chin made him look the least elf-like he possibly could. He looked like a grumpy accountant, but wearing silly Christmas jumpers was their family tradition and Esme wondered what marvellous creation her mother would be wearing. Carol never held back when it came to dressing up.

Alice's car was already parked when they arrived. No doubt Daniel had got up ridiculously early for them to be there already. It was only just after nine. As Carol opened the door, Daniel came running at her, shouting, 'Santa Claus has come, Aunty Esme! He even left me some presents here!'

Esme smiled and hugged him close, breathing in the smell of his shampoo. 'Do you know, he even left a present for you at my house. He told me I could be an elf for him today and give it to you because you were the best boy in the whole world.'

Daniel's face lit up and his eyes opened wide. 'Can I have it now, Aunty Esme? Can I, please?'

Esme looked to Alice stood behind him in the hallway, who nodded. 'Okay, then. I just need to bring it in from the car.'

Daniel ran back inside and Esme brought the presents in. They settled in front of the fake fire with her mother's CD of carols playing in the background. There was no TV allowed on Christmas morning. It was always music mixed with laughter until the Queen's speech. Then an afternoon film with bursting bellies.

Esme shook off her jacket and perched on the end of the sofa, her mum and dad next to her. Carol was wearing a jumper with a giant advent calendar on it, with little flaps for each day, Christmas tree-shaped earrings hung down from her ears and Rudolph antlers were perched high on her head. As per usual, she had a glass of bubbly in her hand. 'Merry Christmas to you, my sweetheart,' she said, reaching over and taking Esme's hand.

'Merry Christmas, Mum.' Her dad handed Esme a glass. Her family were pretty amazing. They watched as Daniel, unable to contain himself, tore off the wrapping paper. As he got to the last little bits, Esme switched her gaze between Daniel and Alice, hoping to catch the exact moment Alice realised what it was.

'A drum kit, Daniel,' said Alice, through gritted teeth. 'How amazing is that?'

Esme gave a cheeky grin and after Alice had shot her a pretend evil glare, they burst out laughing. She turned to Esme. 'I'll get you for that later. As soon as you have kids I'll be buying them every musical instrument I can think of.'

'I know,' laughed Esme. 'I know.' Esme got up and moved to the other sofa to sit next to her sister, then wrapped her arm around her and rested her head on Alice's shoulder.

'I'm glad you're here, sis,' Alice whispered, kissing the top of her head.

'Me too,' Esme replied, refusing to let thoughts of Joe creep in.

They settled down next to the tree with its twinkling multi-coloured lights, and the fake branches decorated with baubles, and began exchanging gifts, sipping Prosecco and eating another batch of sausage rolls and cheese scones that Esme had made a couple of days earlier. When it came to Esme's turn to open her presents, a surge of emotion formed a lump in her throat. Looking around at her family all gathered together, all staring at her with love in their eyes, joy filled her heart. She opened the first gift from Alice and after removing the wrapping paper, unfolded an apron that said, 'When in doubt, add booze!' It was perfect and thinking of her last live vlog, quite apt too.

Her mind tried to replay last night and the drinks she'd shared with Joe, but she shoved the thought away. She was so angry with him that when he'd texted late last night, she'd deleted it without reading a single word. How could he have used her like that knowing everything she'd been through, everything that he'd been through? Clearly the genuine, caring side of him had been fake all along.

'Here's another one, Esme,' said Carol, passing her another present. She opened another and another and, before long, had an array of cooking utensils and cookbooks surrounding her. 'We bought you cookery things,' said her mum, looking uncharacteristically serious, 'because we believe in you. We know you can do this.'

'Hear, hear,' said her father, raising his glass.

'Me too, Aunty Esme,' said Daniel, running and strangling her from the tightness of his embrace.

Esme wiped a tear from her eye. This was the best Christmas Day. Ever. Her family were her sanctuary. Her place to hide and be safe, protected from the rest of the world, which was just what she needed right now. She kissed Daniel's cheek and he let go to begin bashing his drum kit just as Esme's phone pinged with a message. She checked it quickly, wondering if it was Joe. He was spending the day with his family and she hadn't expected to hear from him. Whatever excuse he came up with, she wouldn't believe it. Esme was just preparing a curt response in her head when she saw it was from Leo. He wished her a Merry Christmas, sent his love to her family and hoped she was well. Esme's stomach lurched. Was he sorry for what he'd done and regretting it, or was this just a strange peace offering?

'Everything all right?' asked Alice.

Shoving her phone into her pocket, Esme fixed a smile. 'Yeah, fine. Nothing important.'

Though Esme loved to cook and all the family thought her food better than Carol's, she could never bring herself to cook the big Christmas dinner. She would help out in the kitchen, stirring, chopping, peeling and doing whatever else was required, but Carol always said it was her place to make and serve dinner on Christmas Day, even though she was terrible. It was part of her job as Mum, and no one challenged that because they loved her and her crazy antics so much. Esme remembered the year Carol had messed up the turkey and it was still frozen in the middle so Esme had knocked up an amazing broccoli cheese dish and served it in giant Yorkshire puddings. It was divine and one for the blog, she thought with a grin.

They gathered around the table, squeezed in next to each other with elbows knocking and legs at awkward angles. Helping themselves to the bowls of food, they chatted together, teasing, laughing, joking. Alice tried to get Daniel to eat more sprouts and Esme kept stealing them from his plate whenever Alice wasn't looking, her dad aiding and abetting by distracting Alice if she glanced over.

The only aspect of Christmas dinner Esme was allowed to help with was the Christmas pudding. Made from a traditional recipe of her great-grandma's, it had one secret ingredient no other

235

Christmas pudding had. A good local ale was used instead of stout, and it gave the pudding a lighter flavour. Grandma always used to tell them how when she was a child, she would be given a large white jug from her mother and a purse full of coins and she would walk to the nearby pub to collect the ale. The landlord always gave her an apple for the walk back.

Now that Esme made it, she'd gather everyone around and they would all stir the pudding three times clockwise and make a wish. She'd nipped home for the day in late October, before this whole horrid mess had started, with the contents in a Tupperware box next to her on the train for them to make their wishes. Leo never came. He always said it was her family tradition and she should keep it that way. She'd always believed it to be a kind gesture, but now, looking back, she wasn't sure. The morning she'd packed up her belongings and left the flat, she'd pulled it out from under the spare bed and tucked it under her arm, her suitcase in the other hand. There was no way she was leaving it behind.

Now Daniel was older and she wasn't in London, maybe he would make the puddings with her next year? She wanted to pass on all these family traditions, ensure they didn't die out. And they wouldn't if she had anything to do with it. After a big helping of the pudding with lashings of cream, they flopped on the sofa. Bellies full, tired and sleepy, while Daniel played with his new toys.

'What are you up to tomorrow?' Carol asked Esme. 'Only, you know Mildred and Norman next door have a shindig every Boxing Day? They thought that, as you were back, you might like to come. Their son will be there.' Mildred and Norman's son, James, had been the kid at school who always had a runny nose. Esme blanched at the thought of what he must look like now. 'He's divorced,' continued Carol. 'And I wouldn't say handsome, but he's not unattractive. Could do with some teeth whitening from all the smoking, but he's a very nice man.'

Esme grimaced and Alice hid behind her husband's arm, giggling. 'No, thanks, Mum. I've got plans. I—'

'Are you sure, love? As you've given Leo the old heave-ho, you should be getting back out there again. You could think of him as a practice run. I'm not saying you need to have sex with him but—'

'Mum, stop it! Ewww. I do not want to hear you saying the S word again.' Luckily, Daniel was in the toilet so hadn't heard. Esme could only imagine the emotional damage he'd suffer hearing his granny talk like that. 'Honestly, Mum, it's fine. I've got the gang coming over for a live Boxing Day Bake Off. I thought it'd be a great way to show people how to use up leftovers. Me and Helena are going head-to-head. All in good fun though.'

'Helena?' said Alice. 'Good fun? She's the most competitive person ever, isn't she?'

'Yeah, but it'll be fine. We've already agreed this is to help grow the blog and not a real competition. Plus I plan to soak her in booze so she'll be all chilled out by the time we actually finish.'

'What a fab idea,' Carol said, smiling. 'I'm so proud of my girls.' Her red cheeks told Esme, and from the sly grin on Alice's face, her too, that their mum was edging from tiddly to drunk.

As the afternoon grew dark and Daniel's happy playing turned into overtired tantrums, Alice and Sean went home, dropping Esme off on the way. Before she left, Esme hugged her mum and dad. 'Thank you so much for everything you've done for me since I got home. I don't think I'd have got through it without you.'

Carol cupped her cheek. 'You are wonderful, my girl, and an amazing cook. You can make this work, I know you can. And we will always be here for you.'

Esme felt the tears in her eyes as her dad moved forward and wrapped his arms around her. 'You can do it, little one. We're very proud of you.'

'Thank you.' Esme wiped her nose and climbed into the car,

squished between Daniel's sleepy body and the presents shoved in the back. As he nestled in, she wondered how she could ever have spent Christmas anywhere else, but that didn't stop her heart hurting all over again from Joe's betrayal, or her confusion at Leo's unexpected text.

Chapter 29

Sandchester

Esme was up early, preparing for the Boxing Day Bake Off, still wearing her pyjamas with a giant oversized jumper and her usual fluffy bed socks. Where the oven was on and the log fire burning, the house was warm, and she fidgeted with excitement waiting for her friends to arrive. Outside, shades of purple, navy and grey mixed together as the sun rose lazily. A strong wind had blown the thick cover of dark clouds away and the sky was clearing. She could hear birds singing and see their nests in the bare trees. She loved this time of the day, being up early, pottering around in the cottage, watching the world come to life. Strangely, it didn't make her feel lonely. It made her feel alive and like she was watching something other people missed.

After getting dressed, Esme set up the camera and made sure the place was picture-perfect. She began preparing different ingredients, dividing them in two so that she and Helena could have half each and see what delights they could come up with. Each ingredient was placed in a pretty dish and ordered so they looked good on camera. Before long, the gang had arrived and Esme opened some fizz and filled the waiting glasses.

Mark was the first to hug her, waving a present in the air as he walked in. Helena followed, then Lola, who had given up Boxing Day with Eric to be there. Esme gave her an extra special cuddle. Before they began the broadcast that was supposed to start at eleven, they exchanged gifts and toasted Christmas huddled by the fire.

'How was yesterday?' asked Helena, already tucking into the nougat Esme had made her. It was her favourite, even though she always pronounced it nuggit.

'Do you know, it was one of the best Christmas Days I've ever had.' *Despite Joe,* she thought. 'I really don't know why I've not felt like this before. I think that, the last few years with Leo, it's been a lot of dashing around between his family and mine, and lots of parties with his work colleagues and bosses. Plus he always found Mum so full-on, we never stayed for that long.' Esme frowned. How had she let that happen? She'd let her family down by being so wrapped up in Leo and living the life she thought she should have. 'This time I've been able to really enjoy it, being with my family, cooking and baking here in the cottage.'

'You seem very relaxed,' said Mark. Esme had made him a bottle of homemade Christmas vodka but it was just a tad too early to start on that yet. Even Esme drew the line at consuming hard liquor before lunchtime.

'I am. And thanks for being here, Lola. I know that you're missing out on the day with Eric.'

'Oh, hush, don't be silly,' she said, a chocolate truffle pushing out the side of her cheek as she spoke with her mouthful. 'He can manage without me for one day.'

A playlist of Christmas songs was on repeat on her laptop and after finishing their drinks, Esme stood up. 'Right, before we get started I've got something else for you all for the vlog.' Excitedly, Esme ran to a corner cupboard and pulled out a Christmas gift bag. She brought it over and began giving out Christmas head-bands. Mark's had enormous elf ears and a little hat, Helena had reindeer ears, Lola wore red and white striped candy canes, and Esme proudly put on hers that had two light-up presents, bobbling about on springs.

Mark giggled at Helena, Helena asked Lola to swap but she refused, and Esme couldn't stop laughing at all of them. 'Ready to get started then? It's two minutes to eleven.' Everyone nodded, a tangible excitement filling the cottage as Helena made one last attempt to swipe Lola's headband off her head but only managed to knock it down into her eyes. Lola quickly pushed it up and Esme turned on the camera and gave her introduction like a pro.

'Hi everyone, thanks so much for joining us today for our live Boxing Day Bake Off!' For some reason Esme did jazz hands and the others joined in. She could see they were nervous but Esme was used to this now. So much had gone wrong on previous occasions she couldn't imagine what else could, and so she began safe in the knowledge things would be fine. 'So, Helena here, who is one of my bestest friends, is also a food technologist and an amazing cook. So, what I've done is split the ingredients into two piles. Mark here—' Mark waved and winked at the camera '—is going to work with Helena and the lovely Lola—' Lola gave a small wiggle of her fingers '—is going to work with me and we'll see what we can come up with.' Esme looked directly to camera and leaned over the counter to talk to the audience. 'I'll be honest, guys, I've no idea how this is going to go. We've got Buck's Fizz, this lot are crazy and even more sweary than me sometimes, so I've given you all fair warning. It's going to be noisy and chaotic so all I can say is, pop open the bubbly, put your feet up and try and enjoy it, yeah?' She turned to her friends. 'But guys, it is only 11 a.m., so please try not to swear.' Esme gave a cheeky wink at the camera and the cooking began.

How her viewers heard anything over the laughing she had no idea. Mark spent the entire time either nibbling the supplies or trying to sabotage Esme and Lola, even though Lola mainly sat on a stool drinking bubbly and not doing very much else.

Helena was getting more and more cross with Mark for messing about, and a tiny bit bossy, which was exactly what Esme had expected, but amongst all of this, they were joking and giggling. Mark, now wearing a tinsel scarf as well as his elf ears, threw a tea towel at Lola who nearly fell off her chair trying to catch it. Esme topped up Helena's drink in an effort to slow her down.

Just as Esme was describing the quick cheats chutney she was making, an unexpected knock on the door threw her flow. Faced with the instant decision to keep going or stop the broadcast, Esme's brain froze until Mark said, 'Don't worry, I'll get it, you keep going.' Esme carried on talking, covering the noise of him rushing to the door and pulling it open. Mark was an expert of getting rid of people nicely, so Esme knew it wouldn't take long. But when he opened the door, Esme nearly dropped her mixing bowl as her fingers became weak and she forced her eyes to focus on the figure in the doorway.

'Leo? What are you doing here?' He marched into the cottage, forcing his way into the kitchen and causing Helena to swerve out of his path. Esme's eyes narrowed on him, checking he was really there. Leo tried to smile as his polished brogues tapped on the floor, his hands deep in the pockets of his long coat. She could see the nervousness in his eyes and read it in his simpering smile. As he came nearer, Esme could feel her heartbeat quicken. He was as handsome as ever, even with that strange grin. His sandy blond hair had grown a bit and he brushed it back with a sweep of his hand. He was his normal assertive, focused self but Esme sensed a hint of vulnerability that hadn't been there before.

'Esme,' Leo said, his strong voice overriding the music. He took off his coat, folded it and placed it on the side under the window but not before examining it for dirt. Had he always done things like that? Mark, Helena and Lola were staring at each other. Another Christmas song started playing in the background but it seemed excessively loud to Esme. When she tried to speak, her voice sounded even squeakier than when she heard herself on her videos.

'Leo, what are you doing here?'

He glanced down at his shoes then back at her face. 'I wanted to see you – I had to see you.' His eyes ran up and down the length of her body, appraising her. 'You look amazing. A bit pale, but . . .' Mark tutted and rolled his eyes. Lola was grimacing like she wanted to punch him and Helena placed a hand on her arm as if forcing her back. 'I mean, you still look fantastic. Have you been running more? You look more . . . toned.'

She wasn't more toned, that was a lie. She'd put on a little bit of weight actually, not that she cared. Unable to be swayed by his flattery, Esme said, 'That doesn't answer my question, Leo. What do you want?'

'I've made a dreadful mistake, Esme. Can we talk?'

'Talk about what?'

Mark began whispering something to Esme and motioning towards the living room, but she was so caught up in the moment she couldn't make out what he was getting at, and didn't want to be distracted from Leo's sudden appearance. The large open fire crackled and burned in the grate but despite its heat, Esme's body had gone cold and she shivered. She kept her face blank. She didn't want Leo having any idea what she was thinking, or see how shocked she was. She'd never imagined this would happen. Leo was always so sure of everything he did. He'd always been super-focused, planning out his entire life. He knew what he wanted to achieve by the age of 30, then when he'd hit 30, he started working on 'life goals,' as he liked to call them, for when he was 40, even 50. Looking back, it had been exhausting. Whenever he started having his planning evenings, Esme used to settle down with a good book and a glass of wine and nod at the appropriate moments. His stupid five-year personal plans to 'get where you want to be' were a complete waste of time because life didn't treat you like that. It liked to take you on bizarre twists and turns and derail all your plans and smash you into a million pieces only to make you try and pick yourself up again and again. That he was here now, admitting to having made a mistake, was unbelievable. He'd certainly seemed sure when he told her it was over.

'I miss you.'

Just then there was another knock at the door. Esme turned to Mark who was already moving to get it. 'What the hell is going on?' she said to herself. 'It's like Piccadilly Circus in here today.'

'For the middle of nowhere it is bloody busy,' said Mark as he opened the door again. This time, as he stepped aside, Esme's heart thudded violently like it was trying to punch its way out of her body. It was Joe, standing on her doorstep without a coat, shivering. He must have been watching the broadcast and driven straight here when Leo turned up. Well, if he was here to dish out advice to her he could naff off too. Joe edged into the room but stayed in the living room.

'I've made a mistake, Esme,' Leo said again. 'I really miss you.'

'I thought you were seeing someone else?' There was no way she was going to make this easy for him. 'Veronica? Your boss?'

'I was. I—' He shook his head. 'We finished. It didn't work out. I don't know what I was thinking, Esme. As soon as I let you go, I knew I'd made the biggest mistake of my life. I can't exist without you. Or your cooking,' he joked.

Esme didn't smile. 'You can live without me, Leo. Clearly. You've been doing just that. You were sneaking around behind my back, weren't you? Cheating on me with Veruca, or whatever her name is.'

'Veronica,' he mumbled, keeping his eyes on the floor.

She didn't want to make a scene, but she hadn't had chance to say all this to him and now he was here she wanted him to know how much it had hurt – how much he'd put her through. 'How long were you seeing her behind my back, Leo?'

He raised his head. 'I didn't mean for it to happen like that, Esme. It was just one of those things.'

'It wasn't one of those things, Leo. It was my life – our life!'

'It was an acc—'

'Do not tell me it was an accident.' She felt herself warm up from the fire growing inside her and was jabbing her finger at him. 'No one accidentally starts sleeping with someone else behind their partner's back. You don't accidentally take all your clothes off and end up in bed with someone else, having sex.' For a second she hoped Joe didn't think she was a psycho, but then she reminded herself not to care about him either. And Leo had this coming.

'Listen, Esme, I made a mistake and I'm sorry.'

'So what do you want? What are you doing down here in the sticks, Leo? I live here now. You threw me out of your flat and I've got a place here in Sandchester. What do you expect to happen now?'

He reached out, trying to take her hand but she pulled it away. 'Esme, I've realised what a mistake I made. You can come home with me. We can give it another go.'

Esme couldn't speak. She felt like her world was in a snow globe and someone kept picking it up and shaking it, turning everything upside down. She watched Leo's handsome face and his dark grey eyes that she had stared into so many times, thinking he was the one. She'd wanted so badly to return to her London life when she first arrived. She wanted to be near her friends, be in the city, the centre of the world again. And she'd missed the Leo she'd loved so much before things had started to go wrong. Could she go back now?

Joe suddenly ran around the counter and into the kitchen. Next to Leo he was even more handsome with his dark, slightly fluffy hair and clear green eyes the colour of moss. Exactly the same colour of the moss that grew in the back garden. His eyes were focused on Esme with an intensity she hadn't experienced before and a tightness squeezed her chest. 'Esme—'

'And what are you doing here, Joe? Why haven't you got a coat on?' It was a silly question, she knew, but amongst all the confusion the words were out before she could stop them.

'You can't go back to him, Esme, you can't—'

'Hey,' said Leo, turning to Joe, but seeing the size of him Leo shrank back. Esme knew he wouldn't fight for her physically. He could talk a good game, but he wasn't one for fisticuffs.

'Esme, he doesn't love you. Not like I do.'

'What?' Esme froze, her stomach knotting tighter. *Love her?* What the hell was happening now?

Joe carried on, his face and voice pleading. Leo stared at him, as shocked as Esme was. 'I love you, Esme. More than anything in the world. After Clara, I didn't think I'd ever fall in love again, then you walked back into my life and things started changing. Please, don't go back to this . . .' he looked Leo up and down, '. . . This yuppie.'

Leo's mouth dropped open. 'Now hang on a minute—'

Unfazed, and not in the least bit intimidated, Joe turned to him. 'Listen here, pal, you left Esme because you didn't realise how amazing and special she is. That was your loss. You can't come crawling back now.'

'Crawling back?' Leo's face flooded with embarrassment. 'I wouldn't put it quite like that!'

Esme's eyes pinned on Leo. 'How would you put it then, Leo?'

Just as she'd expected, he ignored her question, too embarrassed to admit the truth. 'Esme, you're not going to listen to this, are you?'

Hearing Joe's words and looking at Leo, Esme felt that she was seeing Leo's true colours for the first time, but her mind was a tidal wave of confusion. Everything Joe was saying seemed like the nice and kind guy she'd seen every time they were together, but then there was everything that had happened at the Christmas Eve party. 'How can you say all this to me, Joe? The other night – your girlfriend!—' She flung her arms in the air, exasperated. This was the craziest situation she'd ever found herself in. And considering she'd once had to hand-paint a burger with melted Vaseline, that was saying something.

Joe stared at her, his brow furrowed. 'My girlfriend?'

Esme raised her eyebrows in disbelief. 'Long chocolate brown hair, gorgeous eyes? You called her your angel.'

Joe's head shot up. 'Her name is Angel. She's my cousin.'

Esme's body froze. 'Angel's her name?'

Joe smiled and nodded.

'What sort of a name is that?'

'It is a bit unconventional,' he conceded. 'Her parents were hippies.'

'But she said she needed to see you.'

'Yeah, she's buying a house and had some questions, that's all.' Suddenly Joe's face betrayed him. 'Did you think she was my girlfriend?' Esme nodded slowly, like he was complete idiot. 'That explains why you ran away on Christmas Eve and didn't answer my texts. I didn't call yesterday because I knew how much you were looking forward to Christmas Day with your family and I didn't want to disturb you.'

'Um, excuse me,' said Leo, stepping slightly forwards. 'Esme, I'm stood here telling you I love you. Won't you come back with me? Try again? Things can be like they were before.'

In the back of her mind she heard her father's voice and remembered his words to her when she first came home. He'd told her to never go back. And he was right. Esme could never trust Leo now. She couldn't go back in time to make him the Leo he'd been before things had started to go wrong. Before they'd begun to grow apart, though she hadn't realised before this moment that that's what had happened. She could never go back to the flat – she would never feel truly safe there. He might toss her out again at a moment's notice if someone else caught his eye. Leo had gone behind her back and cheated and if he'd done it once, he could do it again. No. She could never trust him now. He'd been deceitful and more than anything, it was that she could never forgive.

As she glanced around at the cottage, at the Christmas

decorations everywhere, her tree with its Spiderman-winged, green-faced angel that she'd made with her sweet nephew, she realised she didn't want to go. She liked it here in her crazy cottage. No, not liked – loved. She loved being home, near her family, as mad as they were. Always nearby, ever supportive. And she loved forging her own path in the world. It had been tough. It would always be tough and she wouldn't have much money, but the sense of fulfilment she'd had so far had been more than anything she'd felt working on other people's TV shows. And this was just the start. Who knew where this path would lead her?

Seeing her friends stood in her kitchen, adorned in their silly Christmas headbands, she knew that no matter what the distance between them, they would always be together. They'd come down at weekends or she could go and stay with them in London. Being somewhere else geographically didn't mean they were out of her life. They'd proved that much already. Esme's anger at Leo vanished as a calmness took over – her decision had been made. She was moving on from him but not from here. Esme chewed the inside of her cheek, repressing a smile. In the end, the decision she'd thought would be hard had come so easily for her. Moving back in with Leo, trying to rebuild her life in London, was not what she wanted.

Leo caught her smile and a smugness filled his expression. 'Is that a yes?'

Joe's head lifted, his eyes pleading. Esme turned to Leo and the smile that had always seemed confident and sexy now looked egotistical and superior. 'No, it's not, Leo. It's a no. A hard no.'

'What?'

'I said no, Leo. I don't want to get back together with you. In fact, I'll be quite happy if I never see you again. I'm happy here and this is where I want to stay. So you might as well just leave and get back to London as soon as possible. Maybe you can try again with Veruca.'

He shook his head. 'But why, Esme? I made a mistake. One

248

mistake in all the years we've been together and you won't forgive me?'

'No, Leo I won't. It might only have been one mistake, but it was rather a big one. You cheated on me, then on the worst day of my life, when I'd been sacked and was at my lowest, you decided to dump me.' He stared at her wide-eyed and disbelieving. 'You couldn't even be bothered to hang on for a bit until I'd got back on my feet. You kicked me when I was down, Leo, like it didn't matter. Like *I* didn't matter. I can never forgive you for that.'

Leo opened his mouth to speak then closed it again. His face hardened and he gave a curt nod. 'Fine. But I won't be coming here again, Esme. This is the only time I'll be asking you to come back.'

'Fine with me,' Esme replied with a shrug. 'Cheerio.'

After shooting a quick, distasteful look at Joe, Leo left, the gang all waving as he walked past. Mark followed, closing the door behind him.

Esme turned to Joe and he cleared his throat. 'Esme—'

'Just hang on a minute, Joe.' Esme folded her arms over her chest. She wasn't quite finished with him yet. 'Angel might not be your girlfriend, but what about all the others I've heard about? What about the woman I saw you leave with that night? I can't pretend that the one-night stands haven't bothered me.'

'Esme, I . . .' He faltered, shaking his head as he tried to speak. 'I have had a few, I'll admit that. You know everything that's happened – how much I've struggled. And all I can say is, it was just a way to feel something else, to try and escape this big black hole that was always trying to pull me in. It never meant anything. You're the only person who's meant anything to me since Clara. I never thought I'd love anyone again but then you turned up and . . . I love you.'

Esme stood with her mouth open. 'Oh.'

'But there is one more thing I need to tell you.'

'Oh no! Really?' She wasn't sure how much more of this she could take. And now she'd sent Leo packing and Joe had declared his love, all she could think of was how much she loved him too. And how much she wanted to kiss him.

'Yeah, sorry.' Joe nervously reached a hand up and raked it through his hair, his face a picture of apprehension and worry. Esme felt her own fear mounting. 'The thing is . . . I'm Penny85.'

Mark, Lola and Helena gasped.

'You're what?'Esme shook her head. 'Sorry . . . what did you say?'

'I'm Penny85.'

'You're Penny85?'

'I . . . yes.' Joe stepped forwards, reaching out for Esme and taking her hands in his. They were still cold from where he'd driven here without a coat. 'I didn't mean to lie to you. I just wanted to make you feel better and get other people to give you a break too.'

Again, all Esme could think to say was, 'Oh.' Every thought in her mind had blurred into one. She had no idea how to react and she still really wanted to kiss him.

'Please don't be mad. I was just trying to help.'

Esme thought for a moment and then laughed out loud, her whole body shaking as she flung her head back and giggled. She put a hand to her chest as if it would help her calm down. Leo would never have done anything like that for her.

Joe's face was a mixture of fear and amusement. 'What's so funny?'

'That's the sweetest thing I've ever heard.'

'Is it?' His lopsided grin returned, the fear draining from his face.

Esme noticed he was stood under the bunch of mistletoe Mark had hung on their last trip down, when they'd decorated the cottage. Joe loved her. He loved *her* and that woman hadn't been his girlfriend at all. It had been his cousin. And though she didn't particularly like the fact he'd had a few one-night stands, they hadn't really meant anything. She could understand why he'd sought comfort in that way and they were both in their thirties; there were always going to be skeletons in their closets. Esme stepped forward, wrapping her hands around his neck she pulled him in for a kiss – a kiss under the mistletoe – the most amazing kiss she'd ever had. And when he pulled her close, his fingers in her hair, she never wanted him to let go.

Esme finally remembered this was all being broadcast live but with an internal shrug, she realised she couldn't have cared less. She was in love.

Chapter 30

London

January

'Have you seen this?' announced Felicity, throwing a newspaper onto Sasha's desk. 'This is completely outrageous. How come you haven't issued a statement saying this isn't true?'

Sasha studied the newspaper, keeping her expression placid. Plastered over the front page was a picture of Felicity looking tired after returning from her trip to the Maldives, and a scathing article exposing her stealing recipes from colleagues and even her housekeeper. She'd run off to the Maldives in early December, hiding away after the disastrous day she'd tried to create the triple-layer chocolate chestnut cake she'd supposedly not stolen from Esme. It had been a disaster and Sasha had been furious. Felicity had clearly hoped that by returning in the New Year, it all would be forgotten and she could slip into the country without anyone noticing.

Sasha did her best to hide the wry smile on her face. Esme had been right all along and luckily, the food critic who wrote the article had been able to find out Felicity's arrival time somehow.

252

Keeping her voice calm, Sasha said, 'According to this article, Felicity, you don't have a cookbook from your grandmother. In fact, according to some secret source, you've been stealing recipes from quite a few people.'

Felicity stared at her with barely concealed hatred, tossed her hair and laughed. 'It's all lies, Sasha. Surely you can see that?'

'Was Esme lying?'

Felicity glared.

'And who is this new secret source?'

'I have no idea,' Felicity answered through a tight smile. But Sasha could see in her eyes she did have an idea of who it was. Sasha hoped that person wouldn't be crossing paths with Felicity anytime soon.

'If I were you, Felicity—' Sasha placed the paper flat on the desk'—I'd get onto your agent and PR team straightaway before your reputation is completely ruined. I didn't feel in a confident enough position to issue any sort of statement on behalf of the network.'

'And what about the show?'

'We'll continue filming this series. But we'll have to wait and see whether we commission another one.' She held Felicity's furious gaze. 'It'll depend on how the viewing figures are hit by this.' She gestured to the paper.

'But this is all nonsense,' said Felicity, her voice growing louder.

Sasha wasn't in the least bit intimidated by Felicity's evil glare or her shouting. Sasha had made her career through hard work, sheer grit and determination. She'd never treated anyone the way Felicity had treated her and the fact that she'd lost one of her best, most talented food techs because Felicity couldn't think for herself made her beyond angry.

'You must see this is rubbish, Sasha.'

'Some might call it a revelation.'

Felicity spun in her Louboutins and stomped out of Sasha's office. As soon as she had left, Sasha let the smile she had been holding back spread across her face. *Serves Felicity right*, she thought. But knowing the truth now, having seen and spoken to Felicity face-to-face, Sasha felt a deep regret as to how they had treated Esme. How *she* had treated Esme. Sasha glanced again at the newspaper before opening her weekly email from the research team. It detailed up-and-coming cookery writers they might want to keep an eye on and one name stood out.

Sasha sat back in her chair determining the best course of action. Esme's name was there. It seemed she was carving quite a niche for herself online with what they'd called 'a crazy new presenting style'. She noted her blog was called Grandma's Kitchen and Sasha smiled. Good for Esme not letting herself be kept down and sticking to her guns. They'd done her a disservice and Sasha was determined to put it right if she could. She picked up the phone and called a producer friend at a rival network.

'Richard, it's Sasha.'

'Hey, Sasha, how are you? Have you thought any more about my offer? Our latest offer was very generous.'

'I have actually, now you come to mention it.'

'We'd love to have you here and don't you think the show I pitched sounded great?'

'It does,' Sasha chuckled. She'd been holding out to see if they upped the money they were offering and now they had, and she'd seen Felicity's response, she was sure. 'I liked it very much, but I think I have a better idea.'

'Oh, yeah, what's that?'

'It involves a food tech we had called Esme Kendrick and trust me, this girl's going to be huge. She has a crazy new presenting style, great recipes and she's making quite a name for herself online. We could be in at the very start of a career that I'm sure is going to go places.'

'You're kidding!' Richard laughed. 'Sounds good. Let me get my pencil.'

Chapter 31

Sandchester

Esme opened her laptop to begin work on her blog as a strong golden light poured in through the living-room window. The sun was no longer hidden behind white clouds that rushed across the sky, blown along by a strong wind. The temperature had dropped even further and Esme, who couldn't wear anymore clothes and still move her arms, wore thermals under her jeans, huddling over her computer with the log fire burning.

She and Joe had enjoyed another few dates and things were progressing well. His face looked younger each time she saw him as the lines around his eyes faded. They'd been to his flat and, after some gentle coaxing, had unpacked the remaining boxes in his living room. Amongst his things they had found a picture of him and Clara together. Joe was going to put the photo away, not wanting Esme to feel uncomfortable, but she'd laughed and placed it in the centre of the mantelpiece, saying that Clara had been such a huge part of his life that he should keep her picture out. When they had pictures of their own they wanted to put there, they might think of moving it somewhere else, but she wouldn't let him hide Clara away when he'd only just let his pain go. They spent days walking through the woods with Joe taking photographs and then evenings together eating her food and drinking wine under blankets on the sofa. And once she had some more money, she was determined to show Joe how wonderful London was. She wasn't going to give it up entirely, but now she had someone to share it with.

The new year had started well for the blog too. She still needed money, but a few more cake-making jobs had come in and she had just enough to live on for another month or so. Joe had said she could move in with him, but she didn't want to. She wanted to take it slow and if needed, would move back home, or find a job doing something completely different. But things were looking up. She had some advertising on her blog and was looking into sponsorship opportunities, and her audience was getting bigger every day. The live broadcast on Boxing Day had been a huge hit and had even made it onto YouTube. People had commented how she'd made the right choice, how they wanted more videos of her day-to-day life, how much they admired her for sticking to her guns. It had been a strange experience, and now, every time she posted a new video or blog post, the little community she'd created came together, commenting and discussing their attempts, their lives, their memories, and it filled Esme with hope. Joe wasn't having to comment as Penny85 (a name he'd made up after his own granny whose name was Penny and was 85) anymore as her subscribers grew and the blog took on a life of its own.

Esme decided to check her emails, and a strange one caught her eye. It had no title other than 'Private and Confidential' and was from a name she didn't recognise. Esme felt her eyes widen and her fingers hovered over the keys. She opened the email. It was from an American publisher. He'd heard about her blog and wanted to talk to her about a book deal. Please could she get in touch and arrange a time to speak to one of their editors.

For a moment Esme couldn't move. She'd taken a big breath in when opening the email, thinking it was Felicity suing her, even though the papers had found out what she was like and run a story. Esme had noted with delight today's headline, which indicated she had returned to the Maldives to hideaway again. Which reminded her, Felicity's former housekeeper had been in touch and wondered if Esme would take a guest blog from her. Juanita had quit after the truth about Felicity had come out and reached out to Esme after returning home to Spain. She was sweet and had some great Spanish recipes to share and bonded as they were by Felicity, Esme wanted to help her if she could.

As excitement coursed through Esme's body, her muscles tensed and each breath came in quick gulps. She reached for her phone without taking her eyes from the screen and called her parents. When she explained to her mum what the email meant, Carol screamed and shouted at Stephen to open the champagne they were saving for special occasions. 'We did buy it for your wedding day, but this is so much better seeing as Leo is a useless sack of shit. I like Joe so much more. He's much more suitable for you. So normal. We think he'll fit in with the family very well.'

Poor Joe, thought Esme, rolling her eyes. Her parents had been over the moon when she'd told them they were dating and showed them the Boxing Day broadcast. She'd had to be extremely clear that they were taking it slow, blaming her break-up with Leo. She hadn't told them any more about Clara. Poor Joe might not be able to cope with her mum's mollycoddling if she did.

After saying goodbye to her mother, she called Mark. He also screamed down the phone. 'OMG, sweetie, OMFG! I knew you could do it! I bloody knew you could do it! That shows Felicity.' Esme giggled. 'I'm so proud of you, Ezzy. So, so proud.'

Mark had promised to call Helena and Lola, leaving Esme free to call Joe. Even though he was at work, he said he'd be right over. Esme couldn't contemplate emailing them back just yet. What could she say except for yes, in big capital letters? Underlined. Highlighted. In red. Or purple as that was her favourite colour. It was all so unreal. So strange.

When Joe arrived and opened the door, he took a big step forward, put his hands either side of her face and drew her in for a kiss. She fell into his embrace, elated. The world had gone mad, but Esme didn't care. This time she was quite happy to go along for the ride. 'I'm so proud of you,' said Joe. 'I knew you could do it.' He wrapped his arms around her waist, lifting her and spinning her around.

When he put her down she leaned in and kissed him again. 'I'm glad you knew I could. I didn't.'

'So, what's next for Esme Kendrick then?'

'Hmm.' She stood back and stared into his eyes. 'World domination, maybe?'

Joe glanced at the log fire, and then at Esme's additional jumpers. 'Or you could get central heating installed.'

Acknowledgements

I'm really quite teary writing these acknowledgements for a couple of reasons.

Firstly, this is the story that got me a book deal with HQ Digital and started this whole amazing journey. HQ Digital are an absolute dream to work with and I've enjoyed every second of it. Thank you Emily Kitchin, Abi Fenton and Vikki Moynes for your help and encouragement with this book. And a big thanks to the design team for the amazing cover that made my tummy go all squirmy when I first saw it.

Secondly, I only had the courage to really try and make my dreams come true after my lovely cousin, Dan, passed away. He was only 25 when he died and his loss taught me to stop wishing for things to happen and to actually try and make my dream come true. So I polished up this book and took some chances. You have no idea how long you have on this planet so please, please have the courage to try! I've dedicated this book to him and his mum, Angie, my lovely aunty, who also passed away. They're always in our thoughts, never forgotten.

And of course, I have to thank my family and friends, and every single person who's picked up and read this book! I wouldn't be

able to keep doing this if it weren't for all of you! Thank you
from the bottom of my heart. It really means the world.

The next book from Katie Ginger is coming in March 2020!

Turn the page for an extract from another charming read from Katie Ginger, *The Little Theatre on the Seafront* . . .

Prologue

To my dearest girl,

What a wonderful life we've had together, my darling Lottie. I'm so sorry that I'll miss so many things, such as seeing you get married and have children, but my time has come and I'm off to see your granddad. It's been a long time since we last saw each other so we should have a lot to talk about, which will be a pleasant change from our married life together.

With all this death business I've been thinking about you and what you'll do after I'm gone, and I've decided something – you need a shake up, my girl!

I love you, dear, but all you do is go to work, come home again, and that's it. You're thirty years old and you should be doing more with your life than spending your evenings with a little old lady like me.

If you remember, I have tried to get you enjoying life a bit more, but to no avail. Last year I set you up with that lovely handsome window cleaner, but you didn't bat an eyelid. In fact, I'm not entirely sure you even knew what was happening. And then there was that time at Christmas, when I tried to get you to go to your school reunion . . . but you stubbornly refuse to enjoy anything that takes you out of yourself and out into the world. *To be frank, dear, it's no way to live.*

So, I've decided that a bit of emotional blackmail is in order. And as spending your evenings fussing over me won't be an option anymore, you're going to take over my place as chairman of Greenley Theatre and carry on my, dare I say it, good work, on the 'Save Greenley Theatre' campaign.

Think of it as one of those New Year, New You, type things! Good luck, my dear. I know you'll make me proud.

Lots of love,

Nan

P.S. I haven't actually arranged this with the committee yet so that will be your first job. Have fun!

Chapter One

Lottie waited outside her house for Sid, her colleague and best friend, to pick her up. She checked her watch and rolled her eyes. He was late, as usual. In all the years she'd known him he'd never been able to get anywhere on time – even primary school. After five more minutes of shuffling to stay warm she saw his battered old car round the corner and hid the box behind her back.

'Here you go,' she said as she climbed in.

'You got me an Easter egg,' Sid replied, smiling. It was an *Incredible Hulk* one.

'I couldn't resist.'

'Me neither.' He handed over a large posh box.

Lottie giggled and had a quick look at the huge milk chocolate egg covered in a white chocolate drizzle. Her mouth began to water. 'You're the best.' Sid's grin grew wider. Lottie tucked the egg down by her feet while Sid tossed his onto the backseat where it was cushioned by a mound of rubbish and they headed to the first job of the day.

Lottie leaned forward and peeked at the picture on his top. 'Don't you think that T-shirt's a bit off for meeting an old lady?'

Sid pulled it to his nose and sniffed 'What's wrong with it?'

'I don't mean it's skanky. It's the picture.'

'What's wrong with the picture? Dragon Slaying Vampires are a great band.'

She raised her eyebrows. 'I'm not sure a half-naked woman with enormous breasticles, standing on top of a dragon's severed head in a giant pool of blood, is really appropriate for an octogenarian. Do you?'

'Oh,' said Sid. 'I suppose not.' He shrugged. 'I'll keep my jacket on.'

'Yeah, good luck with that.'

Sid was the reporter on the *Greenley Gazette* and Lottie was his photographer. Over the years they had covered every sort of local issue from the first day at school to hardcore crime and had learnt that old ladies over the age of seventy love to have the heating on. And it was already turning into a surprisingly sunny February day.

Lottie peered up at the clear blue sky and soft white clouds overhead. She loved living in Greenley-On-Sea, especially on days like this. The sun shone brightly, and the air was crisp and clean carrying a hint of salt from the sea. The streets were full of children on their way to school, laughing and giggling at what the day might hold in store.

'You were late again,' she said, teasingly.

Sid pointed to two takeaway cups in the cup holders. 'I stopped to get coffee.'

'Aww, thanks.' She sipped the skinny mocha savouring the tang of coffee and sweet hit of chocolate, then removed the lid to swipe up some of the whipped cream.

'I have no idea why you have it made with skimmed milk and then put cream on top.'

'Because,' said Lottie, popping the lid back on, 'I can convince my brain that whipped cream is mostly air and therefore has no calories and skinny milk is mostly water, so really, it's not that bad for me. In fact, on a day like this it's actually good for me. I'm hydrating.'

Sid's deep set hazel eyes under slightly too bushy eyebrows looked at her sceptically. She'd known him all her life and he knew her better than anyone else in the entire world, especially since Elsie, her nan, had passed away just after Christmas. She felt a familiar stab of grief tighten her throat but pushed it down. 'Do you want to have lunch at mine today?'

'Have you got any decent grub?'

'Sidney Evans, you only ever think about your stomach.' Lottie smiled and considered the sparse remains in the fridge. 'Beans on toast?'

'Yeah, all right.'

They were now in the posh part of town where old white Georgian houses with large sash windows lined the roads, but before long they would be out the other side back to the normal houses. 'So who's this old dear we're seeing this morning?'

He bobbed up and down in excitement. 'Mrs Harker and her opera-singing parrot.'

Lottie stared. 'Opera?'

'Yep.'

She blinked. 'Oh.'

'I know. I love my job,' Sid replied, beaming as if it was Christmas.

Sid parked the car in front of an ordinary mid-terrace house. A neat front garden with a small path led them to a plain white front door. Lottie climbed out first. 'I think I'll get a photo of Mrs Harker outside holding the parrot. It'll be a nice juxtaposition of the ordinary and the extraordinary.'

Sid tutted. 'You take this all far too seriously sometimes.'

They walked to the door and Sid gave a cheerful knock. A petite woman in her eighties wearing a floral dress and long beige cardigan opened the door. 'Good morning.'

'Good morning, Mrs Harker. I'm Sid Evans, from the *Greenley Gazette*, and this is my photographer, Lottie Webster.'

'Come in, won't you?' asked Mrs Harker, leading the way.

Lottie followed Sid into the porch and was immediately struck by the heat. It was like having a boiling hot flannel shoved on her face. She looked at Sid and grinned as a redness crept over his cheeks. It was going to be fun watching him cook, a little bit of payback for last week when they'd done the weekly shop together and he'd kept secretly adding things to other people's baskets. She'd giggled at the time but it was quite embarrassing when he got caught. Of course, he'd come clean and charmed his way out of it while Lottie hid at the end of the aisle, peering round from the pick'n'mix.

As they entered the living room, Lottie slipped her coat from her shoulders and spotted a cage with a bright red parrot perched inside. The bird didn't move and for a moment, Lottie worried it was stuffed. It wouldn't be the first time they'd interviewed a crazy person.

'I understand,' said Sid, 'that you have a very unusual parrot, Mrs Harker?'

'Oh, yes, Mr Neville is very talented.'

'Mr Neville?' repeated Sid. Lottie recognised from the twitch in his cheek a grin was pulling at his mouth.

'Yes, Mr Neville's my parrot. He sings Tosca.'

Sid nodded. 'And can we see this talent in action?'

Lottie readied her camera as Mrs Harker approached the CD player and switched it on. The music started and Mr Neville, as if by magic, came to life. He opened his wings and rocked on his feet as he screeched in unison with the music. Lottie lifted her camera and took some shots. Calling it singing was going a bit far, but it was certainly entertaining. A moment later, Mrs Harker switched off the music and Sid conducted the interview.

'Well, thank you very much, Mrs Harker,' he said when he'd finished. 'That's quite a parrot you've got there.'

'He's great, isn't he?' she replied, opening his cage to take him out. 'Did you want to take your coat off, young man? You look a little bit hot.'

'No, thanks. I'm fine,' said Sid, wiping his top lip.

Lottie repressed a laugh.

'I was so sorry to hear about your grandmother passing, Miss Webster,' said Mrs Harker.

Lottie paused as a shiver ran down her spine. 'You knew my nan?'

'Yes, dear, I went to school with her and we played bingo together for years. She was a lovely woman.'

'Yes, she was.'

'It was wonderful what she was trying to do for the town, she was always working hard to make a difference. Such a shame she never quite got the theatre going again.'

Lottie opened her mouth, but nothing came out. Grabbing the bottle of water Sid offered, she took a big drink.

'Did Mrs Webster talk much about the theatre?' Sid asked. He must have seen her impression of a goldfish and stepped in.

'Oh yes, she had grand plans. Elsie was going to make it like it was when we were young. Get the community involved again. I think that was where she met your granddad, Miss Webster.'

Lottie's eyes darted to Mrs Harker's face. She had no idea that was why the theatre meant so much to her nan. From the depths of her mind she remembered Elsie telling her the story. How she spotted him from across the aisle and that was that. Love at first sight. Lottie had responded by saying how lovely and picking up her book, burying herself in another time, another place. She bit her lip feeling ashamed.

'All the bingo club were behind her, you know. Johnnie, the caller – the guy who calls out legs eleven and two fat ladies, and all that –he said that we could move back there when Elsie finished renovating it.'

Lottie tightened her grip on the water bottle and swallowed. She needed to get outside into the fresh air. 'I think, Mrs Harker, it would be a lovely idea to get a picture of you and Mr Neville in front of your house, if you don't mind?'

'Not at all, dear,' she replied, admiring Mr Neville and stroking his feathers. 'Are you sure you're alright? You look quite pale.'

'Yes, I'm fine, thank you.' Lottie's voice was high and squeaky. Her hand shook as she clicked the camera, but finally, after a few attempts, she had the shot.

Sid escorted Mrs Harker back to her door and said goodbye as Lottie climbed into the car and pulled another bottle of water from her camera bag. She watched Sid remove his jacket and move round to the driver's side to get in.

'Okay, you were right,' he said, wiping his forehead with the back of his hand. 'I was absolutely roasting in there. Why do old dears always have the heating on? I mean, I know it's still chilly, but come on.' He looked at Lottie, his furrowed brow accentuating his crooked nose. 'Are you alright?'

'I am now I'm out of there.'

'Was it the bit about your nan?'

Lottie stared at him in disbelief. 'Of course it was! I wasn't so impressed by an opera-singing parrot I nearly fainted.'

'Alright,' he said sarcastically. 'I was just checking.'

Lottie pushed a stray lock of hair behind her ear. If Sid wasn't so genuinely clueless when it came to women she would have been cross with him. 'Sorry. I know I'm being unbearable at the moment.'

His cheeky grin returned. 'That's okay.'

'It's just that, I knew the theatre meant a lot to Nan, but I . . .'

'What?' asked Sid, softly.

She shook her head, unable to steer her brain into forming a sentence. A familiar wave of grief and sadness washed over her, tinged with panic and fear at what she was being asked to do.

'Listen, Lots. I know you don't want to deal with your nan's letter but I think we have to. You can't keep ignoring it.'

Elsie's final gift to her hadn't been at all what Lottie had expected and she had no idea how to deal with it. 'There's nothing to talk about, Sid. I'm not doing it and that's final.'

'But, Lottie, your nan must have thought this was what you needed. You can't keep shoving your head in the sand and pretending it never happened.'

She crossed her arms over her chest. 'Yes, I can.'

'No, you can't.' Sid ran his hand through dark curls that maintained a stubborn unruliness no matter how short they were cut. If Sid was her type – which he wasn't – she might have thought him handsome in a geeky way. 'I'm not trying to annoy you.'

'I know you're not. You don't need to try.' She gave a weak smile.

Sid started the engine and began to drive off. 'But why leave you a letter? Why not just ask?'

Lottie shrugged. 'Nan knew full well that if she asked me face to face I'd tell her to bog off.'

'And stomp off out of the room,' he said teasingly.

She turned to him and widened her eyes in fake surprise. 'I don't do that.'

'Yes, you do.' He smiled. 'But it's fine, I don't mind. I just don't understand what you're afraid of.'

Lottie opened her Easter egg and broke off a piece of chocolate, waving it in the air as she spoke. 'Oh, I don't know, making a fool of myself in front of the entire town, letting Nan down, everyone laughing at me.'

'No one would laugh at you, Lottie.'

'Despite what Nan thinks—' Lottie felt her heart twinge, the words catching in her throat. 'What Nan thought, I quite like my life.'

Sid looked at her sceptically. 'You like being safe, Lottie, that's not the same thing.'

'But what if I take over the theatre and make things worse?'

'How can you?' Sid glanced at her quickly before turning his eyes back to the road. 'What could you possibly do to make it worse? Burn the place down? Blow it up? You're not planning on blowing it up, are you?'

Lottie scowled.

'Oh, I know,' he continued in a mocking tone. 'You're going to run National Front rallies, or host puppy kicking competitions?'

'No, but—'

'It's a small local theatre for a small quiet town. Not a top notch, swanky London showbiz place.'

Lottie cocked her head and broke off another piece of chocolate. 'But I don't know how to do this.' Her voice was rising and she pulled it back. It wasn't Sid's fault. 'I'm not a project manager, I have no idea how to be a chairman and do chairman-type things. And, I know absolutely nothing about theatres.'

'But you are ridiculously bossy.'

'No I'm not, I'm just . . . organised.'

Sid's face broke into a wide grin and he grabbed her hand, giving it a squeeze. 'You can do this, Lottie, I know you can. Just give it a chance.'

Lottie ate another piece of chocolate.

'The thing is, Lottie,' he continued, 'your nan was right. You do need to get out more. I mean, when was the last time you had a boyfriend?'

'When was the last time you had a girlfriend?' she countered.

'It was 2003, but this isn't about me.'

Lottie repressed a smile. 'You were twelve in 2003.'

'Yep, but I'm perfectly happy with my life; you're not and you haven't been for ages.'

Lottie folded her arms over her chest. It was true. She had been feeling restless for a long time now. But when her nan became ill, she'd retreated even further into her safe, quiet life. It wasn't that she didn't like people, she did. She'd just never quite got around to getting a social life, that was all. 'What's your point?'

'I think if you stopped looking at everything so negatively you'd see this could be good fun.' Sid was always trying to chivvy her up.

Lottie toyed with her camera, opening and closing the lens, her mind racing. 'I've got to do this, haven't I?'

'We have,' said Sid, smiling at her. 'I'll be there for you.' He stopped at a junction. 'Shall we head to yours now? We can have lunch and start coming up with a plan to get you on the committee.'

Lottie checked her watch. 'It's only half eleven.'

'I know, but I'm starving. Please?' He stuck his lower lip out just as her stomach rumbled.

'Alright then. Just for you.'

Hi there, you lovely lot!

I hope you've enjoyed a little bit of festive fun here with me and Esme and the gang! Thank you so much for reading this book. I really hope you enjoyed it! If you did and fancied leaving a review that would be fantabulous and makes a huge difference to us lonely, insecure authors!

HQ Digital is amazing and publishes loads of awesome writers, so if you're looking for what to read next, please check them out.

In the meantime, if you fancied keeping me company it would be lovely to connect on social media. My website is: www.keginger. com; or I'm on Facebook at: www.Facebook.com/KatieGAuthor. And I'm still doing my best to ignore my to-do list with Twitter if you fancied a chat: @KatieGAuthor

Happy reading, everyone!

Best wishes,

Katie

xxx

Dear Reader,

Thank you so much for taking the time to read this book – we hope you enjoyed it! If you did, we'd be so appreciative if you left a review.

Here at HQ Digital we are dedicated to publishing fiction that will keep you turning the pages into the early hours. We publish a variety of genres, from heartwarming romance, to thrilling crime and sweeping historical fiction.

To find out more about our books, enter competitions and discover exclusive content, please join our community of readers by following us at:

@HQDigitalUK

facebook.com/HQDigitalUK

Are you a budding writer? We're also looking for authors to join the HQ Digital family! Please submit your manuscript to:

HQDigital@harpercollins.co.uk.

Hope to hear from you soon!